Tango
Down

A SAM ACQUILLO MYSTERY

Tango
Down

CHRIS KNOPF

WITHDRAWN

THE PERMANENT PRESS
Sag Harbor, NY 11963

For information, address:
The Permanent Press
4170 Noyac Road
Sag Harbor, NY 11963
www.thepermanentpress.com

Library of Congress Cataloging-in-Publication

Knopf, Chris, author.
  Tango down / Chris Knopf.
  Sag Harbor, NY: Permanent Press, [2017]
  ISBN: 978-1-57962-501-6
    1. Acquillo, Sam (Fictitious character)—Fiction. 2. Mystery fiction.

PS3611.N66 T36 2017
813'.6—dc23 LC   2017038505

Printed in the United States of America

CHAPTER ONE

I was trying to maneuver my way across the muddy construction site when Frank Entwhistle ran up to my old Jeep Cherokee and slapped on the windshield. I stopped and rolled down the window.

"Sam, you gotta get in here," he yelled at me.

Entwhistle never yelled. It was one of the things I liked most about him—his calm, steady ways no matter what sort of nutty mayhem was erupting around him. So I left the Jeep where it was and followed him into the half-built house.

A group of workers, wearing loose jeans and sweatshirts, tool belts and nail aprons, made way for us at the front door. I followed Frank over the plywood substrate and up a temporary staircase. He wasn't a slim man, and normally a slow walker, but that morning he moved like an angry bull.

"What's up?" I asked him.

"Don't know," he huffed out as we ran up the stairs. "Something bad. They were afraid to tell me."

On the second floor, a few subcontractors were standing around a wide landing, looking into one of the bedrooms. Frank told them in Spanish to let us by, and they hopped out of the way.

The owner of the new house, a man named Victor Bollings, lay facedown in a slurry of blood, sawdust, and cutoffs from the finish work going on around the windows and door frames. I recognized him immediately, despite the blood that covered the left side of his face, staining most of his grey hair dark red.

An unusually pale white guy, his face had now lost all color. His eyes black in their sockets, as dead as the rest of him. The only thing moving was a swarm of flies in the hot summer air. I took a piece of ply and waved them off, but they came right back.

"Call 911," I said to Frank.

"Of course," he said, fumbling with his smartphone.

He dialed the number, but then handed the phone to me so I could call it in. I kept things to the minimum: my name, the address, location of the dead body on the second floor. The dispatcher told me to hang up and wait there for the responding officers.

"Who found him?" I asked Frank, after I hung up.

"Sanchez is the one who called me."

"Did anyone touch anything, move anything?"

He called back to the men on the landing for Sanchez, who came to the bedroom door. He assured us he touched nothing, he just called Frank the moment he found the body.

"Get all your guys out of the house and keep them in the front yard," I told Frank. "Encourage them to stay put, but don't force it."

I held on to his phone, and he went to gather up his people, leaving me alone in the room with Victor Bollings. I didn't know much about the guy, having only met with him a few times to discuss the built-ins and architectural enhancements I'd been hired to design and fabricate. Frank told me he was a management consultant, getting ready to retire as soon as he had the house in the Hamptons to move into. I assumed he had a wife, and maybe some kids, but I didn't know for sure.

I was hardly a crime scene expert, but I knew enough not to walk around the room. I stood there and tried to get some sense of what happened anyway, with meager results. It was just an empty space under construction. Blood in a big pond around Victor's head and splatter on two of the freshly Sheet-rocked walls.

I thought blow to the head, from behind, but like I said, I'm not an expert.

Frank's phone rang. It was a Southampton Village patrol officer telling me what I'd already heard from the dispatcher—don't disturb anything and keep everyone on the site, if we could. I knew from her voice it was Judy Rensler, an acquaintance of mine.

"It's Sam Acquillo," I told her, before giving as clear a briefing as possible.

"There in five minutes, Sam. Stay where you are and don't discuss anything with anyone."

Victor was pretty lousy company, but five minutes wasn't all that long to wait. I spent the time trying to remember everything I'd done in the preceding twenty-four hours. Having been arrested a few times myself, once for murder, I knew what questions to expect, even if my relationship with the murdered this time was safely remote.

When Judy got there, she told me to step back out of the room the way I'd come in. She moved past me and got close enough to Bollings to squat down and confirm the obvious, reporting what she saw by way of a tiny mic clipped to her shirtfront. Then she stood up and came out to the hall.

"Dead dead," she said.

"Is there any other kind?"

"Maybe dead, when we're not so sure. Which means I can wait a minute to call the paramedics. What do you know?" she asked.

"Only what I already told you. Hardly knew the guy. You need to talk to Frank Entwhistle. It's his job."

"What about the workers?"

"Talk to Frank. I was only here to take some measurements. I do all the work at my shop."

"So nobody you know."

"I know some of them. Sort of."

She didn't have to say that most of the workers were Latino, and a good number of them undocumented. I knew Judy well enough to believe she harbored no particular bias toward any ethnic origin. But she was a veteran cop, well aware of the implications of a murdered rich guy discovered by Southampton's most disenfranchised people.

"Ernesto Mazzotti's on this job," I told her, remembering. "I know him pretty well."

Ernesto was a Colombian finish carpenter of Italian extraction who usually handled the installation of the cabinets and detail work I did for Frank and a few of the other contractors in the area. He was precise and conscientious and I always tried to get him into that phase of the process. Frank usually obliged when he could.

"Is he here?" Judy asked.

"I didn't see him, but this is his work," I said, running my hand down a piece of door trim.

We heard sirens coming from outside, and Judy rolled her eyes, betraying her preference for low-profile policing. She escorted me down the stairs and out to the front lawn, where two more patrol cars, lights blazing, were pulling in. A heavy-faced cop with a substantial beer gut jumped out of his car with surprising agility, his eyes searching the scene for imminent threats. Judy approached him, and explained the situation, her prerogative as the supervising sergeant on the scene. He looked a little disappointed.

There wasn't much for them to do but wait for the medical examiner and the CSIs from the Town HQ, and watch Judy take down information from Frank's crew, since she was the only cop there who could speak Spanish. So the other cops made themselves useful sealing off a wide area around the scene and both ends of the street, and keeping neighbors attracted by the sirens and lights well out of the way.

While watching the cops in action, I noticed a white van pull up at the end of the taped-off street. It was Ernesto. The cops eyed me as I walked over to the van, but didn't interfere.

"Hey, Sam, what the hell is going on?" he asked, in English heavily inflected with his Colombian accent.

"Victor Bollings, the owner. Somebody smashed him over the head."

Ernesto's eyes widened.

"You're kidding. Is he all right?"

"Dead. The cops are interviewing everyone on the job. You might as well get it over with."

"Sure."

I led him through the crime scene defenders and over to where Judy was talking to a slight guy in a blue hoodie, one of the day laborers judging by the caked mud on his boots and gloved hands. He was explaining that he always left his wallet at home so he wouldn't lose it at work. Judy acted like she believed him, but told him he'd have to go get it after they were done with the initial interviews. She told him she couldn't care less about his status. She just wanted his help in figuring out what had happened there. He didn't look convinced.

I introduced her to Ernesto.

"How's your English?" she asked him.

"It's good. Ask Sam."

She asked him where he was before arriving at the site and he said picking up material at the lumberyard.

"It's on Frank's account," he said. "They can show you."

She nodded, thanked him, then asked if he could identify two other guys who said they were part of his operation. He pointed them out and confirmed their names.

We were interrupted by the arrival of the paramedics, lights on the ambulance like a disco. She went over and explained the situation. She knew they had to make their own declaration, but said to please get in and out without contaminating the scene. It was a friendly enough exchange, though no love seemed lost between the first responders.

Not long after the paramedics left, the CSIs showed up in their black box van. The cop with the beer belly approached the van with great purpose and Judy sighed. I caught her eyes and smiled at her.

"I know," she said, before following him over to the van. "Mr. Take Charge."

"This is very disturbing," said Ernesto.

"Any ideas?" I asked.

"I can't believe this. Somebody kill him?"

"That's what it looks like to me. Any ideas on who?"

He stared at me, thinking.

"No. Who would do this? He's the owner."

As if that conveyed a special immunity, which from his perspective, it probably did.

"What was he like?" I asked.

It was likely Ernesto had spoken to Bollings on a few occasions since Frank never put barriers between his customers and subcontractors.

"He enjoy what we did. Appreciate the good work. Said this a lot."

"So he spent time on the site."

"Sure. I ask him all the time if this is okay, or is that okay, and he was always nice. Not everybody is like that. You know that, Sam."

By then the CSIs were in the building and the construction crew had formed into a tighter group. They spoke together in low voices and glanced at the cops with wary eyes. Sanchez was separated, a few yards away, attended by his own village cop.

"Does he have a wife?" I asked Ernesto.

"Oh, sure. Mrs. Bollings. She's not as nice, but try to be. She doesn't come out from the city so much. I think she has a busy job."

"She's about to have a very bad day."

"*Que lastima.*"

What a pity.

One of the CSIs ran out the front door holding a cell phone and was joined by a cop who'd come from the back of the house. They spoke for a moment, then went around the house again. Everyone watched, but no one moved. After a few minutes, I said the hell with it and went on back. The CSI was walking out from behind a giant yew bush holding a golf club by the middle of the shaft. The village cop followed.

They both glared at me, so I made a clear path and stepped out of the way, but then followed them back into the house. We were met by Judy Rensler, the beer belly cop, and another CSI.

Even keeping a discreet distance, I could see dried blood covering the golf club's head and splattered up the shaft. The cop said he found it in the bushes behind the house. Beer belly gripped his shoulder and said, "Good work, son." The CSIs busied themselves tagging the club and scraping the blood into little vials, also carefully documented.

I realized Ernesto was standing behind me when he said, "*Dios mío.*"

I turned around.

"What?"

"That club," he said.

"What about it?"

He moved his head from side to side, as if trying to free himself from the thought.

"I know it," he whispered.

"What do you mean?"

"He was teaching me."

"What are you talking about?" I asked, pulling him back onto the front porch.

"Golf. We were talking about golf and I tell him I really want to learn."

"What's that got to do with the club?"

He moved away, but I closed in, forcing him to look at me. His face was a concert of pleading anxiety.

"Ernesto," I said. "Tell me."

"He gave it to me. To practice."

CHAPTER TWO

I had to nearly drag Ernesto over to his van so he could look inside the golf bag where he'd last stored the driver. It wasn't there. He frantically rummaged around the tools, pieces of trim, and nail boxes, shaking his head, and repeating his conviction that the bloodied club was the one Bollings gave him, the same brand and model, the same scratches along the shaft.

"I've been swinging that thing for two weeks," he said. "I know what it looks like."

I swore under my breath, took out my cell phone, and called Jackie Swaitkowski.

Jackie was a defense attorney who worked for a law firm that only took cases from people who couldn't afford defense attorneys. The bills were all paid by a wealthy benefactor—wealthy enough that even the seemingly limitless clientele on the East End of Long Island barely dented his resources. Or goodwill.

Jackie and I had done a few things together, so she knew who was calling her, which explained the tone of her greeting.

"What is it this time?"

"You have to get over here."

"Where's here?"

I gave her the address and a slightly more enhanced briefing than I'd given the police dispatcher.

"Don't move or talk to anyone till I get there," she said.

"I'm a little tired of people telling me to stay put and shut up."

"Sorry about that. Just shut up and stay put."

She got there from her office in a nearby village in about ten minutes. I used the time to ask Ernesto about the club, which he said he'd last used a few nights before at a driving range out on the highway.

"But you weren't there the night Bollings was killed."

"No. Is that bad?"

"We'll let Jackie be the judge of that."

"I'm sorry, Sam."

"Don't apologize. As long as you didn't do anything wrong."

I thought he was going to melt into the ground.

"No, no, Sam, I didn't do anything. What's going to happen?"

"I don't know, but get ready," I said, then added an expression in Spanish, that roughly translates as, "The shit's about to hit the fan."

"*Santa Madre, sálvame,*" he muttered, his head in his hands.

Jackie was in full client-protection mode when she burst from her Volvo station wagon, not unlike the beer belly cop, only far more agreeable to look at. I was glad to see she was dressed down—jeans, sneakers, and a ratty Oxford cloth shirt. It better suited the environment. I waved her over to Ernesto's van.

She didn't waste any time.

"Do you have an attorney?" she asked him.

"No, miss."

"Can you afford an attorney?"

He nodded, but I said to tell her no. He looked confused, but then shook his head.

"No, miss."

"I will represent you if you agree."

Ernesto looked at me.

"He agrees," I said, but she made him confirm it.

Jackie took a deep breath, then said, "Okay, let's go break the news."

As we walked Ernesto onto the job site, I asked her, "I think you're doing the right thing, but tell me why."

She looked down at the ground as we walked.

"His fingerprints and DNA will be all over that club. The cops might be able to get there on their own, which would make it a lot worse. Though they'll still be plenty pissed."

"Why's that?"

"He's already got a lawyer."

I LOCATED Judy Rensler and asked her to come talk to me for a minute. It annoyed her, but she came along. When she saw Jackie standing with Ernesto, I could almost hear her back stiffen.

"Miss Swaitkowski," she said.

"Officer. We have some important information to share. Voluntarily."

Judy hesitated and looked around. I could read her thoughts: I'm just a sergeant. Where the hell are the brass?

"Yes ma'am," she said.

Jackie told her Ernesto had been in possession of a golf club similar to the one retrieved from the bushes and wanted to report it stolen. Judy lowered her notebook and moved a little closer to Ernesto.

"We'll need to get a complete statement," she said.

"Absolutely," said Jackie, moving in front of her new client.

Judy called over another cop to keep us company while she went back to whatever she was doing. Jackie had a notebook of her own, and out of earshot of the cop, wrote down Ernesto's struggling recollection of the past twenty-four hours. I stepped out of the zone of confidentiality and went to retrieve the mug of coffee, now thoroughly cooled off in my Jeep's cup holder.

A VILLAGE police detective showed up about the time I was finished with the coffee. He was a skinny little guy in a light blue shirt and black trousers. If it weren't for the piece hanging off his belt and plain-wrapper patrol car, I'd think he was a high school science teacher. I watched him talk to Judy Rensler, then with beer belly cop, who was hanging just outside the conversation, then Jackie Swaitkowski and Frank Entwhistle, and finally Ernesto Mazzotti, though Jackie did most of the talking.

A sudden weariness settled on me, and I was tempted to climb back in the Jeep and drive out of there. I'd been through a lot of trouble in the last few years, and the thought of more generated waves of revulsion and an urge for heedless flight. Jackie had the situation well in hand, I told myself. And she was a lot younger, sturdier, and still eager for the game.

It made a lot of sense, and still would have if Ernesto hadn't leaned forward, his hands on his knees, shaking his head, then looking up to catch my eye. Fear lighting up his face. Jackie leaned down close to his ear and said something. They walked off together.

I'm tired, I repeated to myself. Then walked over to where the young detective stood by himself assessing the situation, disappointing him with my presence.

"You're the one who called it in," he said, after I introduced myself.

"I did. And I've got nothing to add."

"How long have you known Mr. Mazzotti?"

"I don't know, eight years maybe."

"Got a temper?" he asked.

"Him? No. Me, yes. But I've been working on that."

"You're a friend of Ross Semple's," he said.

He was referring to the chief of the Southampton Town Police, which was an institutional layer above the village force. I didn't know how they sorted out their jurisdictions, but in effect, Ross was the top cop in that corner of the world.

"Not exactly friends. But I know him, yeah."

"So you know he likes to let people do their jobs. Without interference."

"I do. And I won't."

"What?"

"Interfere."

"The same goes for Attorney Swaitkowski."

"You'll have to take that up with her. She's got a job to do too."

"I'm liking Mr. Mazzotti," he said.

"Me, too. Hell of a craftsman."

"For this," he said, looking at the Bollings house.

"You'll be wasting precious time."

"That sounds like a prelude to interfering."

"You brought it up," I said.

"You know the simplest explanation is almost always the right one."

"That's what Occam thought, though he hadn't heard about quantum mechanics."

"They teach you that in carpenter school?"

"MIT. But think whatever you want. *Cuilibet fatuo placet sua calva.*"

Every fool is pleased with his own folly.

"What the hell does that mean?"

"Ask Ross Semple."

CHAPTER THREE

I live in a cottage in the North Sea section of the Town of Southampton on the tip of Oak Point, a peninsula that sticks out into the Little Peconic Bay. I more or less grew up out there, and after I blew up my marriage and professional life, and my parents had died, it became my home once again. I fixed up and expanded the cottage over time, and installed a woodshop in the basement. A dog lives there, too, but otherwise I have the place to myself.

The only other house at the end of Oak Point is owned by a woman named Amanda Anselma. Her house is a lot nicer than mine, partly because she's a builder and partly because she has a lot more money than I do. But she never lords that over me, and I rarely remind her that she can only get to her house by the right-of-way that runs through my property.

She also prefers sitting in my backyard above the breakwater that defends both our homes from occasional storms, where we eat and drink too much and watch the sunset before crawling into bed together in one or the other of the houses, whichever suits our mood at the moment.

The only thing that renders this arrangement less than perfect is the existential recognition that it can't go on forever.

I got home a little after noon the day Sanchez found Victor Bollings dead in his new house. I never got to take the measurements for the next round of built-ins because Frank told me Mrs. Bollings had put a stop to all the work, and for the time being, I was only getting paid to finish the original commission. The dog, Eddie Van Halen, had little regard for human time frames, so he greeted me the same way he always did, by trying to jump in the car while I was trying to get out. We negotiated this in standard fashion, which ended with him running to our house and me following behind, grumbling over the monotony of the routine.

I would usually go directly down to my shop, but the morning's events had left me feeling enervated and adrift. So instead I spent the afternoon throwing tennis balls for Eddie and loafing on the Adirondack chairs above the breakwater, drinking iced tea and wondering if the translation of Baudelaire I was reading had left too much on the cutting room floor.

This occupied me until Amanda came home from one of her restoration projects, and after transitioning from work boots and paint-splattered clothes to bare feet and silk chemise, she drifted over with a small cooler stuffed with pâté de campagna and fromage d'Affinois, a bottle of wine, and an aluminum shaker filled with vodka on the rocks.

This was another reason Amanda made for an agreeable neighbor.

One of the unspoken ground rules was we rarely discussed the trials and struggles of the day, only the pleasant parts, if there were any. At least until the liquid fortifications had a chance to kick in, and then only if the news was of critical importance. This was one of those times.

"Oh, my," said Amanda, after I ran through the situation. "That's horrible. How is Frank doing?"

It was interesting that she thought of the builder first, one of her own kind.

"He's rattled. How would you feel if one of your customers was found dead in a second-floor bedroom?"

"Somewhere between horrified and relieved. Depending on the customer."

"There's a tough little kid detective from the village on the case. He's already fixed on Ernesto. Jackie's in for some rough sledding."

"In which case, so's the kid detective."

I immediately wanted to return to our standing protocol, which was fine with Amanda. We spent a decent amount of time commenting on the way the moonlight reflected on the ripply bay, agreeing on Eddie's skill at extracting his favorite treats between scheduled meals, exchanging critical views on Baudelaire—and the authenticity of the various translations—and lastly, commenting on the usual lushness of our shared lawn early in the summer. At which point the banality of the conversation collapsed under the weight of the present world and we both fell silent, our strategy of avoidance and denial defeated by the inexorable insistence of the real.

IT TURNED out the skinny young detective's name was Tony Cermanski. I learned that when he called me the next day asking if he could pay a visit. I said sure, it gets a little lonely working all day in the shop by myself.

He asked if we could talk without the chick lawyer, and I said don't call her a chick, unless he was ready to say that kind of thing to her face, and be prepared for the consequences. He said that was pretty tough talk, and I told him if being offensive and antagonistic was his plan of attack, he was in for a difficult time. On the other hand, if he wanted to act like a human being, he'd find us remarkably easy to deal with.

Either way, he was still welcome to come visit me out on Oak Point.

"Just store the attitude somewhere before you come," I said. "They made you detective for a reason. So find some other way to manage your insecurities and feelings of inadequacy."

"They told me you were a hard case," he said.

"Who said that? Bring them along. It's a small shop, but I'll make room."

"What the hell is your story?" he asked, though more a complaint than request.

I used to run R&D for a big hydrocarbon processing company. At one point, they made me go to a company-hired shrink to get therapy for what they said was an anger-management issue. After the first visit, the shrink said there was nothing wrong with my management abilities. But there was little he could do for the anger.

"A long one," I said, and hung up on him.

SOMETIMES COMPLEX woodcraft seems impossible, even when I do it myself. The margin of error is so small, often too small to see, so the work is accomplished through an alchemy of feel, experience, patience, and luck. For me, the beauty is not fully in the finished product, but also the process, which absorbs all my attention, tying up my raggedy brain, thus delivering a kind of solace from the endless nattering of anxiety and regret inside my head.

I was thus engaged when Detective Cermanski banged on the hatch that covered the outdoor stairwell into my shop.

Eddie, who was down there lying on his exhausted sheepskin bed, went nuts with excitement. So my first job was to quiet him before opening the hatch. Eddie's response to the intruder was to run up the stairs and greet him like a person long-lost and beloved. He followed Cermanski down the stairs.

"Hope you're okay with dogs," I said to him.

The detective squatted down and returned Eddie's unabashed attention with an experienced scrunching around the ears.

"I've got two of these critters," he said. "Probably smells them on me."

"One's more than enough, far as I'm concerned. Though I guess it depends on the dogs."

"Fox terriers," he said. "No sane person would have more than one at a time, but they keep each other company when I'm not home."

I pulled an old stool out from under a workbench and offered it to him. He sat down. I leaned against the table saw.

"I'm still liking Mazzotti," he said.

"Have you charged him?"

"Not yet, but I'm talking with the ADA."

"No motive," I said.

"You say that because you don't know Mazzotti as well as you think."

"What does that mean?"

"Assault and battery, ten years ago. Beat a guy to within an inch of his life. Got off somehow. He *does* have a temper, which is the first thing I asked you about, if you happen to remember."

"I remember. What was the beef?"

"A woman, surprise, surprise."

"Okay. So maybe justified. Doesn't convey to killing his rich customer."

"Crazy is as crazy does," he said.

"So why are you talking to me?"

"I don't know. Why not? You know the guy. Maybe you'll remember something that'll help."

"I know he's a skilled craftsman, that he's got five kids and a charming wife. That he's never screwed up any of my jobs, though he can make a mistake, which he always recovers from on his own nickel. That he always acts like a gracious and considerate person, even when dealing with assholes, which we have in good supply around here. Does that help?"

He got off the stool and started walking around the shop, picking up and studying tools and scraps of wood.

"This looks like pretty challenging work," he said.

"Not really, if you're patient and careful."

He looked up at me.

"Good money in it?"

"Enough."

"Pretty big comedown from Con Globe. Senior vice president? Isn't that what you were?"

"They had plenty of vice presidents. And I could argue with the comedown part."

"No one would believe it," he said. "Understand you cold cocked one of the other vice presidents. Got a temper yourself. Though you did tell me that, I admit."

"You want to take that stuff home?" I asked, nodding toward the hand plane and a soft maple cutoff he was holding. "Do a little arts and crafts?"

He put the stuff back on the nearest bench.

"I don't know which end of a screwdriver to use. And never cared to know," he said. "How well did you know Bollings? Any arguments?"

"I work for Frank. Any arguments over my work would go through him. I hardly spoke to the guy, though he did tell me he liked my built-ins."

Cermanski nodded, to show he heard me, not necessarily believing me.

"You have more than a few assault charges of your own," he said.

"No convictions," I said. "Important distinction."

"Your record might be inadmissible in court, but it tells me a lot about how you operate."

"This is the last time I'll say you're wasting your time," I said. "And now you're wasting mine. If there's nothing else, I'd like to get back to work."

He shrugged and started for the hatch door, then turned back around.

"The guy Mazzotti beat the crap out of. Did I tell you their relationship?" he asked.

I shook my head.

"He was Mazzotti's customer. And the woman at issue was the customer's wife."

Then he went back up the hatch and left me alone with my unfinished projects and ruined concentration.

CHAPTER FOUR

etective Cermanski had said I was friends with Ross Semple, the chief of Southampton Town Police. It was impossible to respond to that without committing to a long discourse that no one wanted to hear.

Ross had been known to charge me with various crimes, including murder, manipulate me into doing his job, defend me from criminals both inside and out of the judicial system, and correct my Latin, which had been getting harder to keep straight with all the Spanish flying around.

Suffice it to say the relationship was complicated.

That morning, I had a text message from Ross that said, "Come in." There was a time when I could just show my face at the HQ, but the operation had achieved new levels of sophistication, which meant a granite fortress had been installed to assure minimum contact between citizens and the people hired to protect them.

I called over there and was told by an automated voice to go to their website and fill out a request-for-appointment form. Unless it was connected to an active case, I should expect a minimum of two weeks before receiving a response.

I filled out the form and hit the submit button, but apparently I'd left one of the fields blank, which caused the program to wipe out all the previously filled-out little boxes, requiring me to start all over again.

I did this one more time, with the same result. So I got in my Jeep and drove over like I always did.

I was expecting to run headlong into a ferocious gatekeeper named Janet Orlovsky in the reception area who'd been nearly impossible to get past even before the advent of electronic border control. Instead, a pretty young woman with long, straight black hair was behind the bulletproof glass looking reasonably prepared to have an adult conversation.

"I need to see Ross Semple," I said.

She looked at her computer screen and asked if I'd submitted an online appointment request. I told her I was his half brother and that our Uncle Joe had just been in a serious accident.

She looked appropriately alarmed.

"Your name?"

A few moments later she buzzed me through the door.

"He said you know where to find his office," she said.

"I do. Thanks for your help."

I worked my way down the dull, though freshly maintained hallways, across the open squad room where the officers worked, goofed around, and annoyed each other, to Semple's enclosed office in the back.

He was waiting for me.

"Amusing," he said. "So how is old Uncle Joe?"

"Hanging by a thread. Not that you care."

He lit a cigarette and turned on a fan that blew the smoke out the window. Ross rarely went five minutes without a Winston. He knew I'd quit barely a year before, so it seemed a bit cruel.

"I take it you're unimpressed with our new appointment system," he said.

"What happened to Orlovsky?"

"She's back running the lockup," he said. "Wouldn't learn the new setup."

"She'll be happier. Might get a chance to bash a few heads."

"Speaking of which," he said.

"Has the DA charged Ernesto Mazzotti?"

"Oh, yeah. The club's got his prints all over it. The rest of the set was in his van. Half the crew saw him talking to Bollings toward the end of the day."

"Arguing?"

"Just talking. Not that I need to brief you on our investigation."

"You don't. Unless you want to mention motive."

"None yet," he said, though he seemed unconcerned. "We'll get there."

Ross was wearing a pair of khakis and a polo shirt that bulged around his waist, which surprised me since I'd never seen him out of a suit and tie, albeit something that looked pulled out of a bag. I noted that.

"This is business casual," he said.

"Sounds like an oxymoron."

"Take a seat."

I moved the two piles of paper he was storing on his visitor chair.

"Don't you think it's all a little too easy?" I asked. "Mazzotti's got a little fishing boat. Why not just drop the club in the bay?"

"Criminals aren't all stupid, but crime makes them do stupid things. I see it all the time."

"Before he installs my cabinets, Mazzotti makes a detailed list of every step in the process, with estimated time budgets. In handwriting that looks like it was typeset."

"Things happen in the heat of the moment."

"So you're not thinking premeditated."

"Didn't say that. In fact, I'm not saying anything else."

"So that's why you brought me over here? To not tell me anything?"

"You've met Detective Cermanski?"

I told him I had.

"Don't get in his way," he said.

"No intention to."

"I'm not joking, Sam. You really have to leave this one alone."

"I can't leave it alone. I work for Jackie Swaitkowski."

"Not this time. Article 195, section 7. Obstructing governmental administration in the first degree. Be the easiest case I ever made."

Recently Ross had actually encouraged me and Jackie to mess with an investigation. The reverse in course almost made me lose my balance.

"What is this crap?"

Ross twirled the lit cigarette between his fingers like a miniature baton. Years of undercover work and interrogations had made Ross's mind and mood state an impenetrable thing. Though it never hurt to take him at his word. Unless he was lying.

He put both elbows on his desk and pointed the cigarette at my face. And this time there was nothing inscrutable about his expression.

"I'll do it, Sam. I'll lock you up if you so much as whisper Mazzotti's name in your sleep. And I'll make Swaitkowski an accessory."

"Not so easy," I said.

"Try me."

"Fortis est veritas."

Very rough translation: the truth is a lot stronger than a line of bullshit.

"*Auctoritas non veritas facit legem,*" he said.

Truth is fine, but the cops have a bigger club.

WHEN I got back to the Jeep I checked my cell phone. I had a message from Jackie.

"Don't say anything to Ross Semple until you talk to me."

I called her.

"Too late," I said, when she answered the phone.

"What did he say?"

I took her through it.

"I got a version of the same talk," she said. "Something odd is going on."

"Something odd is always going on."

"Ross has been easier to deal with when the stakes were a lot higher," she said.

"He was wearing a polo shirt. Maybe an alternative reality has emerged and we didn't notice."

"I'm Ernesto's defense attorney, so he can't completely sit on my head. But you're just a citizen. Very different story."

"Hasn't stopped me before."

"You need to get your license," she said.

"What are you talking about?"

"A private investigator license. Get official."

My heart did a slow dive into the ground, and burrowed down from there.

"No. I'm a cabinetmaker. No fucking way."

"It's no cloak of invulnerability, but it'll help. I've read through the test requirements, and I think you can pass."

She started to go down a check list until I interrupted her.

"What is this about?"

"As a defense attorney, I'm entitled to have a staff investigator who can act as my proxy. It's a layer of protection against charges of obstruction. Ross suggested it. He said it was a very good idea. More than once."

"Why would he want to give us a good idea?" I asked.

"I don't know. It's part of the oddness equation."

"I'm not doing it. Ross Semple can kiss my ass."

"Okay. He'll have easy access once it's secured in county jail."

WHEN I'D finally got my workday going down in the shop I saw that Frank Entwhistle was trying to call my cell phone. I'd resisted mobile devices for as long as I could, and only gave my number out to people I actually wanted to talk to, Frank being near the top of the list. But still, what a pain in the ass. I answered.

"I have a command performance scheduled with Mrs. Bollings," he said. "You've been requested to attend."

"You're commanded and I'm a request? Where's the justice in that?"

"I think you'll want to be there. We have to finish this house no matter what, and you'll want to have some say in your part."

"When and where?"

"The Florentine. Private room in the back. Ever set up a meeting with a weeping woman?"

"I'll be there. I'll let you handle the weeping part."

"Feels good to have such a sensitive guy by my side," he said.

"Fuck, yeah."

ROSS'S THREATS to the contrary, they let me accompany Jackie into visit Ernesto Mazzotti at county lockup. On the way up there from Southampton, we compared notes on what we knew, which was a pure act of pooling ignorance. The only thing Jackie had added to the story was a better understanding of Ernesto's prior assault charge, which turned out to be a matter of confused identity.

"The guy thought Ernesto was boinking his wife," she said. "He threw the first punch, and since Ernesto is undocumented, the story quickly switched to the other way around. Until a few Anglos who'd witnessed the whole thing weighed in. They liked Ernesto a lot better than the guy. Turned out the wife had been sleeping with the guy's brother, who'd loaned them money for the house Ernesto was working on. We're not sure about all the transactional elements."

"We live in complicated times."

We were in Jackie's Volvo station wagon. I liked it when she drove, saving me from navigating the road with all that nervous energy emanating from the passenger's seat.

"However, Ernesto did truly beat the crap out of the guy," said Jackie.

"Have you seen his arms? Could easily throw this Volvo through the front door."

"We'll keep that out of the testimony."

Hours before, the day had opened with a twenty-knot wind out of the north that threw up bay waves big enough to hear bashing into the breakwater in front of my cottage. I was sleeping on the screened-in sunporch, which I usually did in the summer, fighting for space with Eddie on an old daybed. The sun, low on the eastern horizon, painted the churning bay gunmetal blue, and the sky was clear, as if stripped of clouds by the wrathful wind.

When Eddie and I went out on the front lawn where I usually had my first cup of coffee, we saw a late-model Chevy

Malibu parked at the end of the street on the western edge of the property. Since most of the people who accessed the beach from that street lived in the neighborhood, parked cars were something of a rarity. And I usually recognized the owners. So I strolled over there, drinking my coffee and tossing one of Eddie's mangled rubber balls for him to retrieve from the dune grass.

The Malibu was a shade of grey designated on the color palette as reliably nondescript. The license plate was US Government. Where I stood on the corner of the breakwater I could see a man at the edge of the bay tossing pebbles into the water. He wore a guayabera—a favored Latino shirt—black pants and black shoes, and a straw trilby hat.

Eddie jumped off the breakwater and ran over to say hello. The man seemed startled, but bent down to scratch the top of his head. Eddie let him do this for a moment, then ran back. The man saw me as he followed Eddie's retreat, but didn't react. He was too far away to accurately judge his age, but I guessed around forty.

"So a guy was tossing rocks in the bay," said Jackie. "What's the big deal?"

"Not a big deal. Just a little odd."

"Like you said. Everything's odd these days."

THE SUFFOLK County Correctional Facility was in Riverhead, the town at the crotch of the East End's twin forks. We'd been up there enough to know the greeters inside the front entrance by name, though few pleasantries were ever exchanged. Jackie let the cop at the metal detector do the work of rummaging through the random objects in the leather sack she used as a purse—enough to stock an average-sized hardware store.

"Did you leave anything at home?" he asked.

"Yeah, yeah, heard it all before."

They brought us to a windowless conference room where Ernesto was waiting in an orange jumpsuit. He usually managed to maintain a scruffy two-day beard, but that morning he was freshly shaved and his wild ball of black hair had been shorn close to the head.

"How are they treating you?" Jackie asked, pulling a legal pad out of the sack.

He said okay, no rough stuff.

"They got a lady to watch me at night so I don't try to kill myself. Why would I do that?"

"They don't want you dying on their watch," said Jackie.

"Don't even know how I'd do it. Run into the wall?"

"We need to go over everything you did that night from the time you left Bollings until you showed up at the job site," she said.

"I did that already," he said.

"Let's do it again."

He repeated that Bollings was helping him learn to play golf. Ernesto had renewed a childhood interest when he was working at the big course in Shinnecock Hills where Bollings was a member. He'd offered to take Ernesto out one day as his guest, but only after Ernesto got down a few basics. So Ernesto had been spending time at the driving range and on practice greens, and with his family at the miniature golf course. That afternoon he showed Bollings his progress, and the other man promised they'd take in a real eighteen holes the next weekend.

"He was a very good man, Victor," said Ernesto. "There is no reason on earth I would kill him. It's crazy."

"What did you do after that last conversation?" I asked.

"I went home. I had dinner. I watched TV. I went to bed. That's it."

"Did you see anyone other than your wife and kids?" Jackie asked.

"No. I was tired. I just wanted a quiet night."

I asked him if he locked his van. He said, no, it was in the garage. He said his dog, a miniature greyhound, barked late that night, but she often did, so he didn't think anything of it.

"Hampton Bays has always been very safe," he said. "I never have to worry."

"Not like back home, I guess," I said.

He nodded.

"My dogs back there were bigger and I listened when they try to tell me something."

"Where did you live?" asked Jackie.

He described his village in the hills above Medellín. It was a farming community, mostly quiet and comfortable, the savage drug wars raging below rarely intruding on their day-to-day lives.

"And when it did?" I asked.

Ernesto wasn't enjoying this line of questioning.

"It's much better now," he said. "Don't believe all that Hollywood stuff."

"Answer him, please," said Jackie, gently delivered.

"Anything could happen. Gunfight in the middle of town. Headless bodies showing up on a family's doorstep. Also, an unexpected gift to the church. Enough to get all new pews. I remember that, since I install them. But all this was infrequent. The really bad things happened in other places."

Jackie bit her lower lip and started clicking her ballpoint pen. I knew what that meant.

"These bad things, Ernesto," she said, "did they ever involve you?"

His eyes, always bigger than his face, opened wide enough to leave the pupils exposed, black disks in a tiny sea of white.

"No, Miss Swee-kowski, I never go near those people. Once you do, you don't get to leave again. It's lifetime employment, whether you like it or not."

"You can call me Jackie. The cops are going to check that story with the *Fuerzas Especiales*, you know that."

That caused a radiant smile.

"That's good. They won't find anything. Unless those bastards lie, in which case, *Dios me salve*."

We talked more about his life in Colombia, then Jackie asked about the angry husband. Ernesto smiled.

"That *guebon*. The only guy in the crew who didn't know his wife was doing the cha-cha with his brother while he was out pounding nails."

"He spent a bit of time in the hospital," I said. "I checked the police report. Said he had three broken ribs and internal bleeding. Lost his spleen. But no damage to his face."

Ernesto looked down at my hands, as if suddenly remembering that I once put them to good use as a professional boxer.

"He was taller than me. I couldn't reach that high," he said, smiling a little, knowing that made little sense.

I mentioned that the guy had swung first.

"Did he connect?" I asked.

Ernesto shook his head.

"I always felt it's better not to get hit if you can avoid it."

"Interesting. What was the punch like? Some cowboy roundhouse?"

"I don't remember. Probably something like that."

"Or was it a jab, like this," I said, standing up and shooting a right directly at his face.

You'd know he successfully blocked the punch if your vision was fast enough to see his left hand come off the table, swat away my arm, then drop back to where it was.

I sat down and waited for the cop outside the door to come in and ask if everything was all right.

"We're fine, officer," said Jackie. "Just doing a little demonstration."

He didn't seem to believe her, but left anyway. I just sat there wondering if Ernesto had fractured anything in my right forearm. Ernesto might have been wondering the same thing.

"You okay, Sam? Sorry. You startle me."

No, I didn't, I thought to myself, but I apologized back.

"I should have warned you."

"Well," said Jackie, after a little quiet settled in the room. "Is there anything else you want to share with us today? I know we're just getting started, but the more you can tell us the better."

Ernesto looked down at the table and shook his head.

"I will think hard about it, I promise."

"What the hell was that about?" said Jackie when we got to her car.

"The difference between a big, strong guy and a trained fighter is the difference between darkness and light. Ernesto is big, strong, and trained."

It was hot in the Volvo, even after Jackie got the motor and air-conditioning going.

"What does that tell you?"

"He hasn't been entirely forthcoming."

"I hate clients who do that."

"Especially when you like them."

"Especially."

CHAPTER FIVE

I always had a hard time calling Eddie my dog, since that implied I owned him, and that was simply not true. We lived in the same house, in a congenial arrangement where I fed him and gave him a place to sleep, while he hung around when I was there, suffering nothing more than the occasional need to retrieve golf balls I hit off the breakwater at the edge of the property.

Unlike other dogs I'd known, he often looked me directly in the eye, as if assessing my reliability in continuing the relationship, understandable since he'd spent his formative years as a feral animal, as had I.

He often seemed to show greater delight in the company of my human friends and family members, though I attributed that more to novelty than unfaithfulness. Though occasionally, he'd surprise me by jumping up on the daybed where I was reading out on my sunporch, shoving his body hard against my thigh and letting loose a deep sigh, as if this was a contentment more profound than joy.

We were spending one of those evenings when my cell phone rang. I was disappointed that I hadn't turned the thing off, but now committed, I answered.

The caller asked if she could speak to Mr. Sam Acquillo.

"That's what you're doing."

She told me she was a reporter with the *New York Times* and asked if I would answer a few questions. I said that depended on the questions.

"How long have you known Victor Bollings?"

"I didn't know Bollings. We just talked about custom built-in cabinets. That started about six months ago. Why?"

"So you never discussed his career as a management consultant?"

"You didn't answer my question," I said.

"I'm looking into the Bollings murder case."

"Then you're talking to the wrong guy. I'm just a cabinet-maker."

"Not according to your history, if you believe Google."

"If you want to talk about the case from an official perspective, call Jackie Swaitkowski. She's representing Ernesto Mazzotti."

"What's your opinion of the prosecutor's case?" she asked.

"I told you to talk to Jackie. What's your name again?"

"I'm with the *Times*."

"Listen," I said, "I'm not talking about Victor Bollings on the phone. I'd rather meet in person."

"Not necessary. I'll check in with Ms. Swaitkowski," she said, and hung up.

I went into the kitchen to refresh my vodka. I definitely wanted another drink, but also a chance to let the call process in my head. I didn't need that much time.

Jackie answered her phone on the first ring.

"Did you get a call from someone claiming to be with the *New York Times*?" I asked her.

I described the call.

"Never happens," she said. "Reporters always identify themselves, and prefer face-to-face, if logistics allow."

"I figured."

"What the hell?"

"What do we know about Victor Bollings?" I asked.

"He worked for O'Connor Consulting, specializing in offshore companies selling into the US. Yale, Harvard MBA, widely published in business magazines, sought-after speaker, almost famous. It's all there online."

"Then why would a *Times* reporter bother asking me?"

"Because she wanted to know what *you* know," she said.

"Like I'd know more than Google?"

"Like I said, what the hell."

THE NEXT day I met with Frank Entwhistle and Rebecca Bollings. We were in a private alcove at the back of an ancient restaurant on Main Street in Southampton. The place was started by a guy named Arlen Rothstein from Brooklyn who'd lived in Paris in the twenties and never got over it. His grandson was the current owner, and like his father before him, had preserved the tables and chairs, appointments, and artwork in the precise state they were in on the day the old man died.

The smell of Gauloises still hung in the air.

Frank and Rebecca were already there, drinking double espressos and ignoring a basket of *petit pain* in the middle of the table. We shook hands.

"I'm very sorry for your loss, Mrs. Bollings," I told her. "A lousy deal."

"Lousy indeed," she said, raking her hand through a head of short, naturally highlighted brunette hair. "Thank you."

She had the kind of delicate hands you'd think might break under a heavy load. Probably twenty years younger than her late husband, you still wouldn't call her a trophy wife. More like a seduced grad student. Small features and skin like

Amanda's, quick to tan. Qualities complemented by her prox-imity to beefy Frank Entwhistle, whose skin was the texture of poorly tanned rawhide, and hands permanently stained by eternal manual labor.

Frank described my part in building the house, throwing in a few examples of other collaborations.

We made some more small talk until Frank said, "Mrs. Bollings is strategizing over what to do with the house."

"Rebecca is fine," she said. "It's really not fair to drag you people through my deliberations. I simply need to know pluses and minuses. From a practical point of view."

"I'd finish the place as planned," I said. "Victor did a good job with the project. If you keep it, you'll have a good house. If you sell it, same thing."

"That would include your part?" she asked me.

"That's up to Frank," I said. "There're plenty of good cabi-netmakers out here. And a bunch of hacks. I think you'll be better off doing it right, but that's your call."

"So doing it wrong might be one of my options?"

What Mrs. Bollings didn't know was I'd been married once, to a woman who'd win an international competition in twisted logic and innuendo. Who could lay bear traps so intricately designed the bear wouldn't know he was a goner until the hunter showed up with his gun.

"I wouldn't call it wrong. Most people don't know the dif-ference between good and bad construction. You could cut a lot of corners and still get a decent price. So that might be the right financial decision. I'm just saying you have a chance to do even better by following through on Victor's intentions."

This really was a subject Frank should have been address-ing, but I knew him, and knew he wanted me there to navigate the situation. He was a strong, brave, and honest man, but client interactions unsettled him. It was the least I could do, given all he'd done for me over the years.

"Good answer," said Rebecca.

"I didn't know it was a test," I said.

"No one ever does," she said.

"So," said Frank, as if waking from a daydream, "let's take a look at the plans and scope of work, what say?"

He rolled out a set of architectural drawings, using tableware to hold down the corners. He also laid out several typed spec sheets.

"Here's what's needed to finish the job."

Rebecca looked up from the plans, and wrecking Frank's hopes for a change of mood, asked me, "Do you know the man accused of killing Victor?"

"I do. He's a friend of mine."

She didn't seem to react, beyond studying my face.

"You think he did it?" she asked.

Frank wriggled in his chair, rocking the table.

"No," I said, "but anything is possible. I know the cops on the case will work it hard. And fair. My friend Jackie Swaitkowski is defending him. She'll do the same."

"Rather an optimistic view," she said.

"Like I said, I know the people involved. Optimism's got nothing to do with it."

"You know the people involved," said Rebecca. "Really."

Frank rapped his knuckles on the plans laid out before us.

"Sorry to be a pain," he said, "but I promised my wife we'd go shopping Up Island, and God knows, she is not to be denied. With all due respect, Rebecca."

"Of course," she said, using both hands to push the plans toward Entwhistle. "Do what you want. Whatever Victor wanted. I couldn't care."

Then she stood up, and after apologizing, said she had commitments of her own to attend to. She handed me a business card on which was printed her name, e-mail, and phone number. Nothing else.

"I know you work for Frank," she said, "but I don't think he'll mind if we speak directly going forward."

Frank agreed heartily, and she left. When she was safely out the door, Frank let out a breath strong enough to fill a main sail.

"That was fun," he said.

"This wasn't about home construction."

"What do you mean," he asked.

"She wanted to talk to me. Make a contact."

"I don't get it."

"Me neither. But for now, you got what you needed. Finish the job, get paid, move on with our lives."

Frank rolled up the plans and stacked up the spec sheets.

"Thanks for doing this," he said. "I admit Rebecca gives me the creeps."

"You don't happen to know what she does for a living?"

He shook his head.

"Not sure, really. Bollings told me she was a numbers cruncher. Said she was the brains of the family."

"Those would be some pretty big brains," I said.

When I worked for Con Globe, O'Connor Consulting, Bollings's employer, was a constant presence. It was the heyday of continuous improvement and corporate reinvention. My part was to ward off attempts to reinvent my R&D division by consultants like O'Connor, who were brought in by people in upper management who knew nothing about R&D. I didn't blame the consultants, who on the whole were as brilliant and driven as their reputations suggested. They even came up with some pretty good ideas, mostly cribbed from other clients, but good nevertheless. These I implemented with enthusiasm and dramatic effect, hoping the corporate intruders would be satisfied enough to leave us alone.

Thus I avoided reinvention, which was helpful for a group of people dedicated to actual invention, making golden eggs for a corporation that often had the goose by the neck.

SINCE I was already in the village, I took the opportunity to visit a Southampton Town detective who I knew had the day off. His name was Joe Sullivan, and I'd known him since his days as a beat patrolman up in North Sea where I lived. I was sorry he hadn't drawn the Bollings case, since he was a friend of mine, and more importantly, very good at what he did.

I found him sitting in a rusty beach chair in front of his garage apartment behind an old house that had escaped modern zoning. Blond hair, blue eyes, and skin to match, he wasn't usually one for sunbathing. I noted as much.

"I was actually headed for the beach, but after testing the beer for temp and freshness, this is as far as I got." He used the neck of the bottle in his hand to point at the cooler. "See for yourself."

I dug out a beer and parked myself in another beach chair.

"I hope you put on sunblock," I said.

"Oh, yeah. Though I don't tan. I just freckle."

Sitting there in his bathing suit, I could see he'd lost much of the extra weight put on after his divorce. Never a lightweight guy, he carried his bulk mostly in his chest and across the shoulders. The better definition looked good on him.

"Not a problem for me," I said. "I'm only about a quarter Italian, but it all went into my complexion. Prompting some racially charged assertions by a few boxing opponents."

"To which you responded?"

"By thanking them for the compliment and breaking a few extra noses."

"So boxers don't just get stupid after they leave the ring."

We devoted the next few minutes to quiet beer consumption and appreciation of the early summer's day, featuring a cool easterly, which in July usually turned predominantly toward the south. Spring had involved an orderly distribution of sun and rain, so the normally fecund landscape along the ocean had gone hysterically floriferous. Even Sullivan's neglected azaleas looked like giant, overflowing snow cones.

"How's it going with Cermanski?" asked Sullivan, breaking the silence.

"Young and cocky," I said. "Though that might be the same thing."

"I'm guessing you think Mazzotti's innocent."

"I don't know what I think. Murder doesn't fit with the guy I know, but how well do I really know him? Medellín makes for an interesting hometown."

I told him about the way Ernesto blocked my right jab.

"Lucky?" he asked.

"What do you think?"

"Not lucky. I've seen your right jab."

Assuming he was mostly out of the loop, I briefed him on the particulars of the case. Including the fake *Times* reporter and sideways meeting with Mrs. Bollings.

"Something's fishy," he said.

"That's the kind of incisive reasoning that makes you the detective you are."

"Even on my day off."

We switched to preliminary assessment of the Yankees' prospects—a frothy brew of irrepressible hope and thwarted expectations. Though we had to admit, the highs had exceeded the lows over the years, and for the thousandth time thanked the Lord we hadn't been born in Boston or Philadelphia.

"Or God forbid, Chicago," said Sullivan.

I was about to take off before another beer completely ruined the day's productivity, when he said, "I'd focus on the old lady."

"Old lady?"

"Mrs. Bollings."

"She's in her early forties, max," I said.

"Whatever. If you start with the assumption that Mazzotti's not guilty, the only solution is to discover who is. I always start with the wife. She lived with the guy. Loved him or hated him, either way, she knows things. I'd try to get close. Make a friend. Nibble on her ear."

"She's a numbers freak. Maybe I could whisper sweet algorithms."

He tossed his empty bottle over his shoulder, and without looking, dug a new one out of the cooler.

"Whatever it takes, MIT-boy."

WHEN I got back to Oak Point, Eddie was waiting on the lawn, barking. This was unsettling, since he rarely barked, and never as a substitute for the ritual climbing-in-the-car greeting.

I popped the hatch of the Jeep and retrieved my pint-sized Harmon Killebrew kids' bat, an aged piece of polished ash proven equally effective at smacking golf balls and hardened skulls.

Eddie ran toward the house, then stopped and turned back toward me. He repeated the maneuver until we were around the front of the house heading toward the Adirondack chairs that sat above the breakwater. By then I could see someone sitting in one of the chairs. I couldn't see his face, but I recognized the hat. I whistled to Eddie to come back to me, which he did, somewhat to my surprise. I stuck the bat in my rear waistband and picked him up, carrying the forty-pound ball of fur the rest of the way to the chairs.

"Man, what a view," said the guy in the trilby hat and guayabera that I'd seen tossing pebbles in the bay. "What's it cost to have a place like this?"

"In the fifties, about $3,000 all in. It's a little more nowadays."

"Hope you don't mind me sitting here," he said, his speech touched by a soft Latin American accent. Too soft for me to place.

"I do mind. It's private property. I've got a front door you're welcome to knock on. And then welcome to leave when I'm not home."

"Understandable," he said. "You let anyone sit here and before you know it, your lawn is crawling with people in bathing suits."

"So what can I help you with before you go."

"I just want a conversation. And maybe a little water?"

"Conversations are sacred out here on Oak Point. It better be a good one."

He looked up at me and cocked the trilby toward the back of his head.

"I think it will be."

"And the only water served out here is frozen."

"That's okay too."

I made Eddie follow me back to the cottage where I sent a text to Amanda asking her to stay away until I gave her the high sign, and one to Jackie telling her to get there as quickly as possible—and bring the Glock. Then I mixed up a tumbler of vodka and ice, and brought it back to the bayside with a pair of cocktail glasses.

The guy was deep in the Adirondack chair with his eyes closed.

"So I guess it's okay to drink on duty," I said, handing him a glass. He opened his eyes and let me fill the glass.

"They encourage it."

Despite his bravado, the jolt of straight Absolut seemed a bit startling. He shook his head like a wet terrier.

"*Dios mio*," he said.

"I wouldn't be invoking Him. He might not approve."

"*¿Español?*"

"Not enough to be sure what I'm saying. I might call you an asshole or something, and then what."

"I'd have to hit you on the head with that little club tucked in your pants."

"Probably not," I said.

He nodded.

"Probably not, if you believe what the Internet says about you."

This was the third time in so many days that someone had referred to my Google history. It was more than annoying, especially for a person who so loathed public display I'd considered boxing professionally under an assumed name. But having been tangled up in a few criminal cases, some with a lot of press coverage, the unwanted exposure was inevitable. Much of it, maybe most of it, was a distortion of the truth, favorable and unfavorable, which made it worse.

Living in a world where your life is an open book would be better if it weren't so full of typos.

I took a long sip of the vodka, and as the cool salve washed over my nerves, I asked him, "What's the federal government's interest in Ernesto Mazzotti?"

He took another sip of his own before answering.

"Who's Ernesto Mazzotti?"

"Right. So who are you?"

"Just a guy," he said.

"So what's this conversation we're supposed to be having?"

"It's about Ernesto Mazzotti."

"Okay. Word games. Love those things. Where in Puerto Rico did you come from?" I asked, making a guess.

"Fajardo. Just a little town, but on a clear day you can see all the way to Saint Thomas. And sail there in a day."

"I know. I've made the trip."

Eddie ran up to us and dropped a tennis ball in the guy's lap. The guy seemed undeterred by the slobber that came along with the ball. A point in his favor.

"So, *perrito*, what am I supposed to do with this?"

"I suggest the dune grass across the street, if you can heave it that far," I told him. "Otherwise, you'll be at it again in a few minutes."

The throw was more than adequate for the purpose. Actually, he threw it like a first-round draft pick. Eddie took off like a shot.

"You have a name?" I asked.

"Mauricio. My mother was a big fan of Maurice Chevalier. Close as she could get."

"So what about Ernesto?"

"You ever hear of behavioral analysis?"

"Not exactly. But I can probably figure out what it is."

"I know that, because I'm a behavioral analyst, and I've studied you."

"There's a waste of time."

"Not if your boss tells you to do it. And you like your job."

Eddie showed up with the ball, a remarkably brisk turn-around, even for him. Mauricio gave it another go, this time standing to give full force to the throw. It looked like the ball was headed for Nassau County.

"Who do you work for?" I asked him. "Major League Baseball?"

"An unspecified government agency," he said. "You pick."

"Does the DOT have behavioral analysts?"

"In the hundreds."

I took the balance of vodka remaining in the tumbler and offered Mauricio the rest. He gamely accepted.

"What did your analysis say about stringing me along?" I asked.

"Not a good tactic."

"Then tell me what the fuck is going on."

"I told my boss that the worst way to persuade you to back off from a case was to tell you to back off. Reverse psychology 101. It's why I tell my son he shouldn't eat his broccoli."

I'd had more significant conversations than this while sitting at the edge of the breakwater looking out on the Little Peconic Bay. And never failed to be lured away by the manifold distractions, especially during the warm months: flying white egrets, tacking sailboats, cloud shadows darkening large swaths of the iridescent water. Mauricio seemed to be succumbing to the same things.

"But you're here anyway," I said.

"Did I mention I have a boss?"

"You told him the worst way, what about the best?"

"Not him, her. I told her persuasion was out of the question. That with some people, the only option is raw force."

I saw Eddie burst out from the dune grass and run across the lawn. He stopped well short of the Adirondack chairs and laid down with the captured tennis ball between his paws. Then he put his mouth close to the ball, breathing hard and ready to snatch it up and flee should anyone attempt to renew the game.

"That sounded remarkably like a threat."

"Did it? I define a threat as a hypothetical, meant to persuade. We already established that this won't work. What I'm describing is an action. A certainty."

Eddie jumped up and started to run toward the house. Then he paused and ran back, retrieving the ball to bring along with him. I turned around and saw Jackie striding across the grass. She wore a light jacket over her khakis, bulky enough to conceal the holster on her hip. She paused to scratch Eddie's head before closing the rest of the distance.

"Hi, Sam," she said. "Who's your friend?"

Mauricio stood up and offered his hand.

"Special Agent Mauricio Something," I said. "Behavioral analyst with the FBI. This is Jackie Swaitkowski, Ernesto Mazzotti's defense attorney."

"He meant to say unspecified government agency," said Mauricio, taking Jackie's hand.

"He's here to intimidate me," I said. "And so, I guess by association, intimidate you."

"Really," said Jackie.

Mauricio gave a sad little smile.

"Not how I'd represent it," he said.

He stood next to my chair in a way that gave me room to stand up behind him. I put my right foot across his ankles and grabbed a handful of the guayabera, pushing forward with enough force to flip him off his feet, smashing his face into the grass. I stuck my knee along his spine and gripped the back of his neck, twisting his head around so he could see Jackie with her Glock pointed at his face. I felt for a wallet, which wasn't there, then around his waist where I found a small pistol under the shirt. I slid it toward Jackie, who picked it up while I felt around his shins, coming up with another, similar gun.

When satisfied that was it, I stood up and let him gather his senses.

"That was not necessary," he said, still prostrate.

"Oh, yes, it was," I said. "You come on my property uninvited, unidentified, armed, and threatening. You're lucky it wasn't worse."

"I was trying to do you a favor."

"You were trying to fuck with my head. Not possible. Already sufficiently fucked up. Go back to your desk job and tell the boss your analysis needs a little work."

I gave him a little kick in the ribs.

"Sam, don't," said Jackie.

"Get lost," I told him.

He stood up and tried to straighten his clothes. I saw a wince or two cross his face as he scooped up his hat and tucked in his shirt. Then he did a little bow to both of us.

"I understand completely. I do," he said. "I predicted something like this, believe it or not. I am sorry I did such a poor job establishing a relationship. But I really did want to help you." He looked out at the darkening sky above the bay. "Black clouds are coming."

As he walked across the yard, we saw him reach into his breast pocket and toss a card on the lawn. Neither of us lowered our weapons until he'd walked down the driveway and passed out of view.

Jackie put her automatic in its holster in the small of her back.

I retrieved the card, blank but for a phone number. I handed it to Jackie, who said, "This is not good."

I held up my hands, both of which held a little .38-caliber revolver.

"What makes you say that?"

"Do you think he's a behavioral analyst for the FBI named Mauricio Something?" she asked.

"I don't know. He's the guy I told you about on our way to visit Ernesto."

"You said he had a government license plate. Did you write down the number?"

I tapped my head. "It's up here."

"Let's make a few calls," she said, sitting in an Adirondack.

I ONLY heard her half of the phone conversation, but it was easy to get the drift. Lots of chummy catching up, thank yous for prior favors—given and received—some reminiscing, and little else. None of Jackie's friends at the bureau had ever heard of a profiler named Mauricio, though acknowledging it was a big place. They thought it unlikely that a behavioral analyst would do field work without a regular agent along, and impossible any would threaten physical force. One of her contacts promised to check the plates, though we'd have to wait for the result.

She also called a reporter at the *New York Times* who'd written about one of her cases. He confirmed that the so-called *Times* reporter who called me had to be a phony. Her part was to confirm she was still seeing her boyfriend, Harry Good-lander, though the offer of dinner and a Broadway show was tempting. She agreed to stay in touch.

"Tempting?"

"Never quell the interest entirely. Key to good press relations."

By this time, the wine and a refresher tumbler of vodka had undermined further ambition, so I called Amanda and told her the coast was clear, and she came over with her own provisions and joined in the appreciation of the garish gold and magenta sunset. She waited until it was dark to ask why I'd warned her away. So we filled her in.

"I could have told the gentleman that persuasion of any kind with Sam was a fruitless enterprise," said Amanda.

"Not true. I'm often persuaded by your fromage d'Affinois and crudités," I said, scooping up a wad of cheese with a celery stick.

"Do you have a theory on what's going on?" Amanda asked.

"No," said Jackie. "Only that forces unknown really want us to stay in our lane. What's perplexing is we probably would have if not for all the warnings."

"They don't know you very well."

"Ross knows us fine," said Jackie.

"Should I be worried?" said Amanda. "I do like Joe Sullivan, but I'd rather not have him move in with me again."

She'd suffered that imposition more than once, so I couldn't blame her. I'm not suicidal, but I care a lot less about my own safety than the people I love. Amanda would say I overreact, but after a lot of dangerous times, she was still sitting there next to me, sipping wine and feeding me fromage d'Affinois.

"Let's see how things play out," I said. "Could be the greatest threat is forced psychoanalysis by a rogue government agent."

"That's not nothing," said Amanda. "I prefer my issues unresolved."

We managed to stay clear of disturbing commentary until Jackie left for Harry's converted gas station apartment and Amanda, Eddie, and I went over to her house, where she had a military-grade security system, shotgun, a brace of Colt .45 semiautomatics, and a purse-scale can of mace. I brought along my Harmon Killebrew three-quarter-sized slugger, just in case.

CHAPTER SIX

It's often the things I dread the most that turn out just fine. Even highly engaging. Such was the course work required for my private investigator's license. Building things in my basement challenged hand skills and brains alike, but I missed the rigor of academic texts and rote memorization.

Jackie had to declare I'd been her assistant in investigations for at least three years. She hadn't paid me, since it was usually hard to tell who was working for whom, but she knew a guy at the governing commission who gave us dispensation.

The test room at the government building in Hauppauge was nearly full. The other participants included several worried-looking guys with T-shirts stretched over their guts. A few others seemed serious and more than qualified. I figured ex-cops and/or military. There were several women, at least one was attractive—a redhead carrying a woven purse with the capacity of a medium-sized duffel bag. Her posture was erect and clothing diaphanous. She chewed her nails as she pondered the questions.

The test giver was crisp and officious, also a meaty guy, with hands that seemed too big to hold the sheets of paper from which he read. He delivered our instructions in vivid and no uncertain terms. He also made a little joke, which I missed, distracted by the redhead who was distracted by a smudge on the sleeve of her delicate cotton top.

I noticed the hum of the air conditioner and the acceleration of a noisy truck somewhere on a distant highway. One of the test takers was still filling out the application form, squeezing the pencil in his fist. He made nearly imperceptible grunting sounds. The professional-looking types tried to hide their disdain.

The experience returned me to the classrooms of my youth, where I was relentlessly proficient, occasionally defiant, and usually bored. My teachers and professors often resented me for this, though a few had the good humor to just let me pass through with nothing more than advice on my general attitude.

I had a good memory for facts. Didn't make me any smarter than the next guy. I had friends at MIT who barely remembered their own names who would stagger me with their analytical skills and mental acuity. Everyone comes with their own wiring.

I was glad to see the PI questions correlated with the test preparation material, which wasn't always the case, leading to a 95 percent score on the exam. For some reason, this annoyed Jackie.

"Nobody can learn all that stuff that quickly," she said.

"Already forgotten it."

"How does it feel to be an official PI?"

"Now that I've learned all that stuff about detective work, I have an uncontrollable urge to investigate something."

"Good. We have Victor and Rebecca Bollings, Ernesto, and the mystery people from the FBI and *New York Times*. Since you speak Spanish, you take Ernesto. For now."

"Roger that, chief."

"Such a pain in the ass."

"Roger that too."

I ACTUALLY didn't start with Ernesto. On my way to his house in Hampton Bays I stopped off to visit Southampton Town Chief of Police Ross Semple. I didn't use the online appointment protocol. Instead I told the pleasant woman at the reception desk my name and that I was there to turn myself in for a dastardly crime, though only if Joe Sullivan or Ross Semple were available. Otherwise I'd leave and carry on with my fugitive life.

"I'll see if either of them are in," she said, with poised efficiency.

Sullivan showed up a few minutes later.

"Do I need cuffs, or will you come along peacefully?" he asked.

"Peaceful sounds fine. Does it include coffee?"

"Our lattes are the talk of the town," said Sullivan, dropping me off at Semple's office.

It turned out the chief was there, which wasn't surprising. In fact, I'd never seen him anywhere else. He'd spent the early part of his career working homicide in New York City, much of the time undercover hanging out with the most evil and ferocious people on earth. Maybe that gave him a hankering for the sanctuary of cluttered, fluorescent-lit office space.

"This is why we instituted the online appointment program," said Ross, waving me into a conference room. "I might have been busy with important department business."

"Yeah, well, kick me out if you want. You're not the only police chief on my dance card."

I got that cup of coffee, as promised, though it wouldn't have passed muster with coffee aficionados. Unless they were looking for a universal solvent.

"To what do I owe the pleasure, if you can call it that," he said.

"I passed the PI exam. I'm official."

He was leaning back in his chair with one hand on the table. On hearing the news, he started to tap his fingers in a convincing jazz rhythm.

"Congratulations. I'd be opening champagne if it weren't against department rules. What brought this about?"

"Our last conversation. Jackie thought I needed some protection from aggressive enforcement of obstruction law. She said you gave her the idea."

"It won't help that much. You still can't get in our way."

"Won't happen. Cooperation is the soul and substance of our operating philosophy," I told him.

"Hmm."

"Though in my new official capacity, I do have a question."

"Fire away."

"What the fuck is going on?"

He brought the two front legs of the chair back to the ground. He stared at me across the desk and restarted the drum roll with his fingers. Catching himself doing this, he reached in his shirt pocket and took out a rumpled pack of Winston cigarettes.

"This is very frustrating," he said. "I have a problem for which there is no solution. So I'm going to do what my alcoholic father would do when confronted with unsolvable situations. Nothing. You're on your own." He lit the cigarette and managed to lean himself back on two legs of the chair. "This is the last time we're going to have this conversation. At least here on earth. We can take it up again when the two of us reach hell."

He continued to stare at me through the veil of cigarette smoke, so I got the message and stood up to leave. I nearly made it out the door before my lesser nature grabbed hold, and forced me to turn around.

"As to that trip to hell," I said, "you first."

ERNESTO'S HOUSE in Hampton Bays was crammed in among others of similar size, mostly well-kept, owned or rented by Latino and Anglo working people, as demonstrated by all the pickups and box vans filling the street and pulled into drive-ways and up on lawns. His wife, Querida, worked most days in an office supply store running copiers and scanners, and taking on occasional administrative work for lone wolf professionals. I knew she was home that day, because I'd called ahead and asked if she could see me.

They had a herd of kids, all boys, the evidence of which littered the front yard. I picked my way over baseball bats, soccer balls, pedal cars, and something that looked like a deflated parachute, and rang the doorbell, which ignited the little greyhound.

Querida's pretty face was taut, but she forced a smile as she pushed the dog out of the way and waved me into the house. Inside it was fresh and orderly, with no sign of the rambunc-tious boys. I asked about them and she said they were all at a day camp up in the pine barrens, under the care of their eldest who worked there as a counselor.

"I don't want them hearing any of this," she said.

"It must be tough on all of you," I said. "I'm sorry."

"It is. Thank you."

She walked us out to a tiny sunporch. We sat at a wrought iron table surrounded by overflowing potted plants and balls of fragrant red and yellow flowers.

"I'm sure Jackie's told you you're protected by spousal immunity and don't have to even talk to the cops if you don't want to."

"She did. And I haven't, though they tried. A young guy came around. Showed me his ID. He was polite and respectful. But I still didn't talk to him."

"Detective Cermanski."

"That was him. The only thing I could tell him anyway was that Ernesto was with me all night. We hardly ever go out, with all these nutty *muchachos* to look after. I don't mind. I'm a homebody. I think Ernesto gets a little tired of the TV. He's got a lot of energy."

Having worked alongside him for a few years, I knew that. I asked her about his interest in golf.

"He had an uncle in Colombia who was like a professional golfer. He died before Ernesto was old enough to learn to play. I think that has something to do with it. But he always liked sports. Plays *fútbol* with the kids."

She looked out the floor-to-ceiling screens as if she could see them out there playing in the backyard. A fair amount younger than Ernesto, she still had a trim figure despite their active family-making. She leaned slightly forward in her chair, clenching strong hands in her lap.

"Did he talk much about Victor Bollings?" I asked.

She shook her head.

"Just that he was a good customer. That he lent us golf clubs so Ernesto could learn. How many customers do you think would do that?"

"Not many."

"This is all so ridiculous. Ernesto's a gentle man. Afraid to hurt a fly."

I told her I'd heard about the altercation with the cuckolded husband, emphasizing the positive outcome for Ernesto.

"He's gentle, but doesn't like to get pushed around," she said. "Who does?"

I tried to steer the conversation toward their lives in Colombia, but she pivoted every question smoothly back to the present time. So I finally said, "What made you decide to come to the US?"

She looked at me as if not understanding the question. Then she put out her hands, presenting their comfortable little home.

"To make a living? To give the kids a better chance? To keep them away from all the trouble in Colombia? This is not a hard decision to make. I have my green card, you know. I came here first and got myself and our first born settled. Ernesto visited and never left."

"But still undocumented," I said.

She looked out through the screens again, this time searching for the right thing to say.

"He said it would be harder for him. He didn't tell me why. It annoyed him when I asked, so I didn't ask. He's a good man, but there're some things he won't talk about."

"Like what?" She looked unwilling to answer that. "Nothing you tell me or Jackie is going anywhere you don't want it to go. You know how serious the situation is."

She nodded, looking down at her hands, which she rested on her thighs, as if suddenly realizing how tightly they'd been gripped together.

"We met when I was working at a ceviche bar in Cartagena. He was building furniture for a designer who sold custom things to the rich people. I've never been to Medellín. He never took me there. It's one thing he never liked to talk about, except to tell me how beautiful his village was above the city. He said we'd go there sometime, but when we had our first boy, he said we need to go to America."

"Had something bad happened?"

"Not at all. You know how he is when he's excited about something. Big joy, lots of plans, it's fun to be around. He wanted our son to grow up learning English. We both learn in school, but it's not the same as being here. It's so much easier, believe me."

"Was that what he did in Medellín, furniture making?"

A cell phone went off somewhere back in the house. Relief crossed her face and she left, bringing back the phone, stuck to her ear. She pointed at the phone and whispered, "*Mi hijo.*"

She told her son in Spanish to stop for groceries on the way home. She gave him a list and told him to go to the big store up in Riverhead. He seemed to be telling her how everything was going at the camp. She smiled and nodded, sharing in the amusement. She thanked him and told him she loved him before hanging up.

"So you're teaching them Spanish," I said.

"Of course. You really need it living here," she said, not missing the irony.

We talked a little more, mostly about her children and her work at the office supply place. She said she was getting more administrative type work and was considering going off on her own so she wouldn't have to share a cut of her take with the store owner.

"I was always good with computers, but I'd feel bad. The people at the store helped me get the green card. They've been good to me."

"They're lucky to have you."

We walked back through the house toward the front door.

"Not everybody thinks like that," she said.

"What do you mean?"

"There are plenty of people who don't want us here. I can tell by the way some look at us. We tell the kids to speak English when we're out in the world. They have no accent, so Ernesto and I let them do most of the talking. Who do these people think are going to build the houses out here? Take care of them? If you're an Anglo and you can work construction," she snapped her fingers, "you got the job. But none of them want to dig in the dirt or carry two-by-fours. Who's going to do that if they chase us all away?"

She took a deep breath and stopped herself.

"I'm sorry. I shouldn't talk like that."

"You can talk any way you want as far as I'm concerned," I said. "The guys I work with don't put up with that racist crap. But, yeah, we got our share of jerks out here."

"Regular jerks I don't worry about," she said, despite herself. "It's the other ones." She could probably tell from my face that I didn't know what she meant. "You wouldn't know, but some people don't just want us gone."

I still didn't know what she meant, so she said, "They want us dead."

JACKIE SWAITKOWSKI's free defense to the poor and defenseless on the East End of Long Island was the result of a billionaire named Burton Lewis. He had a house along the coast of Southampton originally built by his grandfather, where I'd spent a fair amount of time, since he was one of my oldest and closest friends.

We'd met when I was still employed at my old company. My wife at the time had introduced us, back when she had hopes for my career and thought rubbing elbows with the moneyed Wasps comprising her social set would advance my prospects. She didn't count on Burton's complete disinterest in using his social power to further anyone's ambitions (equaling my disinterest in advancing my own), nor his abiding devotion to the New York Yankees, which established the foundation of a friendship that had easily outlasted the marriage.

He also loved to tinker and build things with his own hands, an interest where I clearly held an advantage, leading to many long days covered in mud, or sawdust, or taping compound, followed by nights of semidrunken celebration.

More to the point, I really liked the guy. It wasn't his fault that he inherited so much money. Even after quadrupling the fortune through his own efforts, he never lost touch with his essential humanity.

I can't say I never took advantage of Burton's wealth and goodwill. I did it thinking the benefits accrued not to me, but to people I cared about, for whom I'd do anything, including debasing my own sense of implacable self-reliance. Though I also knew Burton would consider denying his generosity vain and vaguely insulting.

Such is the intricate waltz you have with other human beings, once you decide to engage with the world and expose a trammeled and oft-trampled heart.

A WOMAN named Isabella looked after his professional life, and his house off Gin Lane in Southampton Village, since that's where he mostly ran his legal and real estate operations. She answered the intercom at the end of a long, hedge-lined driveway guarded by a tall gate and mountains of blue hydrangeas.

"I'm glad you're here," she said.

"Glad? That's a first."

"He's been in the woodshop for hours. I went to the door and heard lots of cursing."

"That's what woodshops are for."

The gate buzzed open.

"Just go see what's happening before he cut off something important."

The driveway ran a few hundred feet in a straight line before taking a sudden right turn, where it curved up to the main house, a classic shingle-style mansion full of gables,

Palladian windows, and Doric columns. If you drove past the parking circle, you could follow the drive over to a cluster of out-buildings, one of which was the woodshop. I'd specified the shop's equipment over the years, and not surprisingly, little expense had been spared in the creation. I was plenty happy with my own setup, with which I made my living, though I admit to some envy over his big windows and garage doors, all above ground, in contrast to my subterranean domain.

I waited outside until the power tool running in the shop wound down, precluding the possibility of startling him and causing some grievous injury. He stood at the workbench, leaning over his work and shaking his head. He looked up when I came in.

"Bloody fucking hell," he said.

"There's the spirit."

"I looked up all the calculations online. There's no reason on earth these cuts shouldn't work."

On the bench was a small hip roof. Essentially a pyramid, with four low-pitched sections joining in what should have been a point at the top. Only Burton's point was more of an edge. Other failed efforts lay about the shop, and one appeared to have traveled some distance to a far wall.

"What's it for?" He seemed reluctant to say, but then cast his eyes over to a smaller bench, on which sat a little box with a round hole bored in one side. "A birdhouse?"

"Avian domicile, if you will."

I knew Burton well enough to know even if he could corner the global supply of commercially manufactured birdhouses, it did little to allay his sense of personal frustration and defeat. I also knew that even a birdhouse could be a very tough thing to make if complicated enough. Like Burton's design.

"Show me the math," I said.

He was right. The numbers theoretically should have yielded a perfect pyramid shape. The jig he'd built to run the stock through the table saw was precise and stable. He'd just forgotten one thing.

"Nothing works the way it's supposed to," I said.

"That's heartening."

I picked the best miss-cut piece out of the rejects and used a measuring tape to get a feel for the dimensions. Then I used a few other traditional calibrating tools to reset the table saw.

The first run-through was also out of kilter, but now I knew what to do. I ignored Burton's disappointment with my initial failure, and reset the saw again. The result was perfect and true, like the heart of a young lover before disappointment upends her soul.

"This is annoying," said Burton.

"Statistical noise," I said. "Your numbers only ran to three decimal points. Our machine tools at the company could go up another thirty. That little bit of variation makes all the difference. In a woodshop, you just have to feel your way through the infinitesimal."

He walked the newly shaped roof over to the birdhouse and set it in place.

"Thank you," he said. "You're right, of course. You can't always get there just by the numbers."

"Einstein started with his theories, what he called thought experiments, then applied the equations. Most of which have so far proved correct."

"I could never abide a show-off."

He swept the dust off his threadbare khakis and stained T-shirt and waved me to follow him. We left the shop and walked over the lawn to a stone patio at the back of the big house, where a wet bar and oversized wicker furniture awaited.

"This should have been my reward for a successful venture," he said. "Instead, it's compensation for you and consolation for me."

"Everybody wins."

He assembled our preferred drinks, and after passing me mine, dropped into a wicker chair with a resigned sigh.

"Fucking birdhouse," he said.

"There's no such thing as an easy woodworking job. Even a birdhouse. Frustration lurks around every pencil line and saw cut."

"Almost makes me pine for the law, where everything is ambiguous."

"Don't share that with the public. They think it's hard and fast."

He swiveled his Scotch and soda around in the glass.

"Jackie briefed me on your Ernesto situation," he said.

I asked him what she said, not to challenge her account, but to make sure he'd captured all the details. Burton was a devoted and conscientious employer, but his busy mind had a tendency to drift. Especially when Jackie was in hyperkinetic, info-dump mode.

After he ran through her briefing, I filled in a few details.

"Ernesto assaulted someone?" he asked.

"That was the charge, later dropped once he proved self-defense. He's undocumented, so the greater miracle was avoiding deportation."

"They used to leave people alone if there wasn't a conviction," he said.

"I didn't know," I said.

Isabella showed up with a rolling cart filled with bread baskets, bowls of fruit, and wooden cutting plates straining under mounds of deli meats. She said maybe we'd like a snack. Burton took pains to say none of this was necessary, while expressing heartfelt appreciation. I'd witnessed this before. Isabella had started with Burton as a housekeeper, and over the years worked her way up to chief of staff of a multibillion-dollar operation. Yet she insisted for reasons of her own on retaining her role as the household's mayordomo.

I told Burton about our visit from the shadowy Mauricio, and our failure thus far to locate him within the bureau.

"This is disturbing," he said.

"You think?"

"I've dealt with the FBI quite a bit since opening the criminal practice. It's not how they operate."

"I didn't think so either," I said.

He made a sandwich with two tiny pieces of wheat bread and a wad of smoked salmon. Before stuffing it in his mouth, he said, "The New York field office covers Long Island. I know the man in charge. I'll make a call. Doesn't mean he'll talk to me."

It was a foregone conclusion he would. It's hardly fair that people as wealthy and connected as Burton can talk to anyone they want. It helped that he always used his influence for good, as far as I knew. Though defining good was often a matter of perspective.

"That's great, Burt. We appreciate the help."

I spent some time munching off Isabella's cart before asking another favor.

"Do you know anyone at O'Connor Consulting?" I asked.

"I do indeed. Clever bunch. I get their monthly newsletter. One of the few things I like to read online."

"I want to talk to management. About Bollings."

"Quite doable." He said Isabella could set up meetings in the city with both the FBI field office and O'Connor executives best able to talk about Victor Bollings. Kill two birds with one trip. "When do you want to go?"

"That depends on the boss," I said, taking out my cell phone to call Jackie Swaitkowski.

CHAPTER SEVEN

Several years ago, my former colleagues in R&D had brought a class action suit against the company over a quirk in our intellectual property contract. All I had to do was say, sure, add my name to the plaintiffs, and a proportionate share of the settlement subsequently dropped into my bank account. So I did the intelligent thing and immediately sank the bulk of the money into the *Carpe Mañana*, a custom forty-six-foot cruiser forsaken by Burton Lewis in favor of a sleek racing boat.

My second favorite thing after sailing the *Carpe Mañana* was to stop sailing her and drop the anchor in a sheltered harbor. Especially when I could convince Amanda to come with me, which I did that evening after leaving Burton's house. It wasn't a hard sell. She brought along the usual provisions, and I brought along Eddie, who saw sailing trips as an ideal way to taunt indifferent seabirds.

The sun had mostly set, and dusk was rapidly gathering around the marina as we cast off. The heat of the day had begun to lift, and the light breeze, though warm, cleaned the cabin of stale air and ventilated my encumbered brain paths. The pond just outside the docking area was turning from blue to dark grey, and the cormorants, egrets, and gulls were busy with their evening harvests, much to Eddie's joyful, ever-unrequited exertions.

I motored the rest of the way out into the Little Peconic Bay, and after unfurling the headsail, set a course to an anchorage that was reliably uninhabited during the weekdays.

I followed the GPS into the little harbor, and as hoped, it was clear of boats. I chose my preferred spot and we dropped the hook.

The sky nearly moonless, and once secure in the cockpit, drinks in hand, we sat there watching shooting stars overhead, until I realized the same light show could be seen reflecting off the dead-calm water.

"Will this give us extra wishes?" Amanda asked.

"Yes. But only if you ask in mirror images. Not an easy trick."

"Not for you, captain. I've heard your Latin."

"*Dum anima est, spes est.*"

"Something about hope?"

"Just keep watching."

So that's how we spent those serene hours, punctuated by a tray of sliced sausage and dill cheese and interrupted by a quick trip to shore in the dinghy so Eddie could relieve himself and snuffle around for decaying bivalves. During all this I easily forgot about my cabinetmaking deadlines, the relative happiness of my daughter, Ernesto's legal troubles, and the looming infirmities of a former professional boxer in late middle age.

We passed into sleep to the sounds of insect life in the nearby woods, a rhythmic burr that waxed and waned to the flow of dry, clean wind billowing in from the hatch overhead.

"So if that's what you think, maybe I should just be going," Amanda yelled, sometime in the night.

I crawled back out of sleep and asked her what was up.

It was near black in the V berth at the bow of the boat, but for a soft gleam from the starry sky overhead, so I could barely see her naked form raised up on her side. She was looking toward the stern.

"Darwin should have cut his beard," she said. "That's pretty obvious."

She slithered out of the berth and fell hard on the cabin sole.

"What's going on?"

"Gotta go check," she said, standing up and moving into the cabin. "The game is afoot."

I tumbled after her and caught her about to go up the stairs to the cockpit.

"Hey, wake up. You're dreaming," I said.

She gripped my cheek with her strong right hand.

"Dreams? I have rights, too, you know."

She pulled away and went up through the companionway. I tried to tug her back inside, but she was determined.

"All ashore who's going ashore," she yelled.

Eddie, behind me, started to bark.

"Whose dog is that?" Amanda yelled.

I wrapped my arms around her lower legs and held on. She shook one of her feet free and shot it directly in my face. I'd been punched by professional fighters, but few had the strength of that kick. I fell back into the cabin, and Amanda scrambled up to the cockpit. I yelled to her as I tried to regain my senses. Eddie's barking got more hysterical.

When I made it up to the cockpit, Amanda was nowhere to be seen. I looked around and saw movement toward the bow. I clawed my way up over the cabin top and saw her struggling through the rigging, heading toward the anchor. I yelled to her to stop. Before she reached the far bow, she dropped to her butt, then fell back, her head stuck in the forward hatch.

"Sam?" she asked, in a voice I recognized.

"Stay where you are," I said. "I'm coming."

Before I got there, she was back on her feet. She stepped to the pulpit of the boat, an area above the anchor locker enclosed by chrome railing that offered the last line of defense before going overboard. She sat down again, facing me.

"Say, darling," I said to her. "What's up?"

"This life," she said. "It's all so ridiculous."

"Not your life. It means the world to me."

I crept forward.

She was sitting, facing me. Naked, her long mane of reddish brown hair cascading down over her shoulders. She shook her head.

"Not doing so well at the moment," she said.

"That's okay," I said. "I'll be right there."

"Too late," she said, and then stood up, spread her arms, and toppled backward into the water.

I followed her over the railing, diving slightly to the right to avoid landing on top of her. She'd disappeared below the surface. When I dove under, she wasn't there. I dove deeper and flailed around in the black water, but felt nothing. I'm a lousy swimmer, with the buoyancy of a granite slab, so it was all I could do to get back to the surface to grab a mouthful of air before going back down again. She still wasn't there.

Panic sizzled across my nerves. I screamed her name before diving back down again, this time swimming vertically until my ears cracked inside my head. I hit bottom, a mushy stew of silty mud, dead crustaceans, and pebbly sand. I ran my hands through the concoction until instinct forced me back up again while I still had enough oxygen to remain conscious.

I screamed her name again.

"Honestly, Sam, I'm right here," said Amanda, about ten feet away.

"Stay there," I yelled and swam over to her.

"Whose idea was this?" she asked.

I grabbed her around the middle and started pulling her toward the boat. She squirmed in my embrace.

"Please stop saving me," she said. "I'm much better on my own."

I let her go and followed her around to the stern of the *Carpe Mañana*, where she pulled down the swim ladder and hauled herself up and into the cockpit. I was right behind her, grabbing her again before she had a chance to sit down.

"What's going on?" I asked her. It was too dark in the cockpit to clearly see her expression, but I knew she was studying my face. I moved her gradually toward the companionway. "Let's go below," I said. "Get some towels."

She did as I asked, and stood still while I snapped on the lights. Her long hair hung in strings over her face, and she clenched herself around the middle. I pulled a pair of beach towels out of a cabinet and wrapped her up, stroking her hair away from her face. She shivered.

Eddie, unusually freaked out, whined and tried to jump up on us. I told him to get down and asked Amanda again what was happening, and she said, "I think I can sleep now," and dropped to the floor.

I caught her in time to stop her head from smacking on the wooden sole. I felt her breath with my hand and opened an eyelid. A blank green eye stared back at me.

I scrambled around for my cell phone and called 911. I told the dispatcher where to send an ambulance, with an estimate of when I'd get there. I told him I'd be coming in from the bay by dinghy. He took it all in without fanfare. He asked if I could stay on the line, and I had to tell him no. He said okay, and that he'd be standing by.

I dressed Amanda in a sweat suit I kept onboard, and after yanking on a shirt and shorts, picked her up like a bag of potatoes and carried her down the swim ladder. I used my foot to drag the dinghy close enough to step in and drop Amanda onto the hard bottom in more or less a single movement. I propped her up in the bow and fired up the outboard.

Eddie stood at the stern of the *Carpe Mañana* and looked into the dinghy, preparing to leap. I dragged the boat hard against the swim ladder and reached up to grab him just as he took off. The two of us landed hard on the starboard pontoon, but he was aboard. I unhooked the towline, dropped into the little inflatable, and gunned the throttle.

It took a few seconds to get up on plane, and a few seconds after that to shoot out of the harbor and into the baleful darkness of the Little Peconic Bay. Eddie scrunched up against Amanda's legs and held on. Her head rolled lifeless where it rested on the point of the bow. I held a nylon safety grip with one hand and the throttle with the other, twisting it to full speed. The bay waves were blessedly subdued, though an occasional clump of chop would spontaneously appear as it often did on the Little Peconic and we'd bash about for a few moments, salt spray washing over us and smacking me in the face. Everyone stayed in the boat, and I willed the outboard to greater effort, telling Eddie every few minutes he was a valiant sea dog, and that limitless Big Dog biscuits awaited to reward such courage and forbearance.

I'd lived on those waters most of my life, and could have probably found the right beach blindfolded, but it didn't hurt to suddenly see brilliant flashing lights appear several degrees to starboard. I corrected my aim and drove on.

It took longer to get there than I thought it would, and I had a crazy thought they'd just give up and go back to the hospital. So I somehow retrieved my cell phone from my shorts and called the 911 dispatcher.

"Tell them not to leave," I yelled into the phone. "We're almost there."

"Nobody's leaving," he said, his voice remarkably clear despite the raging outboard and angry slap of bay waves under the dinghy.

"I can see them," I said.

"They can hear you. Just hold your course."

More flashing lights joined the party on the beach. Cops on the North Sea beat, I thought, ready to lend a hand. People I knew.

We hit another band of bigger waves, causing the dinghy to stutter and swerve and the outboard to catch air, whirring like a buzz saw. I let go of the safety line and steadied Amanda, who'd been thrown over to the port side. Eddie started to stand, then thought better of it, and flattened out again, his face turned to me in confused alarm.

"Hey, what's the problem?" I said to him. "You love the dinghy."

And he did, though I'm sure he was thinking, not at the moment.

Distracted by the chop, I didn't see we were closing in fast on the beach. I could see people lined up at water's edge, back-lit by the headlights and strobing red fireworks. I had a plan for coming ashore which was simple and direct. Keep the throttle wide open until I couldn't go any farther.

Luckily the noble first responders were quick enough to get out of the way. The dinghy plowed into the pebble beach and the outboard stalled. Eddie jumped out, and before I had a chance to stand half a dozen people were gathering Amanda up in their arms and moving her to a gurney. Once they had her strapped in, they carried the gurney across the beach and loaded her into the ambulance. Only then did I notice a short woman in an orange windbreaker trying to talk to me.

"Sir, please, I need to know what happened," she barked at me. "Describe her symptoms."

So I did, as I walked away from the dinghy, whistling for Eddie, who was already playfully engaged with some of the emergency crew and neighborhood gawkers.

She kept asking me questions after I'd given my report, so I had to tell her that was all I knew. She didn't seem to believe me, but radioed the ambulance anyway.

Danny Izard, one of the North Sea cops, came up to me.

"Hey, Sam, what the hell?"

"Can you drive me to the hospital," I asked.

"Sure. That was Amanda, right?"

"I think so. Some version."

He didn't react to that, but I often confused him and he didn't take offense. We drove to the hospital in silence, me in front and Eddie in back behind the wire mesh, like any common criminal.

WE QUICKLY caught up to the ambulance and followed it to the hospital, so I was there when they opened the back door. Amanda's head was up and her eyes open.

"How're we doing?" I asked her.

"I have no idea," she said. "What am I doing here?"

The paramedics slid the gurney out of the ambulance and wheeled her into the emergency room. Danny agreed to hold on to Eddie and I followed them all the way to the curtained-off triage area. Amanda got off the gurney and climbed on the bed on her own. Nurses swarmed her, taking her blood pressure, attaching electronics, asking her questions, like what's your mother's name, have you been to France, who was your first boyfriend.

"Why is my hair wet?" Amanda asked me.

"You fell in the water," I said.

"I did? How did that happen?"

"What do you remember?" I asked, but before she could answer, the curtained room suddenly filled up with Dr. Markham Fairchild, a mountainous man and undisputed master of the Southampton ER.

"That's usually you lyin' in one of my beds," he said to me with his soft Jamaican lilt.

"Amanda's filling in for me."

He shook her hand and shot a light into her right eye, then the left. He took a clipboard out from under his arm and read aloud the notes taken by the woman on the beach. I corrected a few things, but she had most of it right. As he read, Amanda stared at me with an ill-concealed mixture of defiance and wonder.

"This can't be," she said.

"How you been feeling lately?" asked Markham. "Any headaches, dizziness, problems with balance, eyesight?"

"Nothing of the sort," she said. "I spent the day climbing around a construction site. Fit as a fiddle."

He asked about alcohol and drugs. She said a bit of wine, and nothing else.

"Any other type of stimulant?"

"Other than Sam? No."

He had her get off the bed and walk out of the room with the nurses following along with the tethered devices, then turn around and walk back. Despite the situation, I couldn't help noticing the nice roll of her hips, one of my favorite features.

After some more of these questions and routines, he said they were going to pull some blood and take pictures of her head. First X-ray, then MRI.

"Just relax," he said. "They'll wheel you around."

"What fun," she said.

I followed him through the curtain.

"I don't know, Sam," he told me before I had a chance to ask. "Something going on for sure. Notice anything different lately? Behavior change?"

Another unanswerable question. Back when I was trouble-shooting for the company, we'd start with an established base-line against which we'd search for deviations. I'd known her for a number of years, yet I couldn't say I had a baseline for normal Amanda behavior. Our relationship had been con-structed around a mutual preference for avoidance and denial. And a belief that the right to love was not predicated on deep knowledge of the other person's past, present ruminations, or future hopes and expectations. We lived most comfortably in the here and now, a state assumed without a moment of Zen instruction.

I didn't have time to explain all this to Markham, so I just said, "No," which was true within the context of the last few years.

"So nothing like this has ever happened before?" he asked.

"No. Never anything like it."

"Any mental illness in the family? Schizophrenia?"

"I have no idea. But I used to spend quality time with a schizophrenic. It was nothing like this."

He read from the tablet device in his hand.

"She's lucky I spent a few years in Africa," he said.

"She is?"

"The area we worked in had never seen a psychiatrist. So when somebody's behavior radically changed they assumed one of two things. Evil spirits or a bang on the head."

"No bangs to the head, that I know of," I said. "Can't speak to the evil spirits."

"My point is, we'll do a psych evaluation, but not let up on a biomedical explanation."

"Meaning what?"

"Let's wait for the tests," he said, giving me a quick squeeze with a hand that encompassed my shoulder and a fair bit beyond that.

I went back to Amanda and did what we did best—talked about nothing and avoided painful subjects and worthless speculation. This was interrupted by the arrival of a slight young man with a handsome face and hair that looked like mine when I was his age, only less unruly. He introduced himself as Dr. Leclercq, though we could call him Pierre. I knew from the accent he was French French, not some questionable Canuck like me.

He said he was the psychiatrist on call and was there to help figure out what was going on with her. He was friendly enough, though letting us know he was there to do a job without a lot of unnecessary melodramatics.

"Oh, God," said Amanda. "I hate this kind of thing."

"Don't worry," he said. "I don't do therapy. I'm just here for a medical evaluation."

"So you don't care about my imaginary friends or fear that I might be growing a penis," she asked him.

He pulled a piece of paper off his clipboard. "I just need to sign off on your mental state from a psychiatric perspective. I ask, you answer, honestly. I fill out my report, we both get to move on with our lives."

I generally disliked shrinks, a prejudice, I realize. Maybe because I'd been forced to see a few, who took an instant dislike to me in return. And then there's that lousy childhood.

But this guy seemed okay.

"Don't be too cavalier," I said to him in French. "She'll make you work for it."

"A smart one, eh?"

"I'll let you be the judge of that. If you're smart enough."

Amanda asked if I could be there when he interviewed her. He said of course not. She said why. He said to protect her privacy. She said she had nothing to hide from me. Hospital rules, he said.

"Oh, so it's not about my privacy, but rather your malpractice insurance," she said. "How often do you lie to your patients?"

He looked at me. I shrugged.

"Madame, this is only to assess your medical condition," said Leclercq. "Like an X-ray or blood test. We can't help you if you don't cooperate."

"Cooperate, is it," she said.

And for a moment I thought we were about to take another magical trip into the loony and hallucinogenic. But she lay back on her pillows and said, okay, bring it on.

"Sam, get the hell out of here. I can brief you later."

The doctor made me shake hands and I withdrew, though not before hearing her say, in French, "I do wonder about this little penis I've been developing. I think I might like it."

After Leclercq left we had another hour while they accomplished the rest of the tests, and nothing to do but wait for Dr. Fairchild.

"Patients hate it when I say, 'I don't know,'" said Markham when he came through the curtain. "But we don't for sure. We need more tests."

"What about the psychiatrist?" I asked.

"He said Amanda was very interesting, but probably not schizophrenic, or otherwise clinically psychotic. So we can eliminate that. For now."

"I like the interesting part," said Amanda. "The 'for now,' not so much."

"I sent the X-rays and MRIs over to our consulting neurologist, who has some theories, but wants you to see a neurosurgeon who specializes in this kind of thing."

"Sudden wacky, nutzoid syndrome?" Amanda asked.

"If you want to get technical on me, yes."

We took a cab to Amanda's house where Danny Izard met us and handed over Eddie. He told us the bay constable had towed my dinghy over to Hawk's Pond Marina where I could find it in my slip. I thanked him and called him a mensch for the ages.

"That's what they pay me for," he said in his dense Long Island accent.

We showered and I put on a bathrobe stored at her house, the only evidence of occasional cohabitation. We went out to her patio and she stopped at the wet bar to dispense our usual drinks.

"Markham said to continue normal daily living," she said, pulling a pair of chaise lounges next to each other.

The neurologist's referral was in New York City. I told her about my planned visits to the FBI and O'Connor Consulting. I thought we could make it a threefer if the scheduling gods were cooperating.

"You want to drive me in," she said.

"I do."

"You can't be with me twenty-four hours a day."

"I won't be. Normal daily living it is. Just wait till I'm around to go nuts."

She gave a vague toast with her wine glass.

"I'm allowed to be a little alarmed by all this, aren't I?" she asked.

"Ask whoever's giving permission."

She let that sit a moment before saying, "Thanks for looking after me."

"No sweat. You'd do it for me."

"I suppose I would, now that you mention it."

CHAPTER EIGHT

$\mathbb{B}$urton had come through with appointments at the FBI and O'Connor Consulting, and Dr. Sean Ng, the NYC neurosurgeon, had a slot the same day at Roosevelt Hospital where he had privileges. My immediate future settled, I filled the intervening time retrieving the *Carpe Mañana* from the anchorage and working on the Bollings's built-ins, and pretending I wasn't grinding my guts over Amanda. She was also back at work, promising to stay off roofs and away from unfinished stairwells. She agreed to tell her number two on the job sites—a seventy-year-old architect who was surprised to learn he couldn't sit still in retirement—that she'd been having some vertigo, so not to be alarmed if she keeled over.

"What about speaking in tongues?" I asked.

"He'll have to discover that on his own."

The only other distraction was the swift indictment of Ernesto Mazzotti for the first-degree murder of Victor Bollings. Along with demonstrating a lot of confidence in their case, the DA's announcement caught the eye of the press, and the story filled up the regional media outlets. Soon after, it made its way into the national discourse, Ernesto being an illegal immigrant and Bollings a business expert with a famous consulting firm. I ignored it all pretty well, since my only news exposure came through NPR and the radio in my shop had a remote control.

Jackie would have to worry about the political pressure and jury selection, but as her humble investigator, I was blessedly ignorant of the sensational blather.

Not so Ernesto's wife, Querida, who called me a few days into the news cycle. She wanted me to come see her at their house. Immediately. Then hung up the phone. I got the message and made it over there in a hurry.

I parked behind a chunky diesel pickup, with four rear wheels, the kind you use to haul heavy trailers that everyone called a dually. It had Kentucky plates. The guy behind the wheel wore a cowboy hat and Sam Elliott moustache. I looked at him as I walked by and he gave me a little salute. I walked back and knocked on the window.

"Can I help you with anything?" I asked.

"Yeah, you can. Is this Hampton Bays?"

"Yup."

"My cousin wants me to go get his old outboard. How do I get there?"

He handed me a tattered brochure for a boat repair shop off the Shinnecock Bay and a road map of the East End. I gave him directions, which he wrote down on the back of his hand.

"Thanks," he said. "You got some confusing roads around here."

"We like it that way," I said, walking off.

I went to the Mazzotti house and Querida met me at the door holding a sign.

It was a piece of cardboard with the words "Swim back to Mexico while you still can" scrawled in red paint.

"Never mind we're Colombian," she said.

As I followed her into the house she told me the kids were back at camp where her eldest could keep an eye on the younger ones. He'd handled a few wisecracks, but so far no fights had broken out.

"But that won't last," she said. "He's Ernesto's son."

"Did you call the cops?"

"They promised to keep an eye on the house, but they can't stop the phone calls." She tossed the sign on the floor and dropped down into the sofa, her hands held tightly between her knees. "We have lots of Anglo and Latino friends in the neighborhood who are watching, but this makes them so angry it's almost worse. I think things could go crazy town."

I had no experience with situations like this, but had to agree. Now that the case was out there in the greater world, a big ugly beast could be aroused, local and imported.

A whole new worry over my own beloveds—Amanda, my daughter, Allison, Eddie—began to ignite, but I stuffed it away and tried to focus on Querida's dilemma.

"You're not safe here," I said.

I could see her weighing the implications.

"I need to be here for Ernesto," she said.

"You need to take your boys and go somewhere else. Find a house far away."

That alarmed her.

"I can't pay for all that."

"Burton Lewis will cover it," I said. I told her about the founder of Jackie's law firm. "He'll find a house and fly you there, with your boys and little greyhound, and bring you back as often as we can."

It was quite a promise to make without asking Burton first, but I already knew the answer, and didn't want to waste the time.

I told her I'd once put my family in danger, not realizing how perilous the situation could be. And the consequences of that lapse. My daughter, Allison, had yet to fully recover from a near fatal beating. She was now living in the South of France, encouraged no doubt by her mother, who owned a chateau in

Eze, the *village perché* overlooking Cap Ferrat and the cerulean Mediterranean Sea.

"What about my job?" she said, as if suddenly remembering she had one.

I let the question hang in the air. It felt a little harsh, but there was no kindness in downplaying the imminent threat.

"What's more important," I said.

"So what do I do now?" she asked.

"Pack."

I let her listen to me call Jackie, who would need to ignite the firm's administrative people to arrange for housing and book the flight. As with Burton, I knew she'd get behind the idea as soon as I explained the situation. I tried to look encouraging for Querida as I talked, though she didn't look all that encouraged.

In fact, tears started to form in her eyes, squeezed through her strained expression.

"This is all so, you know," she said.

"I can't really know, but let's get you and the boys out of here so we can all worry a little less. Especially Ernesto."

She nodded, looking down at her clenched hands, and I took off before she had a chance to come up with a counterargument. On the way back to Oak Point I called Ross Semple and convinced him that keeping a town cop in close proximity to the Mazzotti house for a few days was better than seeing an ethnic battle erupt.

He didn't argue with me. I decided to stop convincing people while I was still ahead and went back to the noisy, dust-filled sanctity of my woodshop in the basement.

ONE OF the joys of going into the city with Amanda was I got to drive her Audi A4, which, after my Jeep and '67 Pontiac, reminded me you could operate a vehicle at a brisk pace without risking permanent kidney damage.

"This car is so smooth," I said. "Are you sure we're actually moving?"

"You say that every time. Once more and I just won't answer."

As we drove I told her about my visit with Querida and our plan for her to get out of Dodge. I was partly sorry I did, since the whole dreary matter of Latino harassment caused her some pain.

"I know some of that trash talk goes on at my job sites," she said, "but I never hear it, since most of the talkers want to avoid my wrath."

"Or in my case, a swift kick in the ass."

"That would go along with the wrath."

"I wish it was that simple," I said.

"Nothing is if you have half a brain. Even one like mine."

"You've got a great brain. I've seen it in action."

"Let's say unconventional and leave it at that."

I then tried distracting her by comparing the various translations of the *Tao Te Ching* I'd been cycling through, with commentary on the relative ability of the translators to transcend historical context. This must have worked, since she fell asleep for the final traffic-clogged third of the trip.

We made it all the way to a parking garage before I nudged her awake.

"Oh, we're here," she said. "The last I knew Lao-tzu was heading west on a water buffalo. What happened after that?"

"Don't worry. I'll catch you up."

"Thank God."

I told security at the FBI field office I was there to see the assistant director in charge. He wasn't that impressed, but called upstairs. Instead of the assistant director, we got Special

Agent Grace Inverness, who said her boss had put her on the Ernesto Mazzotti case as liaison with the local authorities.

"It's not an active bureau investigation, but we're here to help if we can," she said, as we wove our way through the security gauntlet and up the elevator to a big, brightly lit conference room.

I told her Amanda wasn't one of Jackie Swaitkowski's investigators, but had a special role in the operation.

"We never let Sam venture into the city without supervision," she said.

I sat at the conference table so I could look out the big windows. It was a holdover from my years attending meetings at corporate headquarters in Midtown Manhattan, where I needed something to distract me from the plodding slide shows and obsequious prattle.

"You understand I can't discuss any particulars of the investigation," said Agent Inverness as we settled in. "What we share with Mazzotti's defense is up to the ADA as you go through discovery."

"But you're still talking to us," I said.

"The assistant director said I had to. Not that you aren't perfectly nice people."

"We are nice," said Amanda. "If not always perfect."

The special agent had a hard face, though not without warmth. I put her at late forties, a dyed brunette, given to sensible clothing and makeup, with elegant craft jewelry on strong, athletic hands.

"I've reviewed Sam's file," she said. "Didn't include a lot of nice."

"I know you can't talk about the investigation, but that's not why we're here," I said, as nicely as I could.

"Okay."

I described how I'd spotted Mauricio of the trilby and guayabera hanging around my house, and then our encounter in the backyard. I wanted to give her all the detail I could remember, so it took awhile. She had a notepad in front of her, but didn't take notes. I told her about sticking his nose in the grass and disarming him, something Amanda hadn't heard, but she also had her poker face on.

"At no time did this person identify the government agency he claimed to be working for?" the agent asked.

"That's what I told you," I said. "You have his license plate. Just look it up." When she didn't react, I said, "You already know it doesn't exist."

"Do you have a photograph," she asked, "of the man or the vehicle?"

"No. I'd show you if I did."

"And you haven't seen this man since," she said.

"No more questions till I get some answers," I said.

As if I had any leverage. Agent Inverness sat there in her institutional fortress, face set, body language mute, implacable.

"Perhaps if we gave a description of this gentleman to the press, and described the encounter itself, they might be able to lend a hand," said Amanda. "Recruit the public."

"I'm not sure what purpose that would serve," said the special agent.

"Well," I said, picking up on Amanda's strategy. "Nothing ventured, nothing gained."

"Our friend Jackie Swaitkowski has a *Times* reporter on speed dial," said Amanda. "Should she make the call?"

"I'd rather you didn't," said Inverness.

Amanda held her phone with a finger poised over the screen. Inverness relented.

"The story you've related is completely inconsistent with FBI field operations," she said. "The individual in question is not associated with the bureau, nor has ever been in any capacity."

"So you did talk to Jackie," I said.

"A few minutes before you arrived. We just determined the plate was a forgery. And the weapons you," she paused, "confiscated, are nonstandard-issue for any federal personnel authorized to carry arms."

Confession is supposed to bring relief to the confessor, though all Inverness showed was vague annoyance.

"So you don't wonder why a fake operative with fake government plates tried to warn me off the Mazzotti case?" I asked.

"I have no comment beyond what we've already discussed," she said, obviously finished with confessing.

She asked if we had any other questions, not that she'd give any answers.

"So the Southampton police asked for help on the Mazzotti case," I said. "That has to be a yes, otherwise you wouldn't need a liaison."

"I was given that assignment. I've worked with Ross Semple, so I was the obvious choice. Supporting local law enforcement is pretty routine, especially when an undocumented is involved," she said, in a way that was neither dismissive nor condescending, though with a hint of each.

"So when you get out to the Hamptons, you must visit us on Oak Point," said Amanda. "The attractions are manifold."

"Your mystery man apparently thought so," she said.

She stood up, saying our meeting had drawn to a close. With her neglected notepad stuck under her arm, she held the conference door open and we all left. At the front entrance, she shook our hands and gave me her card.

"My cell number is the best way to reach me," she said. "Just in case."

Amanda repeated the courtesy with a card of her own.

"Just let us know when you're coming," she said. "And if you prefer red or white."

SINCE O'CONNOR Consulting's offices were only a few blocks farther downtown, we walked. When I complimented Amanda on the press gambit, she grabbed my arm and put her head on my shoulder.

"Aw, come on. That was the obvious thing to say."

"Not to me. Obviously."

The weather was pleasant enough to lighten the shadowy city as we moved south on Broadway, arm in arm. She didn't ask how I thought the meeting went, which was fine, since I needed time to digest it. Anyway, I just wanted to enjoy the closeness of the walk, made more so by the anonymous streams of humanity swirling around us.

The security wasn't as tight at O'Connor Consulting, but the amenities were a lot better, including a full kitchen where you could grab a croissant and bowl of fruit. The receptionist who brought us there told us Senior Adviser Justin Pincus would pick us up momentarily and bring us upstairs to a meeting lounge.

"I know that guy," I said. "I worked with him at Con Globe. Wasn't a senior then. I think more like Adviser Second Class."

"I'm sure," said the receptionist, whatever that meant.

Pincus wasn't all that pink. In fact, his skin tone was more like Barack Obama's, with a slim frame to match. I recognized him right away, even with the grey hair that had infiltrated what was once jet black. Probably came with the Senior Adviser title.

"Hey, Sam. How you been?" he asked as we shook hands.

"Better and worse. Meet Amanda Anselma. She's the better part."

"He only says that because it's true," said Amanda.

As promised, he took us up the elevator to an area that more resembled a London gentlemen's club than a meeting room. Amanda nearly disappeared into an overstuffed leather chair, but then recovered a more dignified perch at the edge of the cushion. After dishing out coffee from a big chrome machine, Pincus asked what I'd been up to since retiring from Con Globe.

"Didn't retire. They booted me out for some silly infraction."

"What sort of infraction? I heard some things."

"I dragged Mason Thigpin across the table by his tie during a board meeting and planted a right jab in the middle of his face."

"That's what I heard," Pincus admitted. "You might have picked someone more strategic than chief corporate counsel."

"He was closest. So obviously you're still in the guru game."

"I am. Working with your R&D department didn't do permanent harm to my career. Though I got my PhD, just in case."

"You're not the only one we shoved into greatness. You heard about the class action my team brought."

"I testified at the hearing," he said. "On your behalf, by the way. I didn't see you there."

"Had nothing to do with it. And still got a sailboat out of the deal."

"He was actually responsible for developing most of the relevant technology," he said to Amanda, causing her to raise an eyebrow.

"Sam told me his main job was hiding from people in his office."

"Everyone called Sam the smartest guy in the company, when they weren't calling him the biggest asshole."

"Always the overachiever," said Amanda.

I thought this was a good time to redirect the conversation toward Victor Bollings. Pincus said he not only knew Bollings well, he'd worked directly under him for two years out of their offices in Dubai.

"He liked having native Arabic speakers on the team. My mother's Jordanian by way of Nigeria. You remember that, right?"

"No, though I'm sure you told me."

"I did. Right before you told me you weren't interested in personal history."

"What a charming colleague," said Amanda.

Pincus grinned.

"Social skills weren't required in Sam's operation," said Pincus.

"Actually frowned upon. So what about Bollings?"

Pincus said he was a Top Quad, which was O'Connor speak for advisers with the highest hourly billing rate, well into the four figures. Having earned both a BA and an MBA from Harvard in four years, Bollings had gone directly into the consultant business and never came out. An immediate star performer, he was soon brought under Theresa Woodsen, who ran the international division, O'Connor's main profit engine.

"Talk about smart guys," said Pincus, "and not even close to being an asshole."

"It can be done," said Amanda, looking at me.

"What did he specialize in?" I asked.

"Air travel," said Pincus. "The guy lived in jumbo jets. We'd say he had enough frequent flyer points to go to Mars and back. Seriously, his gig was globalized trade strategies. A pretty hot item in those days."

"So I've heard," I said. "Any particular industry? Cars, banking?"

He shook his head.

"The type of business was irrelevant. What he knew were government policies and bureaucracy, currency exchange, logistics, all the plumbing that keeps world trade flowing smoothly."

"And not a lot of enemies," I said.

"None that I knew of. Everybody here loved him. So did his clients. In business and government, which in much of the world is pretty much the same thing."

"Construction crews liked him as well," said Amanda, "or so I understand."

"All but one, it turns out," said Pincus.

"Ernesto didn't do it," I said. "He was a charter member of the Victor Bollings fan club. Bollings was teaching him golf."

Pincus didn't respond to that. Not from any deference toward the legal process. He just didn't have the data.

I confirmed that Bollings was still an employee when he was killed, but set to retire.

"In months, is what I heard," said Pincus. "A full partner for nearly twenty years, you could say he was all set. Shouldn't matter, dead is dead. But it makes you think, don't wait for retirement to live."

"Though maybe not choose Sam's approach," said Amanda.

"It sounds like Bollings was too good to be true," I said.

"The detectives from Southampton thought the same thing," he said. "Victor was a real straight arrow, but also very private. Could make small talk all night long and reveal little about himself. Charming, but reserved. Rebecca would call him a tight-assed WASP."

"So you knew her too," I said.

"Not much. Company events, that sort of thing. They had a jokey sort of relationship. Clever, clever, banter, banter. Stuff you wouldn't hear from Bollings normally. Personally, I hate that stuff. Makes you think they're speaking in code."

"Maybe they were," said Amanda.

He repeated what I'd heard from Frank Entwhistle, that Rebecca was easily as smart as Victor, so maybe they did communicate at a level beyond the understanding of mere mortals. As far as he knew, she never went with him on his assignments, or shared the long-term postings. He thought that might explain why they got along so well.

I asked him where she worked.

"Freelance. Data analytics consulting. You got a lot of numbers, she tells you what they mean."

"Sounds dreadful," said Amanda.

"For her, numbers equal about $800,000 a year," said Pincus.

He said that was all he could tell us. I had to believe him, though I felt unsatisfied. I thanked him and said we'd get out of his hair. On the way to the elevator he had a question for me.

"You never asked me what I thought about Victor," he said. "As a human being."

I hadn't. Maybe because there was always something non-human about the all-business culture at O'Connor.

"You're right. What'd you think?"

Pincus was ready with the answer.

"I liked him a lot. He was a good boss, and a good man. I'm really sorry he's gone. Especially how it happened, just before he had a chance to change his life. To get out of this place."

I asked him what he meant.

"I don't know for sure. Like I said, he was a closed-off person. But I always sensed there was something profound bubbling just below the surface. I don't exactly have a word for it."

"Give it a try," I said.

We were at the main entrance to the building. He smacked a big button to activate the door opener before answering.

"Rage."

CHAPTER NINE

Dr. Ng's office was too far a walk, so we cut over to Sixth Avenue to catch a cab heading uptown. We talked about our conversation while I was busy waving and whistling, so thus distracted I didn't notice Amanda was suddenly gone from my side. I looked up and down the sidewalk, seeing no sign of her. I went through the nearest door into a shoe store where all the customers and sales staff were looking toward the back.

I ran that way, through a curtain into a small office, and then into rows of shelving filled with shoeboxes. Amanda was burrowing into the shelves and tossing the boxes over her shoulder.

I put my arms around her and she leaned back into me.

"Enough pickin' apples for one day," she said. "I need a rest."

"You're right. Let's go find you a place to lie down."

She pushed forward again and tried to climb the shelves. I pulled her back with little resistance. I held her more tightly with my right arm and guided her back out of the store. Everyone watched us, though nothing was said. I got her out on the sidewalk and looked frantically for a cab. She tried to pull away again, this time toward the street, so I had to hold her with both hands.

"Somebody grab me a cab," I yelled to the world at large.

Two men and a woman went out on the street and started hailing. I dragged her as close to the curb as I dared and held on. Seconds later the group effort yielded results. The woman slid open the cab door for us and I called out thank yous as I pulled Amanda in and asked the driver to get to Roosevelt Hospital as quickly as possible.

I tried to ask her what was going on, but she only answered with observations like, "I can't see the sun. Did somebody move it?"

I called 911 and asked the dispatcher to please call the ER at Roosevelt and expect the arrival of a woman experiencing seizures. I didn't know what else to call it. Crazy lady seemed too imprecise.

The dispatcher asked how soon and the cabbie thought about ten minutes, though he was busy lurching and swerving down Sixth Avenue, beeping his horn and cursing everything in his way.

We got there in less than ten, just as a gurney popped out of the wide ER doors. I stuffed a handful of bills in the tray and got her out of the cab and onto the gurney. One nurse held her by the shoulders while the other strapped her in, though at this point, she'd stopped struggling. She looked up at me.

"Sam? Oh shit, not again."

"You just took a little time out for shoe shopping."

"My arm hurts." She held up her right forearm which had a deep scratch oozing blood. "Shoe shopping?"

"I'll explain later."

Dr. Ng joined us at the reception window where they were taking down her personal information. He introduced himself with a calm smile, and in a soothing voice started to prepare us for what was coming next. He invited me to come along as they brought her back to an examination room where they took her vitals and the doctor started asking questions and taking notes from her answers. He said they had the report from Southampton as he looked through the papers attached to his clipboard.

"I know they did an MRI, but I'd like to focus on a certain region," he said. "Would you mind going another round?"

"That's why we're here, Doc," said Amanda. "Anyway, I find that thumping sound sort of soothing."

He looked up at me and said, "So, the sarcasm level is about normal?"

"On a slow day."

"I think we can get you in right away," he said to Amanda. "Try not to run off for at least the next few minutes."

When we were alone, Amanda asked me not to tell her what she did this time, unless it involved something heroic. On her part.

"It wasn't bad," I said. "No possibility of drowning."

She let out a deep sigh, the type that went on for a while.

"I was almost starting to think some form of homey day-to-day contentment was within reach. What fools we mortals be."

"Is that a quote?" I asked.

"Shakespeare. Slightly modified to fit the circumstances."

"You're not a fool," I said.

"A wise broad knows she's a fool. Don't challenge me on Shakespeare. I can allude with the best of them."

"You're a great looking fool. Especially the mussed-up hair. I've seen that look in happier times. Usually in a state of *déshabiller*."

"That word sounds as dirty as it is," she said.

"I would hope so. We'll get through this. We always do."

"Probably not, but it was nice to know you."

The no-nonsense transport crew picked that time to transfer Amanda to another gurney, and we only had a moment to hold hands and exchange pecks on cheeks.

Darkness descended on my mood.

Dr. Ng let me sit in on the presentation. He had pages of MRI images he displayed on a big computer monitor. They were very colorful, and entirely untranslatable to the layman's eye. He used the cursor to direct our attention. And human language to describe the situation.

"Two tumors," he said. "Small, but in unfortunate places." He moved the cursor. "Here and here. The frontal cortex and parietal. Explains the psychotic breaks and memory loss. We need to do a biopsy to confirm if they're malignant or not, but in my experience, these types only get bigger, quickly, and are resistant to treatments like chemo or radiation therapies. Without intervention, the trajectory is rapid deterioration, and the longer we wait, the more the damage and difficulty in achieving a successful surgery. This combination of factors is very rare, though not unheard of. The literature has detailed a few hundred cases in the last twenty years."

"Well, at least there's that," said Amanda. "I'd hate to be ordinary."

I struggled to align the doctor's words with what I thought should be the prevailing reality. Well versed in the art of denial, I turned it into a hypothetical discussion of some other loved-one's brain. Amanda was more pragmatic.

"What are the odds getting them out of there will fix the problem?" she said.

The doctor nodded so deeply, it looked like a series of bows.

"Sixty-forty if you want to be optimistic," he said.

"And if I don't have the surgery?" she asked.

"Probably fatal."

"What about personality and brain function?" Amanda asked.

"No way to predict," said Dr. Ng. "We'll just have to wait and see."

Amanda nodded, in a deliberative way.

"Thank you, doctor," she said. "Excellent honesty."

He seemed flattered by this. He said she needed to stay under observation for a few days while they did some more tests. She didn't like that, but acquiesced. He gave a real bow and left the room, as if ending a modest stage play. The orderlies brought Amanda back to her room with me tagging along.

"What can I get you?" I asked. "I'm here for the duration."

"I'd rather you didn't hang around," she said. "I love you, but your worry is distracting. I want you to go home."

I must have looked ready to resist.

"Listen," she said, with an unfamiliar bite. "I'm not into pity and concern. I find it loathsome. You'd feel the same way."

I admitted I would.

"So get the hell out of here. If I end up dead or lobotomized, it was a great run."

I went to kiss her, but she held back, so I did as she asked and just left. Then I went to a bar I knew nearby and got drunk, because that's what I do. They woke me up at closing time, and I slept that night in the doorway of an art gallery. The place must not have done much business, because it was nearly noon before I was roused by a kid trying to open the door. He was kind, asking if he could take me somewhere, or if I wanted to sleep it off in his storage room behind the gallery. He had a cot and a bathroom back there. I said sure, and slept another four hours. I woke up to bad dreams, fought off images of imminent horror for a few minutes, then got up, took a piss, thanked the kid, and left.

The world had shifted, but I wasn't ready to let it leave me behind. So I found Amanda's car and went back to Southampton, where I fed Eddie, took a long hot shower, and went back to work.

Because that's also what I do.

Chapter Ten

I worked on Victor Bollings's built-ins with an unusual intensity, eager to get the job out of my shop. I wanted done with them and all their painful associations. Not least of which knowing Bollings would never get to see the product of his inspiration. Manual work always took my mind off other things, and I needed a lot of that. This strategy worked until I got a call from Tony Cermanski, who wanted to talk to me again. I told him to go fuck himself and hung up the phone.

An hour later, he called me again.

"What if I told you I'm easing up on your boy Mazzotti," he said. "I'm having doubts."

"I'd say about fucking time."

"I want to work with you on this, but not if you're going to piss all over me."

I went looking for my inner Buddhist and found him crouched in a corner, drunk on fury and frustration. I took a breath.

"Sorry," I said. "I'm a little tense. Shouldn't take it out on you."

"You shouldn't. Let's meet at a neutral location. Mad Martha's at six."

"Okay, but I know the guy who owns the place."

"Jimmy Watruss. My first cousin."

"Fair enough."

As a condition of the deal I made with the Stamford, CT, district attorney after I gutted my ex-wife's house, I had to spend three months in anger management, my favorite treatment. The shrink in charge and I had an instant and abiding dislike for each other. But I did learn a few things. Apparently, when you lose your temper, which I used to do on a nearly daily basis, it's like a short circuit in the brain. The part that evolved back when we were slithering out of the ocean makes a direct connection with the part that was programmed to strangle guys hitting on our caveman wives, leaving out the higher functions that did cave art and wrote *The Iliad*. The technical term was a mental "hijacking." I loved that neuroscience would use a word for uncontrollable wrath that actually made sense.

I could feel myself getting hijacked a lot since Amanda started having her troubles. I knew it would come to no good, so I talked to myself in the words of that little prick shrink, hoping it would work like a mantra to calm down my fevered mind. I also wondered how the shrink would feel about this, since he told me at the end of my enforced sessions to never come back again. An interesting position for a shrink to take, and once a point of pride for me.

Now, not so much. I was older, and slightly evolved past the slithering, snarling lizard I'd once been.

More or less.

MAD MARTHA'S was a dark, cramped seafood place, filled with balding, beer-bellied working guys and their weathered wives, and decorated with artifacts of the fishing trade, like nets, lobster buoys, heavy poles, and a full-sized rowboat hung from the ceiling. They served the best seafood in town, better than the restaurants written up in gourmet magazines, though less celebrated since food writers were afraid to go in there. Afghanistan, fine, Mad Martha's, no way.

The guy behind the bar had been there since I was a kid, and looked no different. Maybe a little greyer, but no less grouchy—expressionless behind a lavish beard and baggy eyes. Arms like twisted metal cable covered in loose fabric.

"What do you want?" he said.

"World peace and eternal life."

"To drink."

"Vodka. On the rocks," I said.

The same drink I'd ordered from him for decades.

"Fruit?" he asked.

"No fruit. Why wreck a perfectly good vodka with your rotten limes?"

Which I said every time.

"Them's good limes," he said.

The anger god started to stir my fragile heart, but then the bartender smiled.

"You should have a lime or two once in a while, Sam," he said. "Gets rid of the scurvy."

"Nobody gets scurvy anymore. But they do die of thirst waiting for their drinks to appear."

"Comin' right up."

Nothing's easy, I thought to myself.

Cermanski came in a few minutes later. He said hello to a few guys, but others shifted away from him. Guilty consciences. He went up to the bar and the bartender was ready with a tall draft beer. They said a few words, and Cermanski turned around to look for me. I waved him over.

"I talked to Jimmy today," said Cermanski. "Said he hasn't seen you much since that thing with the cripple."

"Don't let Jimmy hear talk like that about a veteran. Just say the guy with the disability," I said.

"I never took you for the PC type," said Cermanski.

"How do you feel about people calling cops pigs?"

"Okay, touché and all that shit."

I moved him to a quieter part of the bar. He was dressed like most of the men in the bar, meaning like a builder, including a ragged baseball cap. It made him look even younger, and more self-assured, if that was possible. I asked him why the change of heart on Mazzotti.

"You know Bollings was about to retire from his consulting job," he said. "And do what instead?"

"I don't know. Teach golf to Hispanic carpenters?"

"Close. To head up the North America Progress League. If you don't know them, they push for more favorable treatment of illegal aliens, which out here means Latinos. Mazzotti was aware of this. In fact, he told me, and I confirmed it with the NAPL. Doesn't preclude some other fucked-up personal thing, but it gave me some reasonable doubts."

You always want to trust your local law enforcement, who are supposedly accountable to us taxpayers, but it's hard, since the Supreme Court said they could lie to you all they wanted and lying to them was against the law. I got the logic of that, only it made for difficult one-on-one communications. So I wanted to tell Cermanski all about my encounter with the man in the guayabera, and Semple's order to back off the case, and the FBI lady's reluctance to talk about any of it. But I wasn't sure where that might lead.

"Anything else?" I asked.

"My buddies with the Town police told me a bunch of grey suits paid a call on Ross Semple right after we booked Mazzotti.

When they left, the chief looked like somebody'd sucked out all his blood. Scary fucking undercover hero Ross Semple. My buddies said something's rotten in Denmark, though I don't know what the fuck Denmark's got to do with anything."

Before I got into R&D I was what the public would call a troubleshooter. I'd travel around the world fixing thorny technical problems at our processing plants. My team and I always approached a problem with what we'd call the basic assumptions. This was the most important thing you could do, because it guided everything you did after that. It's how my old man, the mechanic, fixed cars. He'd say, it's not the fuel system, so it has to be in the ignition. If he was wrong, days could go by, with money pouring down the drain, with no good result.

I told Cermanski he had to change his assumption from "Ernesto did it" to "Ernesto didn't." Then the whole thing will look completely different. This is hard to do, because like he told me on the crime scene, the first assumption is almost always the right one. But when it's not, the real answer is usually a tough nut.

"Can people hold two different assumptions in their minds at the same time?" he asked.

"Sure, if they're smart enough."

"I'm smart enough. But you don't have to think so. I like it when I'm underestimated."

"You don't need my approval," I said, "but I think that's a good idea. Keep 'em guessing."

We let a little space in the conversation open up, which prompted another round of drinks and a brief look at the ball game on TV. Then I asked him, "So what are *you* guessing?"

"That everybody knows more than they're saying, which is nothing new. Including Ernesto. Doesn't mean he did it or didn't do it. It just means he's got something to hide. And maybe for good reason. People go down all the time protecting something or somebody for noble purposes, at least in their minds. I also think this thing is way above my pay grade, but I don't give a damn. I'm young and stupid, right? I just need to go on doing my job until somebody tells me not to, then I just keeping doing it anyway until they cap my ass. Which I don't give a damn about either, because I'm young and stupid and immortal."

I looked more closely for signs of too much beer, and didn't see any.

"So what can I do for you?" I asked him.

"I was popping my first zits when you took out that asshole who killed the old lady. You got a degree from MIT and had the world by the balls before you fucked it all up. You been doing this a lot longer than me. You're gonna learn things I won't. I want in. I trust that you're holding up your end, you trust that I follow the evidence where it leads. All assumptions on the table."

I'd wondered if telling him what I knew would be a bad idea. But then I thought, who cares? Amanda's got a couple brain tumors, what could be worse than that?

So I gave him everything I had.

He listened carefully, nodding along the way. He looked a little like the dog who caught the car. I felt some regret that I'd gone against my usual instinct to keep my trap shut until I knew what I was talking about.

"I have an obligation not to compromise Jackie's defense of Ernesto," I said. "I can't violate that."

"Fair enough. If you're right, that won't happen."

There were no handshakes, no clinking glasses. We just finished up our beers and left the bar. Out in the parking lot I told him, for the record, that the rumor about me and the guy and the dead old lady was never substantiated. He said fine, nobody cared anymore.

"Just keep killing the right people."

I DIDN'T have much of an appetite for sitting in the Adirondack chairs after work with no chance that Amanda would be gliding across the lawn to sit with me. I resisted the urge to call her in the hospital, because I knew she didn't want me to, at least not yet.

LUCKILY, JACKIE called me and asked if we could meet with Burton Lewis and talk about the Mazzotti case.

I decided to bring my '67 Grand Prix, which thrilled Eddie, since it was like a rolling playground, with lots of room to bounce between the front and back seats and big windows through which he could criticize the other drivers and talk trash with dogs stuck on leashes walking along the side of the road.

By the time we got to Burton's, he was fully exercised and huffing with glee.

I got Isabella, Burton's Praetorian guard, to open the gate without complaint by telling her Eddie was in the car. If you can't exploit your dog to grease the gears of social commerce, who can you exploit? I just had to wait through her Spanish terms of endearment and Eddie's confusion over where that tinny electronic voice was coming from.

Eddie stayed with Isabella so she could fawn over him and give him traditional Cuban dog treats, which I hoped didn't include cigars. She told me Burton was in the big screened-in porch, where I found him melted into an overstuffed rattan love seat with a tall gin and tonic dripping with condensation and a bowl full of fried calamari in his lap. He struggled to get up, but I told him to stay put, shook his hand, poured myself my usual drink from the wet bar, and dropped my ass in an equally luxurious padded chair.

"What's wrong?" he asked.

"What do you mean what's wrong? I just came to visit."

"It's amazing how otherwise perceptive people can be so blind to their own affect."

"Okay, Sigmund, I'm fucking pissed out of my mind."

"Not at me, I hope," he said.

"Never, Burt."

"So?"

"Amanda's got a brain tumor. Actually two of them. They're little, but in bad places. Odds are bad."

He rose to sit on the edge of the love seat, his face struck with alarm.

"Oh, God."

I told him the story of her going berserk on the boat, and later in the city after Markus sent her in for tests. And what we learned from the neurosurgeon. And since I was on a roll, I told him about the Mazzotti case, even though Jackie hadn't shown up yet, which was a serious break in protocol. I would have told him how furious I was with the political situation and general decay of social norms, but I ran out of breath.

Eddie ran into the room just in time, followed closely by Isabella.

"He want to be with the other boys," she said. "After I show my affections. Typical."

Eddie let Burton ruffle around the top of his head, then trotted over and dropped down at my feet.

"Is there anything I can do?" Burton asked. "About Amanda?"

"Wish there was, but thanks for asking."

A buzzer went off somewhere deep in the house and Isabella left. Eddie panted and looked around the room as if appreciating the aesthetics. Burton and I talked about Amanda's situation a few more minutes before Jackie came in. As she got settled I told her I'd already briefed Burton on the Mazzotti case, from my perspective. It didn't seem to bother her. Maybe because Eddie was dancing all around her, thrilled she was there and providing a useful diversion.

"Thanks for getting us into the FBI office in New York," I said to Burton, "but I think they agreed just to politely tell us to go screw."

Jackie asked about Amanda, and I had the happy task of repeating what I told Burton. She looked slightly horrified, but knew me well enough not to dwell on the subject. So I easily moved to my conversation with Tony Cermanski.

"I'm surprised," said Jackie. "I thought that little shit was going to be nothing but trouble."

"He knows something," said Burton. "More than he told you, Sam."

"Of course he does," I said. "Makes it that much more interesting."

We sat quietly with our individual thoughts until Burton broke the silence.

"We moved Mazzotti's family yesterday," he said. "They're in a secure location with a team of bodyguards."

"At least they're safe," said Jackie.

"Remains to be seen," he said.

Jackie stirred in her seat and said, "You're freaking me out."

"I don't want to insult you," he said.

"What the hell does that mean?"

"You've spent nearly your whole life in Southampton. You don't know what the greater world is capable of. Not your fault, just the way it is," he said.

"I'm insulted," said Jackie.

"What are you saying, Burt?" I asked.

He sighed.

"Local horrors are horrible enough. We've all seen it, even here in our Southampton bubble. But evil scales geographically. By the time you reach the outer limits, it's incomprehensible. I've seen it. You haven't, Jackie, though I know Sam has. I fear this monster has come to call. We might not be up to the consequences."

Jackie seemed to fold into herself, something I'd never seen her do before. Burton had his eyes cast down at the tile floor, grim, oddly resigned.

All I could think of was Amanda at the hospital, roaming the overlit, sterile halls, and out of sheer boredom striking up conversations with anyone who'd listen. Nurses kindly guiding her back to her room, where she impatiently fiddled with the bed's controls and fretted with the institutional linens. Turning on the TV only to turn it off again in disgust.

I saw her in the bathroom brushing out her bountiful hair, and refining her makeup, flicking a tiny comb through her eyelashes and dabbing powder on her cheekbones. Putting on too much lipstick, laughing at herself, then using a Kleenex to wipe off the excess. Striving to be the best-looking corpse in New York City.

"We'll see about that," I said.

Chapter Eleven

Jackie woke me up the next morning with a cold hard voice.

"I'm picking you up in fifteen minutes," she said.

"What the hell for?"

"I'll explain."

Deep sleep clung to my brain like a wet towel. I forced myself up and weaved into the bathroom. I kept the light low to save myself from the unflinching mirror. I pulled on the first clothes at hand and got the coffee going. I let Eddie out, and tossed a pile of food in his bowl for when he came back inside. He was pretty self-sufficient, but I hated to leave him on his own without human supervision, however lax, in the vicinity.

I'd just poured two travel mugs of coffee when Jackie roared into the driveway in her road-weary station wagon.

"Fuckin' hell," I said, as I climbed in the car.

"Ernesto's in Stonybrook Hospital," she said, spinning the wheel and flooring it out of the driveway. "They operated on him last night. He'll live."

"Shit."

"They got him on protective watch, supposedly. I sent over a PI of ours who lives nearby. Can't stop the cops from trying to do an interview until I get there. Who knows what the hell kind of shape Ernesto's in. What he'll say."

I tried to hold myself in the seat as Jackie blasted down the road.

"If you get nailed for speeding, we'll never get there," I said. I felt her back off the accelerator.

"You're right. I'm tense."

"Have some coffee," I said, handing over the mug. "I hear it calms you down."

"Fuck, I knew this was going to happen," she said. "In my mind. I just never said anything. I'm an idiot."

"I love Catholic guilt," I said. "Everything's always your fault. Thanks a lot for global warming and talk radio."

There wasn't much more she could tell me. All she knew was three other prisoners went after Ernesto with knives in the communal shower room, that he'd subdued them while enduring multiple wounds, one of which was serious enough to warrant abdominal surgery.

"Where do they have the other guys?" I asked.

"In the morgue," she said, looking over at me, her face full of questions.

We drove along in silence for a while, then she said, "Sam?"

I took a moment, then said, "You're right."

"About what?"

"This is something different. And no, I don't know what to do."

"That's not what I want to hear," she said.

"Then stop listening."

We drove on for a while, then she said, "Sorry. I'm used to you having answers for everything."

"I have *thoughts* about everything. Rarely answers."

"So what are you thinking?"

"I have no idea."

THE MAN at the reception desk looked like he'd heard it all, and our story was just like the last few thousand. He picked up the phone and talked to someone, then told us to wait nearby for an escort.

Shortly after, a uniformed cop met us and led the way to surgical recovery, where he said Mr. Mazzotti was resting and more or less alert.

"I got a hernia fixed here a couple years ago," he said. "It's like three days before you're entirely aware what planet you're on."

"Earth," said Jackie. "They told you that, right?"

"Good to know."

When we got to Ernesto's room, another cop was standing guard. Our guide told him it was okay to let us in. Ernesto looked completely disinterested in his whereabouts and unconcerned about the tangle of tubes and wires connecting him to expensive-looking machines with inscrutable little pulsating screens.

He barely lightened up when he saw us come into the room.

"Hey, what the hell you doing here?" he asked, his voice slightly slurred.

"I could ask you the same thing," said Jackie.

He frowned.

"Not my idea," he said. "These assholes try to stab me to death. What am I supposed to do?"

"Recognize any of them?" I asked.

He raised his hands to communicate bewilderment, bringing along the whole wiry web.

"Never seen them. *Anglos malparidos.*"

"Bad white guys," I translated.

"Worse than that. Swastika and skull tattoos. Aryans. Call me a murderer and say I'm going back to Mexico in a bag. Do these people know there are other countries in Latin America?"

"This may seem like a stupid question," said Jackie, "but how do you feel? Mentally."

"Fuzzy."

"I'm asking because I need some honest answers."

He nodded.

"I'm sure you do."

"What did you tell the cops?" she asked.

"Nothing to tell them. Guy walks up and sticks a shiv in my gut. Two other guys try to grab my arms. I fight them off."

"Just like that?" she asked.

"Don't remember details. I was too busy fighting."

Jackie asked if that was all he had to say. While she sat silently, I had a question of my own.

"Who are you?"

"You know who I am."

"No, we don't," said Jackie. "I know what you call yourself. According to Colombian census data, Ernesto Mazzotti doesn't exist. Unless you're actually an Italian, with a gift for mimicking a Colombian accent."

"That's funny."

"Either you come clean, or I'm going to fire you as a client. Our mandate is to serve people with limited means. Real people, not phantoms."

Ernesto closed his eyes and slowly shook his head.

"I like you, Ernesto, I really do," I said. "But I hate being bullshitted. Especially if it means my own ass is on the line, which is what I'm feeling."

"My family."

"They're safe," I said. "Burton Lewis has them tucked away. They're in his care, which means forever, client or not. So maybe you could honor that by trusting the only fucking friends you got in this situation, far as I know."

A nurse picked that time to push into the room to look at Ernesto's vitals, check the lines stuck in his body, ask him how he was feeling, and if he wanted anything to drink. He said shots of tequila would be fine, a request I seconded. She didn't think that was funny.

"You know how to work the painkiller drip," she said, pointing to a little thumb-squeezed pump.

"I do, but how do I stick it up your ass?" he said in Spanish.

"Do you want a translator?" she asked.

"He said thanks for all your kind help," I told her.

She left without further comment. Ernesto waited a few moments, then said, "You're right, you need to fire me. I can take care of myself."

"Right," said Jackie.

"You don't understand. It's not for me. It's for you. I shouldn't have let you take on my case. I thought it would just be this Bollings thing. You get stupid when you live like a normal person in a beautiful place with other normal people. You fool yourself. I'm sorry." Then he shut his eyes. "I think that drip is doing its work, because I'm getting really sleepy. Maybe that nurse can come back and tuck me in."

"What the fuck," said Jackie.

His head slumped down on the pillow. Jackie looked like she was about to grab him by the hospital gown, but I moved in front of her.

"Time to go," I said.

"Son of a bitch." I waited her out. She glowered at me. "You have that look."

I jerked my head toward the door.

"After you," I said.

She swiveled around and banged out the door. The cop on duty jumped up from his chair, but we moved on by. I followed her in a contrail of frustration and wrath. I didn't mind.

I'd been back there before. We made it to her car unimpeded. When the car doors were closed, she was about to launch in on me when I told her to shut up.

"I didn't say anything," she snarled.

"Good. Keep it that way. Time to listen to me. We're going back to my house, where we'll sit and have a calm conversation." I checked the time on my phone. "Until then, I need quiet to think. And you need to examine the value of that Irish temper. You might feel it's charming, but I think it makes you stupid."

She made a big show of starting the Volvo and spinning out of the parking space. I could hear her breathing over the sound of the engine and shifting gears. I slid down in my seat and closed my eyes so I didn't have to see impending doom every few seconds. Eventually she slowed down and we drove to Oak Point in apparent silence, though if you had sensitive enough ears, you could have heard the roar inside Jackie's excitable brain.

"That was a first," she said, when she pulled into my driveway. "A client refuses to cooperate in order to protect *me*."

"And your trusty private detective, don't forget."

"I'm not giving up this case. I don't care what anybody says."

"I thought you were firing him."

"I was just trying to twist his arm," she said. "Fat load of good that did."

"Strong arms."

"Maybe we are over our heads. That's what Burton was basically saying."

"You can't go from righteous defiance to abject surrender in less than ten seconds."

"What do you want to do?" she asked.

"We're playing in too small a sandbox. We have to upgrade."

"And how the hell do you do that?"

"You get a guy. No matter what the situation is, there's always a guy."

"My father used to say that, but he was talking about fixing the boiler or getting tickets to the ball game."

"I got a guy. Hadn't thought of it before, but I didn't know what I was supposed to be thinking about."

"You're not serious."

When I was a field engineer specializing in solving intractable problems at our plants around the world, it was the happiest time of my professional life. Every situation was different, every puzzle unique, every plant manager panicked, desperate, and eager to cooperate. It was usually just me and a few supporting engineers, no massive staff to manage, no home office crap to wade through, just these big hydrocarbon processing plants and nice hotels with hot tubs and free-flowing room service.

Since finding the best bar in town was one of my favorite hobbies, it's what I did when I hit a new location. Being American, the first stop was always the English-speaking expat hangout, where I could get the lay of the land and branch out from there. Whether it was Asia, the Middle East, Africa, or South America, these places had a reliable client mix. Salesmen, engineers like me, career embassy people, professors on research sabbaticals, and journalists. If I spent a few hours there, I learned all I needed to slip into the authentic scene with minimal risk of getting fleeced or my throat cut, or both. If I stayed till closing, I'd learn things that often helped solve my assigned problem, since it was often more political than technological.

In those days, Venezuela was an important country for us, sitting on an ocean of oil and generally friendly to American partners before Hugo Chávez turned it into a xenophobic basket case. So I spent a lot of time there fixing refining and transport facilities and prowling the teeming international community drawn by the petro-abundance.

The bar in Caracas was called *El Trópico*, and was like most of these expat places, only so diverse it made the United Nations seem monolithic. Usually on my own, I was always at the bar, where deep in the evening committed regulars began to emerge. Out of this crowd, I'd have steady conversations with an Australian AP reporter named Grant Conkling. A tall man, with an aristocratic face and trim physique, apparently unaffected by a regimen of hard liquor and endless cigarettes, he was graced with abundant energy, much of which he deployed in the service of talk.

His beat extended from Venezuela and Trinidad in a westerly arc across the top of South America to Colombia and slightly south from there. I didn't remember most of what we talked about, but the prevailing theme was the interaction of the various forces controlling the region—economic, social, and political—the approach-avoidance dance between the locals and gringos to the north, and how everyone got the region wrong because they didn't understand there was no whole without the parts banging around in a chaotic, exotic swirl.

Though I did remember him telling me he'd be worthless in his job if he hadn't cultivated, meaning paid off, the intelligence services, foreign and domestic, operating beneath the notice of his benighted readership.

I told all this to Jackie, explaining we first had to determine he was alive, uncertain given his personal habits and profession.

"And how are you going to do that?" she asked.

"A journey of a thousand miles starts with a single step. I'm going to step into my house and work on cabinetry. You and Burton's paralegals are going to get on Google and start to look."

"So we're now investigating our own client, hoping to learn things that will help us save him, which he's trying to hide in order to save us," she said.

"Good summation," I said, getting out of the car. "Keep me posted. You know where I'll be."

I was glad to see Eddie bound across the lawn, tongue out, body animating his long, feathery tail. He turned and jumped on ahead, leading me toward the cottage where he knew a richly deserved bowl of sumptuous dog food was to be had.

THE NEXT day Jackie called to ask if I had a passport.

I said, "Sure. Just way out of date. Why?"

"You're going to the British Virgin Islands."

"I am?"

"Grant Conkling's living in a house near the top of a hill on Tortola. Don't know what kind of shape he's in, beyond alive. Haven't contacted him, since I know you like surprise appearances. We'll make all the travel arrangements as soon as you can pick a date. Look at your e-mail for how to expedite a fresh passport."

"Okay. Nice work."

"Thank Burton. He's picking up the tab."

I DID thank Burton when Eddie and I went over to his house. I'd secured a new passport, packed a bag, and told my customers I'd be gone for a bit, though all projects would be delivered on time. More hope than promise.

Isabella had agreed to take on Eddie's care, which only involved regular meals, room to prowl, and a place to sleep at night. I was still anxious about it, but my rational mind told me this was the best solution, given Amanda's situation.

She was back home on Oak Point, and heartily agreed. She'd be awaiting her surgery for another two weeks, while a constellation of drugs worked on the tumors and her general disposition, improving the odds for success. She didn't need to be responsible for a frolicking mutt, one she might have to abandon on a moment's notice.

The harder part for me was leaving Amanda, but she insisted. Some people really don't want to be catered to in times of duress, and she was one of them. I understood this, because I was one of them too.

I followed Eddie to the front door, opened by Isabella, whom he nearly knocked over in his enthusiasm. She told me Burton was out in the shop, where I went, leaving Eddie to her culinary designs.

Burton was engaged in weaving the seat of a caned chair and far more serene than the last time I saw him at the shop. The smell of a large bouquet of flowers competed with sawdust to perfume the air. Mozart blared from the sound system.

When he saw me come in, he turned down the music and wiped his hands on his shop apron.

"I built the chair, you know," he said. "This isn't all elementary school arts and crafts."

It was a beautiful thing, complex and imaginative. I wasn't sure I could have replicated it. I told him as much.

"I wanted to design and build the most difficult, practical object I could conceive. Turned out to be a comfortable chair. Who knew?"

"Let your ass be the judge of that," I said.

"Is Eddie here?"

"With Isabella. Thanks for looking after him."

"The pleasure's ours."

I told him I was going to the Virgin Islands, and he stood there waiting for me to tell him why. For some reason, I didn't want to. Just an irrational, protective impulse, I guess. Luckily he knew me well enough not to press the issue. Instead he went over to a drawing table and peeled off a piece of graph paper. He wrote down a phone number.

"Friend of mine," he said. "Wired into the Caribbean and South America. Memorize it. Just in case."

"In case of what?"

"You'll know."

CHAPTER TWELVE

I used to spend a lot of time sailing around the Caribbean, mostly the British and American Virgins, but it had been awhile, and I wasn't prepared for the slick little airport on Beef Island someone had put in place of the near-shack that had been there before.

Thank God the pace was the same, so it only took an hour for the twenty people on my flight, the only one at the airport, to clear customs. Once out of the terminal, I looked for the card game I used to interrupt to get a ride into Road Town, but instead found a lineup of crisp, modern cabs.

The trip into town hadn't improved much in terms of road surface and breakneck curves, and the occasional stop along the way to pick up friends and relatives. Air-conditioning was a potential upgrade, though the driver found little reason to use it. I felt lucky to have a window, which blew in a type of sodden air you can suck from a dryer vent.

My hotel was just beyond Road Town, so I was the last to get off. I paid the bill and laid on a big tip. The driver handed me his business card and said he'd take me anywhere, anytime. I think I surprised him when I said to be outside my hotel at eight in the morning, and plan to stay with me for the day. I handed him a hundred-dollar bill.

"Down payment."

The hotel bar was open to the breeze on two sides. Still off-season, it was almost empty, which suited me fine. The last time I'd been there was with my ex-wife, closing out a week-long cruise with a few days on shore. I remembered that we were getting along, which we usually did on sailing trips. Something about the tropical atmosphere cleaned out her abiding pretense and dissatisfaction. Or maybe it was the wall-to-wall rum and pineapple juice, and sexual abandon, that living afloat inspired. I often wondered how life would have been had we never left that blessed world.

Which led to wondering if Amanda would live long enough for me to bring her down there, and if the cosmic order would cause us to break into hostility and wrath, something our relationship had never experienced. This was such an ugly, depressing thought I was suddenly teetering on the brink of despair.

"You all right, mate?" the bartender asked, since my forehead was now resting on the bar.

"Just a little existential crisis," I said. "It'll pass."

"You're supposed to come here to escape that sort of thing."

"I hear vodka has a similar effect," I said, holding up my empty glass.

"Right."

I caught the Australian accent, and when he came back I asked if he knew a countryman named Grant Conkling.

"I do indeed. Randy old bugger. Comes in here during the season to entertain the tourists. Likable. Are you a friend of his?"

"I was, a long time ago," I said. "We hung out together in Venezuela."

"So you're a reporter, then?"

"Design engineer, in those days. Now I build cabinets. It's a long story."

"Most of them are. I used to sell commercial rubbish compactors. My territory was about the size of the American West. The whole time I'm either in my car or sweating in some stinking garbage dump, my wife's dropping her knickers for the upstairs neighbor. No wonder I ended up here."

"My girlfriend's got a brain tumor," I said, surprising myself. "Not sure they can fix her."

"You win, mate."

"Brevis ipsa vita est sed malis fit longior."

"Meaning?"

"Something like, troubles make you live longer."

"Then I'm heading for fucking immortality."

THE CABBIE was waiting there in the morning, conversing in the indecipherable island patois with his fellow drivers. I handed him Conkling's address and asked if he knew where that was. He took out his smartphone, found it on the GPS, and pointed up at the sky.

"Hope you don't get nosebleeds too easy," he said.

One of the charms of traveling around the BVI was driving on the left side of the road, British-style, with the steering wheel on the left side of the vehicle, American-style. This gives the passenger an excellent vantage point for seeing opposing traffic bearing down. With deep rain gullies often to either side of the roadway, drivers used some sort of mystical space perception to avoid routine head-on collisions. In the case of our trip up the tall hill, there was also the matter of tight switchbacks and the persistent possibility of flying off a precipice and into the teal-colored Caribbean Sea.

The cabbie, whose name was Charles Benedict, enhanced the game by maintaining a healthy speed and spending more time than I liked looking over at me as we conversed. Not wanting to be unfriendly, I held on to the strap above my head and talked freely about the current condition of New York City, the only place in America he'd visited, twenty years before.

Nothing like an authentic existential threat to ward off the philosophical.

There wasn't much hill left when we reached Conkling's house—a standard, low-slung masonry cottage surrounded by grey-green foliage, meandering roosters, and pergolas laden with stringy vines. On a patio overlooking the water was the man himself, wearing sandals and a white bathrobe, and reading a tablet device.

"Grant Conkling, I presume?" I asked, as I approached.

He took off his sunglasses to get a better look at me.

"Bloody hell, Sam fucking Acquillo."

He looked to be in his early seventies, holding on to his shaggy white hair and sharp features. He rose like a stork from the nest and shook my hand.

"Good memory," I said.

"It's a curse, actually. Can't forget a thing. What are you doing here, and how the hell did you find me?"

I pointed at his device.

"Hard to hide these days," I said. "Even if you want to."

"Want a latte?"

"Black coffee would be fine."

He told me to grab the other chair and enjoy the view. When he came back with the coffee, he said, "You're not planning on bumping me off, I hope."

"Why would I do that?"

"That's often why people drop by unannounced."

"Sorry, it's a habit of mine. If I called to ask you, you might tell me to stay away, and then what? At least now maybe you'll hear me out."

He first wanted to know what I'd been up to since we'd last been kicked out of *El Trópico* at closing time. I gave him the digest version, though sparing none of the less flattering parts, still suffering from the candor I'd shown the bartender the night before. He listened carefully, asking an occasional question, probing things that caught his interest, all betraying a lifetime in journalism.

"You knew how to throw a punch," he said. "That I remember. I liked being on your good side."

"Some would debate which side that is."

His story followed a more predictable trajectory. One failed marriage, serial girlfriends, a bad scare with melanoma, a brief period of abstinence from alcohol, from which he said he'd fully recovered, postings as a foreign correspondent by various newspapers and magazines, evolving into freelance feature writing, which still sustained him, though always under a pseudonym.

"The prospect of someone showing up with a semiautomatic and muzzle suppressor is actually rather real," he said. "In fact, I've been shot at more than once, without result, and the feeling is hardly exhilarating. Used to be the only thing we had to fear was the competition beating us to the scoop. Nowadays, the subjects of our inspired journalism are liable to chop off our heads. Gets dodgy."

"I get that. I've got some questions you might not want to answer, for good reason. I can only tell you I'll keep your name out of it."

"Unless some bugger's got that automatic stuffed in *you*r face."

"In which case, I'll give him your address, phone number, and exact latitude and longitude."

He enjoyed that, enough to tell me to go ahead and ask. Didn't mean he had to answer.

As with my personal history, he asked pointed questions, guiding the story down several tributaries, before returning to the core narrative. He took in a lot of detail, occasionally recapping in a way that proved his claim to a sturdy memory. He was most interested in Ernesto Mazzotti, far less in Victor Bollings. When I was out of information, I asked him why the difference.

"I knew Bollings. Knew him well."

"Really."

"This is where you remind yourself to forget you got this from me. The last we met, I was puking down a Caracas storm drain."

"Got it."

"You can't even use what I'm about to tell you unless you get it from somebody else. I know it's a devil's deal, but those are the terms. Of course you could go back on that, but then I'd come shoot you myself."

"Seems reasonable," I said.

He still looked undecided, then said, "Fuck it. Bollings was a spook. First rate, deep, deep undercover. Perfect for the job. High level O'Connor consultant, he had access to business and government at every level, and solid reasons for connecting right out in the open. Could easily get in and out of the country, sometimes on a private jet. Worked directly with a liaison at Langley, so little exposure to the embassies, which aren't as secure as your government pretends them to be. No bad habits anybody knew, nothing extortable."

I asked him how he knew this. He laughed.

"Not a chance, Sam. That one stays with me. It's bad enough that I told you anything at all."

I didn't tell Conkling I'd already suspected as much. Not for any one reason, but for all the little things that lacked an explanation. Sitting there on Conkling's patio watching the iridescent glare of the early morning Caribbean soften into a deeper, calmer shade of green, all I felt was confirmation.

And I was fine with the bargain. Secrets can have power without ever being revealed. For me, it was the knowing that mattered.

"What about Ernesto?" I asked. "Any thoughts there?"

"Yeah, but I'm not sure. I can ask some people. Give me your snail mail address and keep an eye out. Turns out to be the safest way to communicate. Good old paper."

I thanked him and stood up to see Charles Benedict leaning back in his seat scrolling through his smartphone. I was about to head over there when Conkling said, "It's not what you think it is, all this cloak-and-dagger routine. The people in the field are on the whole very brave and honorable servants of our safety and welfare. The ones to look out for are all the rest. Bureaucrats who commute to work and labor away in cubicles behind computer screens. They often know not what they do. Neither does anybody else."

He took a small revolver out of his bathrobe pocket and set it on a side table before lifting his tablet and renewing his morning read.

I HAD a chance to hold down my barstool at the hotel one more night before taking off the next morning. A group of people attending a sailing school had arrived during the day, so the bar felt more like a going concern. The bartender was well occupied, so less available for thoughtful deliberation on why we're here on earth when we could be doing something somewhere else. Though we did exchange contact information after he told me he wanted to get up to New York City and maybe take a walk around the Hamptons.

"It is about fifty square miles," I said, "though I guess that's nothing to you Aussies."

"A stroll in the garden, mate."

I was in a better mood, for no particular reason than a successful morning with Grant Conkling, followed by a less harrowing drive around Tortola so I could catch up on things and soak up my surplus time with Mr. Benedict, who proved to be a capable tour guide, a few threatening gestures to other drivers notwithstanding.

"Kill themselves if they want. I got children at home."

The sailing students were earnest and healthy-looking white people, though diverse in age and country of origin, judging by a few of the accents I overheard. One of them, a lovely black-haired woman from Dublin, sat next to me and asked if I was part of the class. I said no, but admitted some envy. I'd sailed the stripped-down, twenty-five-foot training boats out on the waters of the BVI, and loved their responsive tiller and general fearlessness among the big swells of the Sir Francis Drake Channel.

She told me she'd planned to take the course with her fiancé, who turned out to be a right asshole, so she ditched him and kept the plane ride, hotel reservation, and lesson fees, since they were already paid for and in her hand. She thought if I was signed up I could be her buddy, since it looked like everyone else was paired up.

I was glad she hadn't approached me the night before, since by then I'd probably be telling her about Amanda's brain tumors and the long, lost tropical idylls with my wife-turned-reproachful adulteress.

"I have some marjuana," she said, as if a consolation prize. "And the beach is right over there."

"Thanks, but I can't handle that stuff. Just puts me to sleep."

"A pity. You remind me of one of my favorites."

"Really."

"My Uncle George. A little younger than you, but with the same sort of gangster nose and big hands. I thought you'd be a good bodyguard."

I wanted to tell her I'd be the best bodyguard a woman could have, but didn't want to encourage her. I did buy her a few drinks and helped her through her evening's loneliness and isolation, hopefully to be purged of the necessity of fellowship out on the water.

"You know I've done all the talking and don't know a fecking thing about you," she said, as I got up to pay our bill.

"*Nescis quid non nocebit*," I said, hoping she wasn't a Latin scholar, since I wasn't sure if I'd said "What you don't know won't hurt you," or something insulting about her intelligence.

Then I fumbled my way to my room, where I hoped the insistent winds would interfere with the bright paint on the walls and quell my rising anxieties enough to let me get a good night's sleep.

CHAPTER THIRTEEN

I checked on Amanda as soon as I hit ground and learned she was back in the hospital for more tests. Her foreman had driven her in with no incidents along the way.

"I nearly have the nursing staff trained," she said, "but they're a headstrong bunch. They've taken so many blood samples I'm beginning to feel like a pin cushion. No, I am a pin cushion."

"Tell them to leave some blood behind. You'll need it later."

"They might keep me here and just do the surgery after the test results come through," she said. "The doctor looks revved up to go."

"Let me know, would you?" I said.

"If you don't hear from me, you'll know."

Jackie called when I was in the car leaving the airport parking lot.

"We have another situation," she said, then turned the phone toward what sounded like a crowd of sports fans chanting for their team. I couldn't make out what they were saying, but it didn't sound friendly.

I asked her when she came back on the line.

" 'Illegals kill,' " she said. "The signs are worse."

"Where are you?"

"At my place," she said, meaning her second-story combination office/apartment over a Japanese restaurant in Water

Mill, the hamlet east of Southampton Village. "I don't know how many are out there, but they've just about stopped traffic on Montauk Highway. The cops are busy."

"I'll come in from the back roads. Can I bring you anything?"

"Do they still make Gatling guns?"

I hit some traffic winding through the fields and woodlands north of Water Mill, probably locals trying to bypass the logjam. I got to within about two blocks when I gave up, pulled the Jeep off the road, and walked the rest of the way.

Jackie's place was directly on Montauk Highway overlooking the town green which featured an ancient windmill. It was a big, open area and now looked full of people and parked cars. Everyone was facing the highway brandishing their signs, proclaiming a variety of hostile sentiments against immigrants, illegal immigrants, and attorneys who represent illegal immigrants. The tone varied from simple declarations to nakedly racist and obscene.

I crossed the highway, and walked into the crowd. Contrary to the belligerence on the signs, they seemed to be having a nice time, as if pleased by the closeness of so many likeminded. I did my best to look part of the tribe as I worked my way toward where most of the cars were parked. The state cops had cordoned it off, leaving a single opening for cars to leave, and none to get in. Likewise, access to the green from Halsey Lane, which paralleled Montauk Highway, was blocked. I could see the strategy—contain the people who were there, move any newcomers along down the highway.

I scanned the license plates. It wasn't a scientific study, but it looked like more than half the cars had come from out of state, and the New York plates were mostly held there by frames from dealers outside the metro area.

When I wormed my way back toward Jackie's place, I spotted the guy in the cowboy hat who'd been parked on Ernesto's street the day I went to see Querida. He was just standing there looking toward Jackie's, with no sign, no companions. I went up to him.

"Did you find the repair shop?" I asked him.

It took a moment for him to place me. A grin formed somewhere under his moustache.

"I did. Thank you for that."

He wore a plain white T-shirt, jeans, and banged-up cowboy boots. Not much younger than me, but a lot bigger across the shoulders, with well-developed arms and thick, rough hands. Long reach. Heavy thighs to help keep him upright in a brawl. All things I noted by reflex, a fighter's habit.

"Enjoying the show?" I asked.

"Not really. Just curious. I came up here to visit my cousin, not hang around these knuckleheads. No offense to you."

"Not offended. I'm just curious too. It's a curse."

He nodded.

"Ain't that the truth." He looked around at the crowd.

"Who's your cousin?" I asked. "I know most of the people around here."

"You wouldn't know him. He's just a guy. Any idea what this is about?" he asked, switching the subject.

"No, you?"

"I'm guessing somebody in that building across the street has pissed these people off. Wouldn't want to be her."

"You knew it was a her," I said.

He just looked at me for a moment, then jammed his meaty hands into the pockets of his jeans.

"Ain't it always?"

I left the cowboy and jostled my way over to Jackie's place where I was met by a pair of Town cops who were guarding the door that led to the second floor. I showed them my PI card.

A small cluster of protesters was standing about twenty paces away. Lucky for them the cops were there. The first protesters to breach the door would have learned how accurate Jackie was with that Glock of hers.

I called her and told her where I was.

"I see you," she said, having an eye on the security monitor I'd installed for her years before. "I'll be down."

When we were inside the office, I said, "So otherwise, how're things going?"

"I doubt you know much about social media," she said, sitting down in front of her computer.

"It's a mystery to the unsociable."

She turned the screen so I could see better. It was a website with a photo that ran across the top of the page. The photo was of a rectangular banner on which the words "Illegals Kill" were artlessly painted. Jackie told me it was home base for the people who incited the crowds outside, a vehicle for spreading the word about when and where to show up. She said it was only posted a few days ago.

"Pretty effective," I said.

She pointed at a box that showed the number of members who'd signed on to the page. One million, four hundred and thirty-two. She refreshed the page, and the number went up to more than three million.

"We're going to need a bigger town green," I said.

"It's called a flash mob. Mob being the operative word."

The story about Ernesto's arrest for Victor Bollings's murder was bad enough when it went national. But that paved the way for news of the prison fight that ended with three dead white guys. The whole thing made me feel like I'd been dropped down into an alternate universe. I said as much to Jackie.

"Mounting an effective defense is hard enough without all this baloney," she said.

I debriefed her on my trip to the BVI and subsequent cliff-side conversation with Grant Conkling. Before I got into the details we heard a thud on the outside wall, followed by a cheer from the crowd. I went to the window and saw a Town cop drag a guy out onto Montauk Highway and whack him over the head with a nightstick. Two other protesters went after the cop and suddenly there was a swarm of fists and nightsticks and signs redeployed as weapons. Then, as if by magic, the staties moved in and quelled the action, while other police formed a phalanx in front of the crowd at large. Several of the protesters were handcuffed and led from the green.

I noticed Jackie standing by my side and told her to get back from the window.

"You get back," she said. "This is my mob scene."

I did as she asked and watched over her shoulder as a semblance of order descended on the throng.

"I'm not telling you," I said.

"What?"

"The things I learned from Conkling. I can't tell you. I promised him it would stay with me."

She looked at me with angry eyes.

"Jesus Christ."

"You have an overriding responsibility to Ernesto's defense," I said. "You'd have to use the information, which could endanger Conkling's life."

She used both hands to squeeze her head, her eyes shut.

"You're such an impossible man," she said.

"I'll figure something out," I said.

Jackie's phone rang. It was her boyfriend, Harry Goodlander, calling from San Francisco. He'd just turned on the news.

"I'm okay," said Jackie. "Sam's here. So are most of the police on the South Fork." She listened for a while, then said,

"You don't have to do that. I'm fine." She looked at me and shook her head. "Okay, if you insist. It will be nice to see you. It always is." When she signed off, she said, "He's such a darling. I don't deserve him."

"You don't."

"You're not supposed to say that."

"Then you stop saying it."

The rabble outside began to dissipate as darkness started to fall, though police remained at full strength. We checked the security monitor and it looked like the two cops were alone at the bottom of the stairway.

"How are you at disguises?" I asked Jackie.

It took some effort to cram her frizzy mound of hair into a baseball cap, which she covered with a baggy old hoodie. It didn't change her appearance that much to me, but I knew what she looked like. When we got to the outside door, she waved over one of the cops.

"Do you think we could sneak out of here without anyone seeing?"

He looked around.

"If you don't mind walking through the woods behind the parking lot, then cutting over to Old Mill Road. I can lend you a flashlight."

We thought that would draw attention, so we braved it in the dark, stumbling and thrashing our way over to Old Mill. We fell in with a file of protesters who were heading north as well, and no one bothered us the rest of the way to where I'd parked my Jeep.

NOT LONG after, we were out on Amanda's patio with Eddie, whom we had to wrest away from Isabella. She said he'd been a very good boy, except for making little yipping noises and wiggling his feet while sleeping at the foot of her bed.

"Visions of tennis balls and eviscerated water fowl," I told her.

When we'd settled on the patio, Jackie said she felt bad sitting there when Amanda was in the hospital.

"She'd feel bad if we weren't," I said. "Likes to make good use of the place."

I fought off her efforts to get more information about my talk with Grant Conkling out of me, until I remembered something I could tell her.

"He didn't know anything about Ernesto," I said, "but he's looking into it."

"Oh, great, more crucial information I don't get to know."

"Not sure that's true, so hold the outrage until we know more."

It was a clear night with a steady breeze off the bay. A motorboat was streaking across the water, too far away to hear, but you could see a red running light as it moved east toward the channel that demarcated the Little Peconic from Noyac Bay next door. I felt a twinge of longing as I put myself in the place of the helmsman, feeling the subtle chop under the hull, listening to the burr of powerful outboards and straining to see other boats in the pale moonlight.

I far preferred sailboats, but there was something about speed over the water that held some appeal. A different form of escape. Purposeful and direct.

I noticed Eddie was lying next to my lounge chair when he sat up and growled. He was staring over at my cottage. I grabbed his collar before he jumped to his feet. He snapped out a bark, in a tone I recognized. Warning.

I clamped my hand around his muzzle and listened. Nothing. Jackie said, "What?"

I shushed her and continued listening, squinting to see in the near blackness. I thought I saw movement. Eddie lurched forward and I pulled him back.

"What?" Jackie whispered.

"I don't know. Let's get Eddie into the house."

I scooped him up and he tried to wriggle out of my grasp, his attention focused on our cottage. I kept him in a bear hug until we were inside, where I slid him into a downstairs bedroom and shut the door. He barked again, indignant.

I told Jackie to follow me, and we went upstairs to another bedroom, converted to office space, where Amanda ran her security array. Joe Sullivan had installed it back when we faced another potential threat and he'd volunteered to secure Amanda's house. I turned on her desktop and fought to remember how to boot everything up.

There was a lot to remember. Outdoor cameras you could switch from normal light to infrared, motion sensors that triggered alarms set to individual tones, a switch that locked all the windows and doors, and a panic button that went directly to Southampton Town police.

There was also a switch that fired up a swarm of floodlights, mounted on the house and nearby trees, but I held off on that. I showed Jackie the basic controls, which she picked up quickly.

"Turn off the lights and close the shade," I said. "Then look."

"What am I looking for?" she asked.

"I don't know," I said. "Anything that doesn't belong here."

"What are you going to do?"

"See for myself."

Before I left the house, I stuck in an earpiece connected to my phone. I also retrieved one of Amanda's Colt .45s from its hiding place, gave it to Jackie, and asked for her Glock.

"It's easier to carry in my pocket," I said.

"Why aren't I calling the police?" she asked.

"Not yet."

I wore a dark green T-shirt and blue jeans. Not exactly Ninja wear, but good enough. I stopped to retrieve my Harmon Killebrew bat from the Jeep, risking the hatch light, and moved along a strip of grass that ran between our common driveway and a stand of woods buffering us from the neighbor behind our houses. I came up to the big shed at the back of my property where I kept the Grand Prix inside my father's mechanic's shop. I paused at the corner and listened while peering at the back of my house. I saw more movement, but it was so indistinct it was like watching a black pulse against a black velvet background. The driveway was clear to the road. I went around the front of the shed and slid into a squat. A silhouette appeared on the east side of the house. I could see an arm move, as if directing something, against the faint moonlight reflecting off the Little Peconic.

Now fixed on the form, I could see it moving, running in a low crouch. In a moment both unexpected and harrowing, it looked like it was heading straight for me. I was just inside the corner of the shed, I hoped out of the view of night-vision goggles, which I had to assume the silent wraith possessed. I slid the three-quarter-sized baseball bat out of my rear waistband and waited.

It wasn't the first time I had the bat ready for someone running at me across my backyard, only then it was in broad daylight, an advantage for both of us. My advantage that night was this guy didn't know I was waiting in a spot he wanted to occupy.

As he got closer I could hear soft footfalls on the damp grass. It helped me gauge the closing distance, so he was about where I'd want him to be when I stepped out and swung the bat as hard as I could, aiming for the bleachers.

The shock of the blow ran up my arms all the way to my shoulders. The guy spun halfway around, but the momentum of his run carried him right into me, and we went down, him on top.

He was dead weight. I rolled him off and scrambled up, pulling the Glock out of my pocket. I stood and listened. Nothing. Other shapes moved outside my cottage, none in my direction. Then I heard a mechanical sound—faint and indistinct. It seemed to come from nowhere, until I realized it was coming from the guy on the ground. I leaned down and put my ear to his chest. I heard the sound again, and knew what it was.

Earbuds.

I pulled them out and stuck one in my ear.

"Merlin, repeat, report your location," said a whispered voice out of the bud. "We can't read you." There was a pause, then the voice said, "Report your status."

I yanked him up into a fireman's carry and got him through a side door into the shed. I dropped him on the floor and put my cheek up to his mouth. Still breathing. I dug out clothesline and tied his wrists and ankles, then put a strip of duct tape over his mouth. I popped open the trunk of the Grand Prix and dropped him in. Then I called Jackie and told her to hit the panic button and stay in place.

Immediately after, the world went crazy. I'd forgotten the panic button was wired to the floodlights and a firehouse-grade siren. I went out the side door and looked around the corner. Amanda's house was lit up like a ballpark, with my cottage in its proximate glare. Three guys in black jumpsuits were running around my backyard, discarding all pretense of stealth and yelling for Merlin. In the lee of the shed, I was still in shadow. I lay on the ground, propped up on my elbows, and aimed the Glock in their direction.

There was a lot more yelling and running around until the flickering sign of headlights lit up the trees overhead. I started firing across the lawn, too far away to take decent aim on the scurrying figures, though I didn't want to actually hit anybody unless I had to. One of them must have spotted the muzzle flash, since a tight cluster splattered into the shed above my head. It would have cut me in half if I'd been standing. In the strobing red, white, and blue light, I saw the black jumpsuits race toward the bay and disappear over the breakwater. I heard an outboard motor.

Then headlights flooded the yard as the Town patrol cars slid into our driveway, racing toward Amanda's house. I tucked the Glock under a workbench in the shed and followed the frenzied cops down my driveway. The siren went silent. When I got within eyeshot I raised my hands above my head and yelled don't shoot until I was told to lie facedown on the ground with my hands where they could see them.

I did as they said, and when they came over to frisk me, I asked if Danny Izard was in Amanda's house. One of them had his gun trained on my head. He said who wants to know, and I told him the guy who's going to stick that thing up his ass if he didn't point it somewhere else. His partner put his hand on the gun and lowered it.

"He's the owner of the house next door. Go get Izard."

When the hothead left, his partner helped me to my feet.

"Sorry, Sam. Rookie. What the hell happened here?"

I told him I was staying at Amanda's and saw people trying to break into my house. So I hit the alarm and they showed up in impressive time. I thanked him for that, and reminded him that Joe Sullivan had set up the rig.

"Why the hell would somebody try that out here with people all around? And why your place, no offense?"

"You're the cops. You figure it out."

The hothead came out and told me Danny wanted to see me inside. He stood at the head of the path, making me walk around him. I used my anger management skills to quell the urge to shove him out of the way.

Danny and Jackie were in the living room. I repeated what I told the officers outside, talking over Eddie's frantic barking from the nearby downstairs bedroom. I asked if I could let him out, and Danny said please do before he had a nervous breakdown from all the noise. The two of them had a nice reunion, so that calmed some nerves.

"Stay here while we check your house," said Danny. "Keep the dog inside."

I gave him my keys and we went back out to the patio. I put Eddie on a leash made out of my belt. He took it well enough.

"Sam, what the hell," said Jackie, her voice low and hoarse.

I put my finger to my lips.

We watched their flashlights bob around my yard, and then inside the cottage. Eddie sat up, alert and eager to run, but restrained by a gentle hand on his back.

"Just cool it, man," I said. "You did your part."

When Danny came back, he reported that my side door was busted in and the house ransacked. He told me to check through my valuables and let him know if anything had been stolen. That would be easy, I thought to myself, since I didn't have much in the way of valuables.

He said he'd leave one of his crew there for a few hours, just to be on the safe side.

After a lot of handshaking and thank-yous and reassurances, Danny and the other cop left. It was getting late at this point, but it seemed reasonable for Jackie and me to have a nightcap on the patio. When we got comfortable I told her I caught one.

"What do you mean?"

"He's in the trunk of the Grand Prix. In the shed."

"You're joking."

"He was alive when I tossed him in there, but no guarantees. I gave him a pretty good smack on the head with that little bat."

"Oh, my God."

I gave her a quick rundown on how it happened. When I was finished, she walked to a side window and looked down the driveway at the patrol car.

"We got to get him out of there," she said. "He could die."

"How do we do that?"

Ten minutes later she was leaning in the cop's driver's side window offering a cold soda and snacks, saying I had to move the Grand Prix to Amanda's house to unload some perishables, which was true enough. I backed the car up to a hatchway leading to the basement. I hoped it was positioned to block the view of me gathering up our house guest and hauling him down the hole.

I rested him on the floor and checked his pulse. Still working, though he looked a little pasty for a young, fit guy. I stripped the duct tape off his mouth and untied his hands. Under the basement lights I could see an angry red welt oozing blood on the side of his head. I relieved him of his sidearm and can of pepper spray while searching for identification. There wasn't any.

I picked him up again and laid him on a couch that had belonged to Amanda's mother, and had yet to be disposed of. Jackie showed up soon after, and knelt to take a look.

"We need to get him to a hospital," she said.

"We need to pour a bucket of water on his head and see if he wakes up."

He decided the choice by moving his lips, saying what I thought I heard as 'what the fuck.' I held his sidearm on him as he emerged from unconsciousness. Jackie went upstairs to get a bottle of water. When she came back, we pulled him into a seated position. She put the bottle to his lips and he grabbed it, taking a long swig. He felt around the wound on his head.

"You want to start explaining?" Jackie asked.

He looked at her impassively.

"Your friends are gone," I said, "chased off by the cops, who don't know you're here."

"You're not going to say anything, are you?" said Jackie.

He didn't respond.

"I guess I'll have to shoot him and toss him in the bay," I said.

The Sphinx had more affect.

"You're not allowed to do that, Sam," said Jackie. "We have to give him to the cops." She looked at him. "You're sure you don't want to tell us anything before we do that?"

Apparently, he didn't.

"Louis Armstrong," I said. He stared at me. "Donald Duck. Yitzhak Rabin. Ford Madox Ford. Victor Bollings."

He jumped up. Jackie screamed. The gun went off.

That's all I remembered.

Chapter Fourteen

I woke up to a ferocious headache and Jackie telling our cover story to the hotheaded cop. I said ours because I wasn't going to get a chance to weigh in, so it would have to stand. Like most good stories, it held elements of the truth. I'd encountered the guy as he was breaking into Amanda's hatchway and hit him with the bat. He seemed unconscious when Jackie let me into the basement and we dragged him under the light. I was covering him with his gun and about to call hothead when I got a little too close and he sprang to life, swatted away the gun, causing it to fire, and ran.

He didn't look convinced, but not much would have changed that. Jackie saw me struggle to stand and ran over to help.

"You're going to the hospital," she said.

"Just shoot me and toss me in the bay."

The cop wouldn't let us go until I corroborated her story, which I'd heard enough to accomplish. He pressed with other questions, but Jackie told him to call in the incident and have a detective meet us at the hospital. She dragged me by the arm across the lawn, which wasn't a bad thing, since I didn't feel all that steady on my feet.

I heard a bark.

"Where's Eddie?" I said.

She stopped.

"I tied him to the dining room table."

"Go get him, please. He hates being cooped up."

I sat on the ground while she ran back to the house. I took stock. I could see fine, but my mind was blurry. Memory unsure. Things were coming back in fragments, as if frames had been cut out of a film. I had a jolt when I remembered Amanda in the hospital in the city, but then the current situation came back to me and I felt my nerves steady themselves.

Eddie stopped to fuss over me, but Jackie managed to herd him to the Jeep, where he jumped through the hatch. I followed under my own power and she shoved me in the passenger side, slid behind the wheel, and we took off.

"Next time I catch a commando in my backyard," I said, "I'm keeping him tied up."

"Sam, I've never seen anything happen so fast."

"What did he hit me with?"

"I think his elbow. Right in the freaking forehead. I was watching the gun, which he swatted toward the ground before he hit you. Or maybe it was simultaneous. Like I said, freaking fast. Amanda's got a new bullet hole in the basement tile."

"I wonder why he didn't kill us both," I said.

She clenched the steering wheel with two hands and shook her head.

"He just dropped the clip out of his gun, checked the rounds, and snapped it back in again. Then he put it in his pocket and walked out the basement door," said Jackie. "Not a word, not a look back."

"Lousy conversationalist. I wonder if Ross Semple would have been more persuasive. Lost opportunity."

"Not exactly," said Jackie, handing me her smartphone. "Check the photos." There he was, sitting on Amanda's mother's couch looking up at me. "And, we got his fingerprints and DNA." She burrowed around in her bag and pulled out the water bottle, holding it by the cap. "If that doesn't do it, I used a Kleenex to dab some blood off the basement floor."

"All while I was out cold."

"That was the nice part. Working in silence."

"Not that we can do anything with it. 'Hey, Ross, can you ID this guy I cracked over the head and kidnapped?'"

"Good point."

Eddie jumped into the back seat and barked at the window. I let it down for him, and he stuck his head out. The wind noise inhibited further conversation, which was fine with me.

I wouldn't say Markham was happy to see me, mostly because the ER had just processed a bump in business caused by the protest in Water Mill. Twisted ankles, a few cracked heads, opioid overdoses, two heart attacks, and at least one badly cut hand the result of poor sign construction.

"I suggested to him next time use wood instead of aluminum," said the doctor. "Or at least polish up those edges."

He didn't bother explaining what was next, since I'd been through it so many times. I just let them poke and prod, draw blood, and wheel me over to X-ray and subsequently the MRI machine. It was hard not to notice the technicians were the same who took care of Amanda. One of them recognized me.

"We got a two-for-one deal," I told her.

When they brought me back to the ER, Jackie told me Joe Sullivan and Tony Cermanski were in the waiting room. I asked her to go find Markham to see if he'd spring me and follow up later. The twenty minutes waiting in the curtained-off examination room without a book or ball game counted among the longest minutes of my life.

"You know what I'm going to tell you," said Markham, when he finally pulled open the curtain, Jackie hovering behind him.

"I do," I said. "I'm trying, Doc, honestly I am. It keeps happening. Maybe the world will be a better place if the dementia finally gets me. I'll be drooling in some rat hole nursing home and you can use these beds for more deserving patients."

The fact was, nobody knew how many concussions a brain could absorb before systems started to break down. I was already well past the limit, and so far so good. At least that's what I thought, and probably always would, well into the long visit to la-la land.

"I hope you donate all those MRIs we been takin' of you to science," said Markham. "Get dressed. We'll call you when we know something."

They made me ride a wheelchair out to the waiting room, yet another petty indignity.

Sullivan and Cermanski stood up when they saw us come through the double doors. The contrast was laughable, the skinny little Cermanski standing next to meaty Sullivan. We took the meeting outside, where I could sit on a park bench, still unsteady on my feet.

"Joe thought it was good to let me know what happened out in North Sea, in that you two are involved in one of my active cases," said Cermanski. "Which I appreciate."

"He's not telling you my douche bag colleagues didn't think it was worth letting him know," said Sullivan.

"I didn't say that."

Jackie huffed.

"I love jurisdictional bullshit. Who's going to interview us?"

Sullivan cocked his head at Cermanski and told him to go ahead.

So we took him through it, cleaving to our cover story, which sounded more credible in the second telling. Separated from his friends, our guy tried to find cover in Amanda's basement hatchway, I interrupted him, the rest followed as described.

"Any idea about why?" said Cermanski. "Why they were there?"

Jackie deferred to me with a single look.

"No," I said. "But it's related to the Victor Bollings murder and Ernesto and the whole fucking mess. You'd be an idiot not to see that."

"No idiots here," said Sullivan.

"Except those who've had repeated blows to the head," I said.

"I say we sleep on this and regroup in the morning," said Jackie, resting a light hand on my shoulder. "It's been a day."

SHE DROVE us back to Oak Point and I checked on my cottage. I flicked on the lights and saw the carnage. All the kitchen drawers and cabinets were open and the contents strewn on the floor. I walked carefully over the mess to the screened-in porch, which was also thoroughly tossed, the bookcase emptied, and the daybed flipped over. The scene was repeated throughout the rest of the house.

The basement door had a deadbolt, which had valiantly held off a crowbar long enough for me to interrupt the intruders, to my great relief. Now twisted in the door jamb, it took some effort to unlock. Downstairs the shop was intact and handcrafted woodwork unmolested.

I went back to Amanda's and told Jackie what I'd found.

"Why vandalize your house?" she asked.

"It was purposeful," I said. "They were looking for something."

"What?"

"I have no idea."

"So they weren't here to kill you."

"I don't know that either."

WE SPENT the waning night hunkered down in Amanda's house. Me and Eddie on the living room couch, a shotgun squeezed between the cushions and backrest, Jackie in the first-floor bedroom, equipped in the same fashion.

For some reason, I slept fine, dreaming of giant cracking towers, where we separated asphalt, gasoline, and lighter fluid from crude oil, towers I climbed on tiny ladders, far above fields of grass and desert sand, tangled urban neighborhoods and swampy meadowlands, frigid and tropical, exhilaration the unifying force.

"I DON'T want you driving in here just to watch them wheel me into surgery," said Amanda, when she called the next morning. "Plus, they'll probably shave my head. I'm not ready to introduce that just yet."

"I don't care."

"Wait until you see me. I have a rather small head."

"When is it happening?" I asked.

"In a few hours. They've already given me something for anxiety. Though what's to be anxious about? They bore holes in my skull and cut out pieces of brain. The good parts that play chess and discuss Baudelaire. Nothing important."

I felt a grip tighten somewhere inside my chest.

"Make sure they leave in the parts that like your next-door neighbor," I said.

"I love my next-door neighbor, as it turns out. What a surprise."

We didn't usually go in for that kind of talk, so it was a surprise.

"He loves you back."

"I've named you my health proxy, by the way," she said. "Which means you can decide what to do with me if things go south. I have a lot of money in the bank, but don't spend it all keeping a brainless body alive. I also wrote a will, so you'll know what to do with everything."

"Got it."

"Thank you."

My father abused our family. As part of her defense strategy, my mother put a high premium on unsentimental resistance to his barbarity. No bending, no capitulation, and never tears. I fought my way through school, literally, and would rather cut off my own limbs than show any sign of weakness. So the greatest surprise of that moment was feeling wetness in my eyes. I had no memory of such a thing, and didn't think it possible.

"I'm expecting you to come through this," I said. "So don't disappoint me."

"That's the plan, sailor. Okay, gotta go."

And that was that.

I spent the next hour sitting with the phone in my lap, trying to figure out what to do with myself. I pictured the Bollings project in my basement and what was needed to bring it to completion. Which led me to think about Rebecca Bollings, whom I remembered living somewhere on the Upper East

Side. Amanda's hospital was on the Upper West Side. So that decided it.

I found the card she gave me with her phone number and called her.

WHILE NOT the capacious adventure land afforded by the Grand Prix, there was plenty of room in the back of the Jeep, especially with the seat down, for Eddie to dash about and interact with the passing world outside.

I rarely brought him into the city, since it always meant putting him on a leash, an indignity at best. But there was no other choice.

I timed the trip to avoid the worst of the traffic heading into town, so I made it to the Upper East Eighties in about two hours. Mrs. Bollings had directed me to park in her building's garage, saying the guard would be on alert. That proved to be true, though he seemed suspicious of my muddy Jeep and exuberant dog. Probably not the typical caller to the Bollings's Manhattan fortress.

The front desk expressed the same reserve, but they called her apartment on the second floor, then escorted us to the elevator, watching Eddie the whole time as if expecting antisocial behavior at any second.

There were only three apartments on Rebecca's floor, which was one up from the lobby. He'd repeated her number several times to make sure I knocked on the right one. It mostly made me want to knock on the other two just to see what would happen.

"Mr. Acquillo," she said, when she opened the door.

"Call me Sam. This is Eddie. I hope you're okay with dogs."

She swept us into a small foyer.

"I love dogs. Pets aren't allowed as permanent residents. We had to smuggle our miniature dachshund in and out of here for years. Never a bark."

She was a lot smaller than I remembered. She wore a flannel shirt, long pants, and hiking boots, an unusual choice for summer, until I noticed how cool it was in the apartment. She led me into an ostensible living area, which would be better described as a book repository. Floor-to-ceiling bookcases on two walls, books stuffed under side tables and stacked on the floor, and papers in neat piles on every available horizontal surface. A computer workstation with two monitors faced picture windows that viewed a slice of Central Park through two other buildings. A kitchen and dining area, less cluttered, completed the space.

Without asking, she poured a bowl of water for Eddie, who lapped it up.

"Victor called this data central," she said, using two hands to display the room. "He wasn't far wrong."

She brought a stiff wooden chair for me out from the dining table and set it several feet from her computer station, where she sat in a swivel office chair.

"Somebody likes to read," I said.

"Both of us. It's an affliction. Not just the reading. The keeping. You never know when you might want to read a book again, but if you've thrown it out, then what? Intolerable."

She studied me with her folded hands clenched between her knees.

"So why are you here?" she asked.

"As I told you on the phone, I'd like to know more about your husband. I'm just an investigator working for the lawyer defending Victor's accused killer. You don't have to tell me anything. But we don't think our client did it, so maybe you could help us get the bastards who did."

"I suppose that's what you tell all the widows."

"I'm not here to sword fight, Mrs. Bollings. Talk to me if you want. If not, I'll get out of your hair."

She seemed satisfied with that, and took another tack.

"I was married to Victor for twenty-three years. Two hundred and seventy-six months. Of that time, we spent about eighty-six months in each other's company, on a cumulative basis. That works out to about 31 percent of the marriage. Say a bit less than a third. I haven't done the analysis, but if you counted the number of associations he had in his professional life, and correlated time spent with those people, I'm guessing hundreds of people lived with him far more than I did. You should maybe start with them."

She leapt up out of her chair and walked over to one of the colossal bookcases. She peered at the shelves for a moment, then pulled down a book. She held it up.

"*Seven Pillars of Wisdom*," she said.

"Lawrence of Arabia."

"You want to know Victor, this is a good reference. Loved the foreign and exotic. And like Lawrence, found it easy to slide into their cultures, adapt without losing his own identity, his Americanness."

She went back to her chair and curled into it like a satisfied cat.

"Though hard for you," I said.

She smiled. I'd noticed over recent times, much of it spent prying information out of the unwilling, that people usually think smiling is their best defense. As if they're indulging your efforts, but have no interest in playing along.

"Not in the least," she said. "Victor and I were entirely self-sufficient and unentangled. The perfect match. What else did you want to know?"

"Why did you give me your card?"

She made a little clicking sound that caught Eddie's attention. He got up from where he was lying on a throw rug and trotted over to her. She scratched the side of his head.

"In case you had something you wanted to share with me," she said. "About my husband."

Mexican standoff.

It was my turn to smile. In fact, I gave a little laugh.

"Ernesto Mazzotti, the accused killer, said Victor was teaching him how to play golf," I said. "Does that sound like him?"

"No. Victor was the only person I knew who preferred playing eighteen holes of golf by himself. A good metaphor, though, if you think about it. Always the man apart, with only himself to compete with, and getting the job done in the most efficient way possible."

"What about his planned line of work," I asked, "heading up the North America Progress League?"

"What on earth is the North America Progress League?"

She didn't look curious so much as annoyed.

"It's a nonprofit on Long Island that advocates for Latino immigrants. Like Ernesto."

A disturbance flicked across her controlled reserve, then as quickly vanished.

"You did have something to share," she said. "You just didn't know it. As I said, Victor and I lived such distinct lives, I could easily lose track of him. I once learned they'd moved him from Istanbul to New Zealand from a press release on Google Alerts."

I told her I understood.

"I don't think you do. I've never been on an airplane in my life. Barely been outside New York City. Victor hadn't the faintest idea of what I did for a living, nor the curiosity, and vice versa. It just didn't matter to us. That must seem awfully peculiar to you."

"Not to me. Two people can do anything they want as long as they're both in on it."

She asked if there was anything else I could tell her, and there wasn't, as far as I knew. She looked poised to dismiss me, so I beat her to it by standing up and giving Eddie a quick whistle.

"There's one thing you've never asked me," she said, guiding me to the door.

"What's that?"

"Did I love him."

"Did you?"

"Painfully so."

CHAPTER FIFTEEN

When I called Dr. Ng, he said I could pick up Amanda in about two hours.

"Just like that?"

"New technology. Yesterday we shaved a small patch of hair, made a tiny hole, went in with a probe, took a biopsy, then followed in with the laser. Zap, zap. Would you like that in layman's terms?"

I told him I was an engineer and could handle a little more tech talk. But that was the gist of it. Amanda turned out to be an ideal candidate for the procedure, since the tumors were small, but in typically hard-to-get places, unfriendly for scalpels. Minimally invasive as it was, the brain still didn't like getting probed and ablated, so he wanted to observe her overnight.

Braced as I was, the news was almost hard to absorb.

"What's the prognosis?" I asked him.

"She'll be tired and fuzzy for a few days. Maybe a little nauseous from the post-op meds, but otherwise, should be fine."

"I mean long-term."

We'd already established that full candor was the best approach for both of us, so he didn't hesitate to say, "I have no idea. These tumors are gone, but others could appear. In a year, ten years, twenty, or never. I also can't predict the psychological effects. Mood state, behavior, cognitive functions. I'm optimistic, but the brain is a very complicated thing. We'll have to wait and see."

We settled on a time for me to be at the discharge exit where they'd be waiting with Amanda. I thanked him and he said the pleasure was all his.

"I asked her to keep a log on emotions, mental clarity, mobility, sensual acuity, that kind of thing. I'd like you to observe her and do the same. As health proxy, it's not a violation of her privacy."

"Will do. Especially the sensual acuity part."

"That reminds me," he said.

"What?"

"I think the sarcasm's still intact."

"Best news yet."

She looked great. I knew there were two bald patches somewhere under her hair, but she had a lot of hair left to cover them up. Her olive complexion had a tint of salubrious pink and those green eyes looked ready to foment rebellion.

"Why, Sam," she said, "you're on time."

"I'm always on time. It's you that's breaking tradition."

"It's the hospital staff. Sticklers for efficiency."

She nearly leaped out of the wheelchair, to show she could, and jumped into the Jeep. Eddie did his best to greet her back into our private three-cornered world, manifest even in the narrow confines of the old SUV, while I threw her stuff into the back.

"Well, that was interesting," she said, as I pulled out into traffic.

"How do you feel?"

"Strangely mellow, though the sedatives are playing a part."

"You might get a little sick when they wear off," I said.

"Killjoy."

By silent consent, we talked about everything but her medical condition, so I had plenty of airspace to tell her about the protest on Water Mill Green and subsequent encounter with a team of commandos in black jumpsuits, leading me back into the tender mercies of Markham Fairchild.

"Oh my," she said. "See what happens when I leave you alone for a few days."

I also told her about my meeting with Rebecca Bollings. Amanda found their marriage of parallel paths amusing, as did I, since it bore some resemblance to our own situation. And some profound differences.

"At least I get to see you every day," she said. "I think I lack the attention span for a long-distance affair."

"If we were they, I'd bring you with me. We'd travel pock-marked desert roads and smelly stone alleys together. Not to mention sugar-white beaches and slinky sports cars."

"I'm not sure I have the wardrobe for that much adventure." She reached over and squeezed my shoulder. "Though I love what you're trying to say. I'd do that with you, Sam. I might not have said that a few months ago, but perspectives change."

I remembered I'd shut my phone off the day before, so I turned it on and saw a text message from Jackie: "Google Grant Conkling."

I took the next exit off Sunrise Highway and drove into a gas station. I spent a frustrating minute trying to operate the tiny keyboard with my rough thumbs.

Journalist Grant Conkling Missing, Leaving Signs of Struggle

The Royal Virgin Islands Police are investigating the disappearance of Australian journalist Grant Conkling, seventy-two, after neighbors reported hearing gunfire coming from his hilltop home on Tortola, the main island in the British archipelago. On arriving they discovered the house in disarray, with damage to furniture and blood spatter in several of the rooms.

Mr. Conkling's vehicle, a late model Nissan Pathfinder, was also missing. Neighbors said the journalist, who has had a long career as a foreign correspondent covering stories in the Caribbean and South America, had lived in the BVI for several years, and was a well-known figure in social settings around the islands.

The article went on to describe some of his better-known features, a handful of awards, and his reporting on major stories of the era. Along with no further comment from the police, citing the ongoing investigation.

"Oh no."

"Bad news?" Amanda asked.

"Very. I might've gotten a friend of mine killed."

"Oh no. Might've?"

I handed her the phone so she could read the news piece, and got back on the highway. As we drove I told her about my trip down to the BVI, and all that I described to Jackie, leaving out the same critical piece of information. Withholding from her was hardly a violation of our intimacy. I'd known her by then for years, and much of her life remained undisclosed. She didn't like talking about it, and I didn't ask.

"What can you do?" she asked.

"Nothing. That's the worst part."

When we made it out to Oak Point, I pulled into a sandy access road to the lagoon on the eastern side of our properties. I asked her to wait with Eddie while I checked everything out. I handed her my phone.

"If I'm not back in fifteen minutes, call in the cavalry."

I took a path from the lagoon to where it came out behind Amanda's house. I did a walk around and took a pass through her house, then repeated the same at my cottage. The only thing out of the ordinary was a FedEx envelope leaning against my back door. The return address was the hotel where I stayed in the BVI.

I ripped it open and took out a single sheet of paper.

"Your mate on the hill is okay. Await further word."

It was signed by the Australian bartender.

I DIDN'T have to wait long for further word.

Finally having time to pull together my ripped-apart house, I was almost finished when another FedEx package arrived. Also sent from the hotel in the BVI, this time it was a box. Inside was a prepaid cell phone and a note:

"Please call when you get a chance," along with a phone number.

I parked myself out on the screened-in porch and called.

"Hello, Sam," said Conkling.

"What the hell happened?"

"I told you we were fucking with fire."

"Are you all right?" I asked him.

"I got a big bloody gash on my forehead, busted a toe, and lost a tooth, but better than the other bloke."

He'd been home working at his computer when a guy showed up at the door claiming to be a messenger with a package. First off, he wasn't holding a package. Secondly, he spoke English with a thick Spanish accent Conkling felt pretty sure was Colombian. When he asked who the package was from, the guy said a friend. Conkling said he had a message of his own, which was to piss off.

He got the door shut before the gun came out and put a hole through it approximately where Conkling was last standing. He had his little revolver in the pocket of his bathrobe, but thought the occasion warranted heavier ordnance, so he ran for the bedroom while the guy kicked in the door.

Conkling retrieved his .45 semiautomatic from the bedside table and listened to the guy moving through the house. It was hard to pinpoint exactly where he was, but Conkling took a guess it was the living room, which turned out to be sadly wrong. Halfway down the hall, the guy burst out of the powder room and cracked Conkling in the face with a freestanding toilet paper holder. Conkling fell back, but managed to get off a shot, hitting the guy in the foot. Now they were both on the floor, Conkling trying to regain his senses and find the .45 that had flown out of his hand. Meanwhile, the guy is screaming in Spanish and holding his foot, and unfortunately, blocking the path out of the tight confines of the hall. Conkling literally ran over the guy and made a dash for the door, but the guy scrambled after him and they ended up wrestling in the living room, Conkling trying to get his little gun out of the bathrobe pocket, the guy half trying to strangle him, and half using his much taller opponent as support as he hopped up and down on one foot.

Grasping the situation, Conkling used two hands to grab the guy's shirt, and shoved him into a glass-topped side table holding a lamp made out of a giant vase. In the crashing chaos that ensued, the guy's ass went through the glass top, a shard of which, still affixed, sliced open his left side. The guy had regained control of his gun and started firing at Conkling at nearly point-blank range. Though remarkably, with no apparent effect. Conkling finally dug out the little .38, and used a single round to shoot the guy through the heart.

He wrapped the body in a thick, and hopefully absorbent, rug and secured it with duct tape. Then he dragged it out to the patio, shoved it over the cliff, and watched it pitch pole into the Caribbean Sea.

"By this time, I'm bloody knackered."

He saw to the wound on his forehead, got dressed, and packed up essentials for a hasty departure. He drove the Pathfinder to a friend's house, who hid it in an outbuilding and took Conkling by boat over to Puerto Rico, where he was holed up with another friend on Vieques, an island off the southeastern coast.

"I'm sorry, Conkling," I said. "I guess it's my fault."

"Indirectly. The truly offending party is this wanker source of mine who decided to tell the wrong people I was looking into your friend Mazzotti."

"Which people?"

"I don't know. Colombian for certain. Could be Farc, or any number of gangs, or corrupt officials, the intelligence service, though the last one I doubt. They'd have sent someone capable of doing the job."

"I don't know, Conkling. With you it would take a full hit squad. What did your source tell you?"

"Not much, except that Bollings was busy down there for a long time when a lot of important things happened. Without blowing his identity, no easy feat. Though the thing about deep, deep cover, reporting only to his handler, is nobody on the ground knows who you are or what the hell you're doing. This breeds resentment and suspicion, should the field office catch wind, no surprise."

"Must've been a pretty good source to know that," I said.

"That's the fuck of it. The best. Gold plated. But he's the only one I talked to. Had to be him."

"So now what?" I asked.

"I don't know. I like my little house on Tortola, but I still have a flat in Melbourne. Maybe the travel expenses would be too high to kill me there. Or I could just squat here in PR. Or go to London and spend all my money pub crawling until they catch up with me. It's a quandary, I'll admit."

"Tell me who the source is," I said.

He didn't answer right away, but then said, "Can't do that."

"Listen to me. He forfeited your professional obligations when he gave you up. I got you into this, I need to get you out. That's my obligation. Not to mention Ernesto. I owe him too. I've honored my promise not to reveal Bollings's true identity, at great personal cost. If I can get corroboration, you're off the hook, and I'm free to pursue."

"I don't give a damn about the source. It's you. Waltzing into that cesspool is an easy way to get yourself killed."

Though hardly equivalent, I remembered similar cautions when I decided to become a professional fighter. They said I was too small for my weight class, too inexperienced. Too smart to risk getting my head beat in. Not heedlessly crazy enough to overcome a street-hardened kid from the projects.

I did it anyway, and proved them all wrong. At least the heedless crazy part.

"Tell me who he is," I said, "and you can have an exclusive to the Ernesto Mazzotti, Victor Bollings story. However it turns out. I'll keep careful notes."

"Well," he said, without hesitation, "if you put it like that."

Chapter Sixteen

I waited for a third FedEx package to arrive, then told Amanda I had to leave town for a while. Way out of town. I told her she and Eddie could either move in with Burton, or let Joe Sullivan reclaim his first-floor bedroom.

She sighed. "Is that really necessary?"

"Have I showed you the bullet hole in the basement floor?"

"I like Joe. He can just be, well, overly protective."

"Darling, that's the idea. I won't be gone long."

She reminded me I said I'd bring her along if I went international. That wasn't like her, which I stored in the back of my mind.

"Next trip," I said. "You pick the country."

There wasn't much else to do before leaving. Ernesto's next hearing was in a few weeks and Jackie was buried in other case work. I turned over most of the Bollings built-ins to my second-choice finisher/installer. There was plenty of time to complete the balance.

I was free and holding a fresh passport.

I'D BEEN to Cartagena a few times, though rarely went beyond the oil refinery where I was jiggering several of our technologies.

I'd never made it into the Walled City, the old town, where the tourists swarmed and my quarry owned a townhouse.

I got a room in a hotel nearby that used to be a princely townhouse surrounded by gardens, now enveloped in red stucco-covered masonry buildings. You got there through a tunnel that opened on a courtyard engorged with tropical foliage and humidified by an enormous fountain.

My room was high enough to clear the impediments, so I could open the window to the sea breeze. A ceiling fan did its part, and another window looked out over the fecund extravagance at the center of the building. Floral scents followed the breeze and birds threatened to flap into my room.

The man's name was Tomas Maldonado, an Argentine-born, naturalized American citizen. He worked for the embassy in Bogotá, though since his brief was trade relations, he had his own office in the port city of Cartagena.

Conkling said his parents had been wealthy, but the terrors of the Dirty War forced them out of the country, first to Puerto Rico, then Washington, DC, where they established themselves as political consultants and effective liaisons between the United States and Latin America. Tomas joined the family business and eventually found himself attached to the embassy in Colombia. Conkling knew little of his competence at international trade, but could attest to his proficiency at drinking, gambling, consumption of illegal substances, and procurement of expensive women.

In the morning, I made my first run by Tomas's house, which was a block in from one of the major thoroughfares, thus still within the zone of enterprising street merchants who aggressively cajoled every passing tourist into a contest between wariness and salesmanship. One of these operations looked well-established within a choice alcove it shared with a big shade tree, and directly across the street from Tomas's place. He sold cowboy hats made of white straw, maracas, and knock-offs of Colombian Arhuaca mochila bags. As I walked by, the vendor approached me holding out an arm slung with the mochilas, but I briskly shook my head and moved along.

I wandered around for an hour, then came back for another pass, this time stopping to look over the vendor's merchandise. He closed in fast with a pair of maracas. I asked him in Spanish how much they cost. It turned out they were usually twenty American dollars, but could be had that day for only ten.

I asked about the hats and bags, and miraculously, these were also on a special 50-percent markdown, though only for that day.

Still in Spanish, I asked him what he'd take for everything on display. He thought I was joking, so I had to repeat the question. He looked it over and did some fast calculations, and came up with something like $350. I took $500 out of my wallet.

"I'll take everything, but I want a chance to sell it myself. You can take the rest of the day off. Whatever I don't sell, will still be here tonight."

He asked if I was crazy.

"I'm an American journalist," I said. "I'm doing a story on street commerce in Cartagena. I think it's important to have the real experience for myself, so I can tell an authentic story and do honor to your profession."

He still thought I was crazy, but bought the fiction. He volunteered to stay with me to offer advice, but I said I wanted to jump in cold, though maybe I could join him the next day once I had some selling under my belt.

The reluctance creeping into his face quickly abated when I handed him the 500 bucks. We shook hands and I was in business.

I introduced a completely different marketing strategy. As my prospects strolled by, I picked out American and European couples and called out to them in English with my best Bronx inflection, "Yo, I got a good deal over here, can't hurt to at least hear me out."

About every fourth couple took the bait.

"I'm having a clearance sale," I'd tell them. "Buy one of them things at a 30-percent discount and you can have another thing for free. Just don't tell any of the other guys on the street. They'll cut my throat."

Sales were brisk, which interfered more than I wanted with my surveillance activities. One of the distractions was constantly repeating a credible reason for a guy from the Bronx working as a street vendor in Cartagena. Luckily, nothing was happening over at Tomas's, understandable since it was a workday.

As it grew later in the afternoon and I'd cleared about half my inventory, I reverted to another approach—sitting on the curb and ignoring all passersby, surrendering to the competition on either side of me. This let me concentrate on Tomas's house, though I couldn't have missed the black S Series Mercedes sedan that pulled up to the front door.

A large man in a black suit and white shirt got out from behind the wheel and went around the front of the car. He opened the back door to let out another man, this one in a white linen suit and what looked like a cape. The two of them went through the front door. A few minutes later, the driver reemerged and drove away in the Mercedes.

Not long after, he returned, by foot, and used a key to let himself in. The sun was setting, and light shone around curtains and louvered shades covering the windows of the house.

A woman in shorts and a University of Rhode Island T-shirt walked up to me, blocking my view, and said, "How much for a hat?"

"Depends on the size of your head," I said, in Spanish.

"Do you speak English?" she asked, her voice slightly raised as if that would improve my command of her language.

"A leetle."

"How much for a hat," she repeated.

"*Sombrero?*" I asked.

"No, one of these hats," she said, lifting it up.

"*Sombrero bonito.*"

"Sombrero? What is this, Mexico? I'll give you this much."

She held up both hands with her fingers spread. I gave her a double high five.

"Okay, keep your fucking hat," she said, and stalked off.

Customer service. The key to successful commerce.

Soon after I heard a loud click-click of high heels coming down the sidewalk across the street. Those heels supported a lot of long, slender leg. Her bountiful black hair caught the street-lights, as did her sunglasses, a brave accessory for the dimly lit streets. She wore a short jacket on top, which she clenched to her throat.

I guessed her destination and wasn't disappointed. The guy in the black suit let her in, after giving each of her cheeks a quick kiss. It wasn't long before the glow of light faded from the downstairs windows, though two tiny windows on the third floor stayed alight. I kept watching, but nothing else happened, so I was happy when my business partner showed up.

He was pleased with my sales success, and equally joyful over how much remained on the table. He gripped my shoulder when he shook my hand, and laughing, told me as much. The air filled with metabolized alcohol.

"I hope your bosses love your newspaper article," he said. "You deserve a great triumph."

I laughed as well and shook his hand even harder.

"It was a great day," I said. "Thank you for entrusting me with your reputation. I think you'd be proud. Can I come back tomorrow? I want to learn from you."

He threw his hands out with great magnanimity.

"Of course. I'll share all my secrets, and you can take them back to New York and make a million dollars."

I thanked him again and retreated to my hotel, where I stumbled into bed. It only took two hours to overcome a jagged wakefulness and slip into unsatisfying sleep.

THE NEXT day was a Friday and I had high hopes. I arrived at the vendor's table across the street well before he showed up with his wares, so I got to see Tomas and his bodyguard leave for work. It was an orderly and precise exit, though as with the day before, I only caught a glimpse of Tomas, again dressed in fresh linen, an ascot, and matching pocket handkerchief.

No sign of the woman in high heels and sunglasses.

When the vendor pulled up in his little van, I helped him unload and set out the day's offerings. He thanked me for standing guard while he found a place to park the van. Before he made it back, I'd sold a set of maracas at list price to a pair of gay Swedes who stood a foot taller than I and spoke in impeccable Castilian Spanish.

"I have nothing to teach you," said the vendor when I handed him the take. "You were placed on earth to do this work."

I replied with a Spanish idiom that meant, roughly translated, "dumb luck."

That morning, I switched my promotional strategy again, this time focusing on Latinas, suggesting in English that their partners would look very manly in one of our fine white hats. The profit margin went down, but I made up the difference in volume. The male victims, many of whom showed animus toward our enterprise, sucked it up and paid full freight.

Meanwhile, my partner, seized with inspiration, stood in the middle of the street and sang famous songs from Spanish opera, his arms spread wide and laced with Arhuaca mochilas bags. We started to gather a crowd.

The front door of Tomas's house opened and the woman stepped out. She wore a floral housecoat and sandals. Her hair poured down her shoulders in turbulent waves. She sat on the doorstep and lit a cigarette. I realized I was staring when our eyes locked. She winked at me, and I immediately looked away, putting my hands in prayer and bowing my head. Forgive me, my lady, for staring at you.

Two hours after that, we'd nearly cleared the day's stock. My partner put his fleshy arm around my shoulders and gave a squeeze.

He said something completely incomprehensible, even to Spanish speakers, and I answered in English, "Fuckin' A, brother." And he laughed as if he knew what I was saying.

After he left, I hung in the back of the alcove, my black jacket zipped to the throat, and watched.

Well into the night, the black Mercedes pulled up across the street. Tomas and another guy got out before the driver could open the back. The driver unlocked the front door of the house and the two other men, arm-in-arm to steady themselves, went inside.

After the driver disposed of the Mercedes, he came back and took up position in front of the house. Unlike the night before, music joined the light seeping out the windows on the third floor. The driver, after pacing back and forth in front of the house for a few hours, finally relented and sat on the small front stoop. He lit a series of cigarettes while scanning up and down the street. I moved away from the alcove and took another position down the block, where I could see the driver without him seeing me, I hoped.

By midnight, the street was nearly deserted. I crossed over and started walking toward Tomas's, weaving a little and singing my own Spanish version of "The Times They Are A-Changin'." When I reached the driver I asked him if I could bum a match. He looked a little disgusted, but reached in his inside jacket pocket, at which point I punched him in the left temple. He wobbled where he sat, but stayed conscious. I hit him again, which sent him into the sidewalk. I grabbed him by the hair, covered his face with my hand, and slammed his head into the stone.

I looked up and down the street. No one there. I relieved him of his keys, wallet, and an old-fashioned automatic pistol, then arranged him in a curled-up position next to the stoop.

I let myself into the house. The music was coming from upstairs, which judging from the lights in the windows, was two flights up. I flicked off the gun's safety then moved as quietly as I could up the stairs.

There was a night-light in the hall on the second floor, but the doors of the rooms were open and dark inside. I moved to the bottom of the next flight and could see lots of light up there. The music covered the sound of my footsteps as I climbed about halfway up the stairs, paused to listen, then trotted the rest of the way up.

The third floor was a single open room. Sofas and small tables cluttered with bottles, glasses, ashtrays, the remnants of coke lines, and articles of clothing. Directly in front of me was a king-sized bed. Tomas was in the middle, with the guy to the right, and the woman to the left, all apparently naked. I pointed the gun at Tomas's head and said, "Hi."

The woman screamed, then the guy to the right screamed, and Tomas tried to pull the sheet up to his chin. I told his playmates to get out and crawl under the bed. They complied, the woman taking the sheet with her, after a brief contest with the guy. This left Tomas alone and fully exposed. He covered his genitals with both hands.

I took a few quick steps and jumped on his stomach, pinching his arms between my legs. His face had little definition, but enough to express wretched terror. His head was mostly bald, and he had a goatee, as futile compensation. I held the muzzle of the gun to his forehead and said, in English, "Victor Bollings. What was his real job? Get it wrong, and I pull the trigger."

He shook his head. I started to count backward from ten. At three, he said, "Intelligence!"

"Very good. That made this whole trip worth the effort. Who did he work for?"

"I don't know. It didn't matter to me. Probably CIA, but he was so deep, who knows for sure. Better not to know."

"What did he do? Remember, I know the answer. Be precise."

"Counterinsurgency."

"Farc?" I asked.

He shook his head.

"Los Rastrojos. Worse than Farc. Fanatics. You are one of them."

"What did you say?"

I racked the slide, tossing a live round out of the chamber, then put the muzzle back on his forehead. It had the desired result.

"I'm sorry!" he yelled. "I was only speculating."

"Do you know Ernesto Mazzotti?" I asked.

He flinched and squeezed his eyes shut, as if expecting a blow.

"I have never betrayed him. I swear. Never. You must know that, or I'd already be dead."

"Who is Ernesto Mazzotti?" I asked.

It wasn't much of a reaction, but I saw something different flit across his face. Somehow Tomas's lifetime of connivance and venality got the better of his survival instincts.

"This is why you're here," he said. "You're testing me. Or you really don't know."

I took the gun away from his head and aimed it where his hands sheltered his crotch.

"The bullets will go right through tissue and bone," I said. "All the way to the mattress."

"*Madre.*"

"Think about your social life," I said. "Those kids under the bed are going to be really disappointed."

He looked oddly thoughtful, working the equations. Probably weighing short- and long-term potentials, and like most hedonists, leaning toward the immediate.

"That's all I'm saying," he said. "What does it matter. You're going to kill me and my friends anyway. Go ahead, start shooting. I can finish myself off if necessary."

I heard a burst of crying from under the bed. I guessed they had more fluency with English than I'd hoped for. A new mood settled on Tomas's face. Fatalism, worse than defiance. I reminded myself that this asshole had dropped a dime on my friend Grant Conkling. A friend who was put in that position because of me. The terrified people under the bed were not my quarrel. I would never hurt them. I'd never hurt Tomas either, even if he'd had the balls to keep his mouth shut. The implications of the moment circled my mind like the inside of a windstorm.

I let it all go and got off Tomas, sticking the gun into my rear waistband. I told him to resign his position. The State Department had no more use for his services. If he was still there on Monday, I said, someone else would come visit and finish the job. It was all pure fantasy, but I felt better saying it.

I walked down the stairs and out of the house.

The driver was still out cold. I checked his breath and it was steady. His pulse was good, his face warm. I apologized for the headache he'd have in a few hours, and left for my hotel.

I had what I needed, though I didn't feel all that good about it.

CHAPTER SEVENTEEN

My plane home left at noon, so I had time to eat breakfast at the hotel. I was told by the woman at the front desk that I could sit in the restaurant where they had a buffet, or out on the patio that lined the center garden, or get a table right in the middle of the little jungle, with table service. I opted for that.

I was reading a copy of *El Universal*, the local paper, and working my way through a pile of Colombian breakfast specialties when I saw three cops through the foliage, *Fuerzas Especiales,* talking to the man at the front desk. They were showing him something, and he was nodding. He pointed to the maître d' standing in front of the inside restaurant.

I checked my pockets to be sure I had my passport, wallet, and smartphone, then I got up from the table and moved away from the maître d' stand toward the opposite corner. Two huge double doors were open to a conference room where a group was holding an event. I walked past a long table filled with name badges and poked my head in the room. There was a door to the left of the podium. I tried to look casual and unconcerned as I wound through the partially filled room.

The door led to a hall off which hotel staff worked in kitchens and storage areas filled with tables and chairs and rolling service trays. I followed the hall until I came to a freight elevator, of the old style where you shut the wire mesh gates manually. I went one floor down to street level, guessing the elevator served a loading area off the back of the hotel.

I was right. Two men were pulling a big dolly full of boxes across the floor. One told me the area was off-limits to guests. I said I was with hotel management and was expecting a delivery. He said he'd never seen me before, and I just said Bogotá. It's a little like saying New York to guys working in Saint Louis. They watched me walk over to the dock and jump down to the street. I waited to get my bearings, then headed up to a cross street. It was busy and crowded and lined with my fellow street vendors. I bought a white hat without haggling and a tuxedo jacket with a floral pattern to put over my black T-shirt. A few minutes later I hailed one of the ubiquitous horse-drawn carriages and asked if he could take me to Gestsemani, another old district, but less crowded with tourists and the pleasure trades that served them.

In English, he said that was a long ride and would mean a higher fare. I asked in Spanish if he hated making money. He laughed and said he liked making money very much.

I slumped down in the carriage and put my feet up on the opposite seat, pulling the white hat down to my nose. It was a long ride, and the clop-clop of the horse monotonous, but no one from law enforcement thought to intercept an escaping fugitive in a horse-drawn carriage.

When we were just inside Gestsemani, he asked where next. I looked at the GPS on my smartphone, and gave him an address of a hotel that found it useful to advertise with people who made the maps. I paid the fare and threw in a few extra pesos, thanking the driver for the effort.

"Okay for me. Next time I take you to Chicago," he said, in English.

I went in the hotel and was happy to see they had a restaurant filled with a good mix of locals and outsiders. I found a booth away from most of the noise and called the number Burton gave me when I was in his shop admiring his custom-built chair.

"Aberdeen," said the woman answering the phone.

"Burton Lewis gave me your number," I said.

"He must have, because I surely didn't. No one calls this number."

"I'm in Cartagena. I need to get out."

"They have an airport."

"Can't do that. Police are looking for me."

"Oh, dear. Something you did?"

"Yes. If you're Burton's friend I hope you'll trust it was the right thing to do."

"I trust Burton," she said.

"My name is Sam Acquillo. Call him to confirm he'd rather have me in the states than buried in a Colombian jail."

"I will do that. Meanwhile, where are you now exactly?"

"I'm in a bar in Gestsemani. I have my passport and plenty of cash, but had to leave everything else at the hotel."

"They have an American consulate in Cartagena."

"Can't go there either. It's related to the thing I did."

"Interesting. So that means the embassy in Bogotá is out."

"Yes."

"I'll be back in a moment," she said.

The line went quiet, though the phone said I was still connected. I waved over a waiter and ordered a cup of coffee and a few of the dishes I'd left uneaten in the Walled City. He suggested one addition, and I gladly complied.

"Your friend extends his regards," the woman said when she came back on the line. "You need to get to the Cartagena airport. I have no way to help you do that within the time horizon."

She told me to go to the private jet terminal and ask for a Mr. Sandoval.

I finished most of my meal and left. I stood on the street and pondered my options. There was light street traffic, with cabs drifting along looking for fares, and undoubtedly Uber drivers were in the mix. I had no way of knowing how much effort the cops were putting into finding me, though a road stop near the airport wasn't out of the question.

I saw a row of motorcycles parked in a designated area. I could see most were locked with the front wheel cocked, or chained to a metal rack. I leaned up against a storefront and continued to ponder.

I was about to resort to Uber when a kid pulled up on a beat-up, small-block Honda. I approached him and asked how he liked the bike. He said he wished for something bigger, but it was cheap to run and never broke down. I asked if he could tell me what he paid for it, and he did.

I didn't have time to weave an elaborate story that would innocently explain why I wanted his motorcycle, so I just gave him a version of the truth—that I had to get out of Cartagena in a hurry, and would pay him twice what the bike was worth, in American dollars, if I could take it immediately. Along with his helmet.

I knew it was a big risk, but I decided to take it. If that failed, I'd try something else. But I was lucky. The kid was a cheerful sort, who thought the idea was pretty cool. Still, he didn't jump at the deal right away, until I told him I'd only need it a few days. If he gave me his phone number, I'd text him where I left the bike.

This proved irresistible. I counted out the bills while he unhooked a pair of saddle bags. He did his own count, then handed me the key.

For the second time in so many days a Cartagenan said I was loco. Or in really big trouble with somebody. I said both, and took off.

It had been a few years since I'd ridden a motorcycle, but as the adage goes, once you get on a bike, it all comes back. Everything seemed to be mechanically sound and well adjusted. It wasn't the snappiest performer, but my intent was to stay well within legal limits, avoiding unwanted notice.

I stopped at the first gas station I came to and filled the tank. Before leaving, I checked a map and plotted a course, not the most direct, but easiest to maneuver on the way to the airport. Soon I was in the flow of traffic, well disguised, I hoped, by the helmet and visor.

On the main road to the airport, traffic bunched and opened up in a reliable, normal rhythm. A few of the cars came uncomfortably close when in front of me, or behind, but I was used to that from the Long Island Expressway. I kept calm and alert.

At the entrance to the airport, traffic slowed significantly, then came to a near halt. Blue lights flashed up ahead, though I couldn't see where they came from. I carefully extracted the motorcycle from my lane and went back the other direction, taking a previous exit that led to the maintenance hangars and freight operators. Most of the buildings were secured behind tall, chain-link fences and check-in booths. I drove around until I saw a gravel side road. I took it, and pulled off onto the shoulder, where I could check my GPS.

The gravel road appeared to wrap around the back of the hangar area, then connect with a main artery within a few hundred feet of the terminal. This encouraging prospect lasted until I reached the end of the road and saw a locked gate blocking the way.

I scanned the area and saw a parking lot that seemed to connect unimpeded with the paved road on the other side of the gate. Unfortunately, I'd have to cross a patch of weedy grass about the length of a football field to get there. It was either drive over there or go back to look for another way out. An immediate gross exposure versus more prowling around, drawing suspicion, and subsequently, the cops.

So I went for it. The grass was a lot rougher than it looked, composed of thick clumps and stalks more like trunks than stems. The Honda pitched around, forcing me to stand dirtbike style on the foot rests, and ratchet up the RPMs, all in all creating a noisy, raucous display designed to attract the maximum amount of attention.

At least it was a short ride. As soon as I hit the hard surface of the parking lot, I raced toward the entrance and shot into the traffic moving toward the terminal. Before I got there, I drove into short-term parking and into an open space. I took a photo of the sign marking the location so I could send it to the kid, and joined a line of people crossing the main road to enter the terminal.

I split off at the automatic glass doors and followed signs to a taxi stand, where I disappointed a cabbie by asking him to take me to the private jet terminal. I told him it was worth a big tip. He was still surly all the way there, which I preferred anyway, recovering from my scrambled nerves and the physical effects of the recent off-road jaunt.

Though I didn't think he deserved it, I gave the cabbie twice the fare, and ignored him as he muttered something like "rich assholes" under his breath.

The terminal was more like a luxurious lounge, with a pair of modern desks instead of a counter. I asked the two women sitting there if I could see Mr. Sandoval. They asked for my name and I said I needed to see him first. One of them nodded solemnly and left her desk and disappeared through a tall mahogany door. The other suggested I help myself to coffee and pastries, which I took her up on, though when I spotted a little wet bar, and saw that it was after twelve, I just opted for a vodka on the rocks.

Mr. Sandoval was an elegant man with a bald head who spoke Spanish with an eastern Caribbean lilt. Probably Jamaican, like Dr. Fairchild's.

"Mr. Acquillo," he said, as we shook hands, "please join me in my office."

I followed him through the door and then into an office that more resembled a reading room at the New York Public Library. We sat in a pair of red leather club chairs.

"The procedure is simple," he said. "In about ten minutes you will leave this office and turn left. You will go straight until you reach a door that leads to the tarmac. You will walk unaccompanied to the jet waiting there. I expect no interference during this time, but if so, I apologize that it's beyond my ability to come to your aid."

"Fair enough. I appreciate your help."

"Not necessary. I am merely providing a service," he said. He didn't have to say well compensated.

He rose from his seat and left the office. The AC was set to low, emitting a quiet whir, the only sound other than jets taking off and landing. I admired his book collection, the titles in various languages.

As directed by Sandoval, I waited ten minutes, then went out and followed an empty hall to a heavy steel door you opened by slapping a chrome button on the wall. Hot air and the whine from the engines of a Learjet 45 rushed through the door. The airstairs were rolled in place, and the hatch was open, but no one stood waiting. The only other vehicle in sight was a fueling truck, and in the distance a box van traveling down a runway. I looked over my shoulder at the terminal, with its low, flat roof. Perfect sniper position.

It was a short walk to the jet, but it felt a lot longer.

I climbed the stairs and entered an empty plane. The door swished closed behind me and the cockpit door opened.

Mr. Sandoval stepped out and secured the hatch. He'd stripped off his suit jacket and wore a pilot's headset.

"Make yourself comfortable, Mr. Acquillo. Our food service is spare, but there is ice and a selection of spirits."

"Good enough for me."

"Then as they say, please sit back and enjoy the flight."

There's nothing quite like taking off in a light jet. No long, rumbling heave down the runway. The acceleration is almost immediate, followed by a near vertical launch. Sandoval came on the intercom and told me when we'd arrive at JFK. I just sat back and enjoyed the fact that I'd made it out of Colombia alive, intact, and only somewhat seared by moral ambiguities.

CHAPTER EIGHTEEN

When I checked my phone after landing at JFK, I saw that Joe Sullivan had left a text.

"Call me when you can. Something's up."

I did, but no answer. So I left my own message. Technology ping-pong. It wasn't until I was halfway home that he called back.

"Where the hell are you?" he asked.

"On the Southern State Highway. Where the hell are you?"

"Hampton Bays, walking around smoldering ruins with the state police arson squad."

"What ruins?"

"Ernesto and Querida's house. Burned to the ground. Neighbors called it in around four A.M. When the firemen got here, it was totally engaged. They just hosed down the houses next door and waited for it to burn itself out. No one was home, though I guess you know that."

"I do, but I bet the arsonists didn't."

"I bet you're right. Can you meet me here?"

"On the way."

I tried reaching Jackie, but she didn't answer. Neither did Amanda. "What the fuck good are these phones if nobody ever answers?" I said out loud, immediately feeling foolish for doing so.

I hated the forced isolation because it gave me time to think. I had a professor back at MIT who described the process of solving seemingly implacable quandaries as Plunging Into The Void. He used a cane, and would walk up and down the classroom aisles striking our chair legs to punctuate his points. Do you have enough data? Yes, whack. Of course you do. You might need more. Data are good, but it is hardly the most important element. Heresy, my colleagues would say! Data is God! No, no, no. It is a lead vault into which we lock our most powerful intellectual potential. Whack!

Engineers, he'd say, his voice dripping with mockery and derision. "It's amazing the right side of your heads haven't shriveled into tiny walnuts your brains are so out of balance."

He'd pull a clown mask out of his desk drawer and put it on, then walk up to one of us and ask what he or she was thinking about at that exact moment.

"With respect, sir, that you are behaving strangely."

"Exactly! Are you thinking about data?"

"No, sir."

"Data is what you know. The Void is what you don't know. It's the blackest black, an absolute vacuum. You can't see, can't hear, can't breathe. What's left?" he yelled at me.

"I think it might be that cane of yours, professor," I said.

"Exactly," he said, bringing the cane down on the top of my desk hard enough to bounce my notebook onto the floor.

"What else?" he said.

"Our minds," I said. "Unfettered, out of control. Free to make random associations. The Void is the realm of creativity and imagination."

"And why do I call it The Void?"

"Because it's terrifying and no one wants to go there. As engineers, we're trained not to. Which is mostly a good thing, since the precision of our calculations can be a matter of life or death. Your point, if I understand it correctly, is that empirically based evaluations often fail, at which time most engineers will recalculate with basically the same data, and then eventually give up. Whereas those who resist the fear of the unknown, and tap into our intuition, often prevail."

He sat on my desk and nodded with appreciation, adding, "Though just as often, commit some colossal fuckup."

"Yeah, but so what, as long as nobody gets hurt."

So there I was in The Void. I knew lots of things, yet understood nothing. I just had a bagful of undifferentiated facts, with no connective tissue. No interdependencies. No logic chain.

I couldn't see, couldn't hear, couldn't breathe. And unlike the abstract thought problems we solved in the classroom, or the real life system failures we solved in the field, the unanswered questions before me could get me killed.

Whack.

THE COP guarding the yellow tape at the end of Ernesto's street called Joe Sullivan to confirm I was allowed in. When I got to the burned-out house, Tony Cermanski was there with Sullivan watching the state police fire investigators do their work in tan and yellow protective gear. All jurisdictions represented.

"We need the arson people to make the call," said Sullivan, "but the detective and me don't believe in coincidences."

Cermanski nodded.

"The neighbors reported seeing an out-of-state pickup prowling around lately," he said. "A dark blue dually. The driver wore a cowboy hat, and nobody knew which state issued the plates, so he's likely from way out of town."

"And probably long gone," said Sullivan. "Our staties are looking, but without a better description, that's the best we can hope for."

I told them I'd seen the guy too. Parked on Ernesto's street, then later at the protest in front of Jackie's place. I gave them as thorough a description as I could, including the Kentucky plates. I didn't remember the number.

"Said he was visiting his cousin," I told them. "Didn't get a name."

"That's okay," said Sullivan. "This helps."

"You don't happen to know where Ernesto's family is?" Cermanski asked.

"I don't," I said. "Just that they're safe."

"Good move on somebody's part."

One of the staties came up to us holding a black wad of something, and not unlike other experts I've known, made us play the guessing game.

"I don't know," said Sullivan. "A bag of potatoes?"

The statie looked at Cermanski.

"A solid accelerant," he said, "and I bet it was outside the house walls. In the back."

The statie nodded with appreciation.

"The kid wins a trip to Disneyland."

"Visco-elastic polyurethane," I said. "Memory foam mattress. Hard to get started, but in combustion, will off-gas methyl ethyl ketones, toluene, and other aromatics that burn hot, supported by the denser hydrocarbons over the duration of the fire. Look for a charcoal lighter stuck in the on position."

He looked down at the glob in his hand as if that would confirm its chemical composition.

"All righty, then," he said, and went back to his crime scene.

Sullivan looked happy with me.

"Sometimes that MIT shit comes in handy," he said.

"That's what they say at MIT."

"Any idea on the perpetrator?" Sullivan asked me.

I wasn't ready to entangle them in my web of confusion, but I could honestly say I had no idea. Instead I told them something they already knew.

"The blue pickup is probably your best bet, weak as it is. It leans toward the protesters, some of whom are still around, I'm sure. Though there are other possibilities."

Sullivan looked annoyed.

"Now's not a good time to hold out on us," he said.

"I'm not holding out, exactly, I'm just trying to process what I think I know, but I'm not sure. Give me a couple days and we'll confer. You were right, detective," I said to Cermanski. "This thing is above everybody's pay grade. Be careful."

"I told you I don't care about the fucking politics."

"I don't mean that. I mean be careful." I looked pointedly at Joe Sullivan. "Lock the doors at night and cozy up with your service weapons."

Both of them looked excited at the prospect of needing guns in the middle of the night. I hoped those wishes would never be realized.

JACKIE, AMANDA, Eddie, and I were gathered with Burton on his capacious glassed-in patio, screened for the summer. The night was starry and the sea breeze sprightly, stirred up further by the monstrous paddle-wheel fan overhead. Isabella had dispensed drinks and comestibles, and Burton, finally convincing her we were well cared for, shooed her out of the room.

I'd given Amanda a few headlines when she finally picked up the phone while I was driving back from Ernesto's, but this was the first chance I had to brief Burton and Jackie.

Before I dove into the story, I thanked Burton for that phone number he gave me.

"To say it saved my ass is putting it mildly."

He nodded and held up his drink.

"I have information for everyone," I went on, "which I had to withhold from Jackie, but now I can share it with all of you. We just need to talk seriously about how to handle it. It comes with implications."

Jackie still looked perturbed about it, but kept her peace.

For the benefit of Burton, I described my visit with Grant Conkling at his house on Tortola. That he'd been pretty forthcoming, though concerned what he was telling me could come back at him. Which it did, as it turned out. Jackie looked braced for what was to follow, but I quickly eased her fears.

"He's alive," I said to her. "Unlike the guy who attacked him. Conkling's hiding out in Puerto Rico. I called him on the way in from the airport, but no answer. I assume he's still okay."

"What's so radioactive?" Burton asked.

Sometimes a secret is so hard to keep, when you finally let it go, it sticks in your throat. I forced it out.

"Victor Bollings was a highly successful international management consultant. He was also an operative for US intelligence. Which agency, and in what capacity, I don't know. This is the intel Conkling gave me, and made me promise not to divulge it. I had to hear it directly from his source, who Conkling gave up after being attacked in his house."

This puzzled Burton.

"How would they know if it was just a conversation you had with Conkling on his patio? Was he bugged?"

I shook my head.

"No. I also asked him if he could look into Ernesto Mazzotti. We knew that wasn't his real name. It seemed remotely possible that Bollings and Ernesto knew each other in Colombia.

Conkling went back to his source to find out, and soon after, a Colombian *asesino* paid him a visit."

Quiet descended on our little gathering as each absorbed and mulled what they'd heard.

"Interesting," said Burton, "but not definitive."

"Hardly," I said. "Still just a hypothesis."

"Nothing hypothetical about the guns," said Jackie.

"I think I warned you about this," said Burton.

Jackie slid her chair closer to Burton so she could put her hand on his shoulder.

"What were we supposed to do, boss?" she said. "You always tell me the only thing that matters is a full and vigorous defense of our clients, no matter what. That's all we're doing here."

He took her hand and kissed it.

"I care about our clients. But I care far more about you and Sam. You'll do what you will do. Doesn't mean I can't worry."

I'd said more or less the same thing to Joe Sullivan, and by extension, Tony Cermanski. Now I knew how they felt.

"Thanks, Burt, but the real bogeyman here is the unknown," I said. "We're stumbling around in the dark. We're used to our own homegrown thugs and sociopaths, not strange actors from afar. It's biological. Fear increases in proportion to the distance of the feared."

Burton nodded.

"That is true," he said. "But it doesn't change the central dilemma. You may have inoculated Conkling by corroborating his claim about Bollings, but it's still unusable in open court. We can't out an American agent, even a dead one. It could compromise God knows how many current operations. And, if you think Mazzotti's case is challenging now, what would happen if he's linked to Bollings's activities in Colombia? Do you expect our intelligence services to come rushing to his defense? Not bloody likely. You better pray none of that ever sees the light of day."

Jackie nearly glowed with frustration, while I sat there wishing Burton hadn't said that, right out in the open where the humorous God could hear him.

Chapter Nineteen

(O)ne of my least favorite things is waking up to someone pounding on my kitchen door. It was Jackie.

I picked up Eddie to stop his enthusiastic barking and asked her what the fuck.

"I got a bad phone call," she said. "Where's the coffee?"

"Sorry. I usually don't make it in my sleep."

She set to work at the coffeemaker. I tied up my bathrobe while regaining my faculties.

"Roger Angstrom, *New York Times*, called me to confirm a story. Guess what about? Think murder victim."

"Victor Bollings?"

"Bingo. An anonymous source told him Bollings was a deep-cover intelligence operative, with extensive experience in South America, in particular Colombia. The source told him attorney Jacqueline Swaitkowski could corroborate, and provide additional information about her client Ernesto Mazzotti, if I was willing to divulge. As if."

She thrashed together the coffee like the process deserved punishment.

"I don't think the *Times* would out an American operative," I said.

"Angstrom called the CIA. They said Bollings never worked for the agency, so go ahead and run the story if they wanted to print fabrications. That's why he's calling me. And you, by the way."

"This makes no sense," I said.

"Not to us, Sam, because we don't know what the fuck we're doing."

I stumbled back to the sunporch where I hoped I'd left my phone. I called Grant Conkling.

"Did you drop a dime to the *New York Times*?" I said, when he picked up.

"Beg your pardon? Sam?"

"They have the Bollings story. Specifically, Roger Angstrom has the story, a reporter closely associated with Jackie Swait-kowski, and by extension, me. Who else knows that?"

"Bloody hell."

"Tell me."

"You think I'd give that one up to another paper, even if I wanted to? Which I don't."

"Angstrom's coming out here to try to get corroboration," I said. "He's not getting it from us."

"Have you checked for bugs?" he asked, as if inquiring after termites. My nerves lit up like I'd stuck my finger in a 220-amp socket.

The black jumpsuits.

"Fuck, shit."

Jackie was yelling something to me as I ran back through the house, "How the hell would anybody put you, me, and Bollings . . ."

I put my hand over her mouth. She reflexively tried to wrench away, but I held firm. Her eyes were lit with furious intensity, until I managed to lock on. I shook my head and put my finger to my lips. She sagged in my grasp. I twirled my finger in the air and she nodded.

I took the phone out of my bathrobe pocket.

"Still there?" I asked.

"I am," said Conkling. "Have nothing else to do."

"Go take a swim. I'll be in touch."

"Cheers."

I held on to Jackie and guided her out the door, and out to the lawn.

"Conkling asked if we'd been bugged," I told her. "Would explain a few things."

"Oh, no."

"The special ops visit," I said. "They weren't searching, they were leaving a few things behind."

"I am so confused," she said. "Why out their own agent, and then connect it to us?"

"The world's changed. We just don't know how."

"Great," said Jackie. "And I didn't understand the one we already had."

I PAID a little woman with a blonde ponytail to sweep my cottage. I got her name from Sullivan, who said she was the go-to for local detectives suspecting the feds of operating a parallel investigation, usually on drug or racketeering cases. It's not that the local boys were looking for a turf battle, it just helped to know some big dog agency was playing in their sandbox.

To me she looked a lot more like a cosmetology student, or second-string cheerleader at the high school. In fact, she'd learned her craft as an army intelligence officer in Iraq and Afghanistan. Another lesson in the foolishness of stereotyping, reinforced by her tone of voice, which more resembled a small-arms instructor.

"You'd be most useful sitting outside and out of the way," she said. "I'll let you know if I have questions."

She'd brought along a chocolate lab, and asked if she could let the dog out of her van so he could commune with Eddie. After the usual introductory rituals, the dogs spent the time trotting up and down the breakwater chasing seagulls, and wrestling over wads of seaweed, giving me something to watch while the young woman did her work.

About an hour later she walked across the lawn shaking a coffee can that sounded like a percussion instrument.

"I'll make one more pass through, but I found the repeater, so any mics or cams still in there will be worthless. You can keep all of these in case you want to bug somebody else. You'll just need the software. I can spec it for you."

"Full service."

"Affirmative."

After wrapping up, she handed me the bill, which I paid on the spot, and she gave me a handshake that took some doing to equal.

"You have my card," she said. "Please visit the website to be aware of my other countersurveillance services."

I tossed her a set of keys and asked her to go to Hawk Pond and sweep my boat. She said yes, sir, right away, sir. I thanked her, resisting the urge to salute.

She whistled for her dog, who ran across the lawn and leaped into the open van door. Eddie watched, bemused.

"That's what obedient dogs do," I told him. "I know it's a foreign concept."

THE NEXT morning, Jackie and a slim little guy with delicate hands and soft curls met me at the boat. Jackie made introductions then climbed down from the dock into the cockpit so she could help Angstrom accomplish the perilous descent.

"Ever been on a sailboat before?" she asked.

"I've ridden the Staten Island Ferry. Does that count?"

I had them go below so I could leave the dock and prep the boat without having to climb all over human impediments. In about fifteen minutes, I told them to come on up as I piloted my way through the last segments of the channel.

"It's a very beautiful bay," said Angstrom, taking pictures with his smartphone. "And nearly empty. Hard to believe we're only two hours from downtown Manhattan."

"Don't tell anybody," I said.

"Oh, great. Another confidential source."

The breeze was placid, but enough to move the boat, which was all I wanted. I raised the sails, turned on the autopilot, and flopped down in the cockpit.

"Okay," said Angstrom, "you know why I'm here. Not just to ride on a boat in a place I'll never be able to afford."

"We thought, since you weren't going to get what you wanted, we could at least show you a nice time," said Jackie.

"I don't think you'd go to this much trouble," he said.

"Not if we just wanted to throw you overboard," I said.

He grinned, but not all the way.

"He's kidding," said Jackie. "Aren't you, Sam."

"You want a beer?" I asked. "It's after twelve."

"Sure," he said, as if casting caution to the winds.

"Here's the thing," said Jackie, as I provisioned the cockpit. "You want corroboration, but we can't give it to you, because for you it's a story. For us, it's federal prison for breaching national security. On the other hand, we'd love to know who put you onto this in the first place, which you can't do, since revealing a source would violate a principal canon of your profession."

"A fine mess," I said, before slurping down half my beer.

"As you said, I won't reveal a source," said Angstrom. "That includes you guys."

"Ah, but when the FBI grills us, which they will, we'd have to either lie, or fess up, either of which could lead to very bad things happening," said Jackie.

"Which might be why whoever told you about Bollings wanted you to involve us, to ensnare our asses," I said. "Not your fault, but you can see the problem."

"The bigger question is why burn Bollings," said Jackie.

"The CIA denies he was an operative," said Angstrom.

Jackie put her hand on her heart.

"You don't think the CIA would ever deny the truth," she said. "What a horrifying thought."

"How will this affect your defense of Ernesto Mazzotti?" Angstrom asked.

"All good attorneys adjust strategy based on new or changing information," she said.

"Jesus Christ, Jackie. What's the point of talking if neither of us can say anything?"

"He's right," I said to Jackie. "We're going to travel out to the bow. Why don't you stay here and mind the helm."

"No, Sam," she said.

I climbed up on the cabin top and helped Angstrom follow me. I told Jackie to keep her eye on the depth finder and try not to crash into anything. She sputtered, but the wind quickly blew away the words. When we went out to the far end of the bow, known as the pulpit, he went to sit down, but I grabbed him and did a thorough frisk.

"You know, I don't usually fondle on the first date," he said.

I took a smartphone out of his pocket and turned it off.

"Ever heard of quid pro quo?" I asked him. "It's Latin, meaning 'tit for tat.'"

He allowed that he had.

"It happens a lot in journalism."

"You're going to run the story whether we corroborate or not, right?"

"Yes," he said. "The CIA denial clears the way."

"Can you keep our names out of it? At least Jackie's?"

"The person who called me said you two have special knowledge about Victor Bollings. You're defending his accused murderer. Hard to keep that out."

"You like the truth, right?" I asked. "Just say you requested comment from Jackie Swaitkowski, but she declined. That is true." He stipulated that. "I'm the one who knows something, not her. But I won't tell you where I got it and you can't use my name. If you give me up, I'll deny it and it'll be your word against mine."

"It's a deal," he said. "You first."

"The story's true."

"You want to add some details?"

"I don't have any, but the information came from Colombia. I don't know what he did in the rest of the world. When you go digging, I can give you a place to start."

"Which is?" he asked.

"You got your quid. Now give me some quo."

He sighed.

"Are we running through a minefield, or juggling grenades?"

"Both."

"I can't name my source, but I can tell you who the person isn't," he said.

"Okay."

"Anyone working for the government. Unless they're lying to me, which is always possible."

I noticed he didn't specify gender, but pointing that out was a waste of time.

"Good enough. Remember the name Tomas Maldonado. A diplomat at the US Embassy in Colombia."

"I'll remember."

"And be careful," I said.

"I won't expose you, Sam. If you knew me better, you'd know that."

"That's not what I mean. I mean be careful yourself. The people we're dealing with don't give a whit about the sanctity of the Fourth Estate. Shooting a reporter would just be another day's work."

Before he could respond, I led the way back to the cockpit and a fuming Jackie Swaitkowski.

"Ever sail a sailboat?" I asked Angstrom, when Jackie stepped away from the helm. He shook his head, watching the wheel start to turn back and forth. "Go ahead, take it."

He stumbled behind the helm and grabbed the big wheel. I lay back in the cockpit and waited to see what would happen. About twenty minutes later, after some lurching and near broaching, Angstrom got the boat under control.

"Holy crap," he said.

"Nice work," I said. "Most people couldn't do that."

"I can't do it," he yelled. "Take back the wheel."

I reset the sails, then sat behind him, though I didn't take the wheel.

"Relax," I said. "You're doing fine. The boat knows what she's doing, you just have to keep the extremes in check. Keep a light hand. The boat will move a few seconds after you turn the wheel, so don't oversteer."

"This is not what I expected."

"Nothing is. If you want to live in the world, sometimes you need to take a leap of faith."

We were closing in on a lee shore, and I saw the depth finder inching down toward the impassable, so I took over and tacked 180 degrees, leaving Jackie to pull in and reset the sails. When the boat settled back into a comfortable cruise, I punched in the auto helm and fell back into the cockpit.

"There's a lot about this pursuit that I clearly need to learn," said Angstrom. For some reason, Jackie reached over and ran her hand through his hair.

"I feel that way about life," she said. "The sad part is it keeps getting worse the harder I try."

"I'm getting more beer," I said. "That I know how to do."

ANGSTROM LEFT the boat without committing to anything, but Jackie and I knew the story would run, and we were right. Page one, above the fold. I was reading it on my computer when Ross Semple called.

"Should I have Joe Sullivan come get you, or can I trust you to show up in the next half hour?" he said.

"What for?"

"What do you think? Get over here as soon as you can. I want some quality time with you before the FBI shows up. They're on their way."

"Not unless Jackie's there," I said.

"She's on her way too. So's the ADA. Gonna be crowded. Help me recall, Sam, did I happen to mention that this was one case to steer clear of?"

"You did. And you knew what I'd do."

"I won't be able to protect you."

"I don't want your protection."

He hung up on me.

ROSS WAS right about the crowd. Joe Sullivan and Tony Cermanski were there, along with Cermanski's boss, the village chief of police, a slim blonde woman in civilian clothes. ADA

Andy Frost and an assistant were better dressed, though Grace Inverness and another FBI special agent were a close second. Jackie had chosen her jeans, flannel shirt, and hiking boots motif, which I called her pugnacity ensemble.

With so many jurisdictions represented, I could see Ross wondering how to kick things off. Inverness decided the issue.

"We want the name of your source, the means by which you obtained this alleged information," she said to me, before my ass had barely hit the hard seat of my chair, "and the names of any others you have communicated with in the course of this unauthorized activity."

"We say nothing until you explain the nature of this interview," said Jackie.

"Miss Swaitkowski," Frost started to say, but Inverness cut him off.

"This is a very serious matter," she said. "Be very careful what you say."

"I'm always careful what I say," said Jackie, which wasn't all that true. "Chief Semple asked us here. So we're here. Why?"

Ross picked his pack of Winstons out of his shirt pocket, looked around the room, then put them back. I grinned at him.

"You're interfering with national security," said Inverness. "There will be consequences."

"What a ridiculous accusation," said Jackie.

"She's referring to the article in the *Times* about Victor Bollings," said Frost. "The consensus here is you two are among the reporter's sources. All we want to know is who gave you the information you passed along. And by the way, no one here is confirming the *Times* piece to be accurate or factual."

"I always thought accurate and factual were the same thing," I said. "But I'm not all that modern a person."

"Me neither," said the other special agent. "I'm more medieval."

"For the record," said Jackie, "I count that statement as an attempt at intimidation."

"Really, Miss Swaitkowski," said Frost.

"Ms.," she said to him. "Ms. Swaitkowski. Or just plain counselor. That'll work."

"Care to comment on this *Times* thing, Jackie?" said Ross.

"No."

"You know," said Cermanski, forcing all eyes to turn his way, where we saw him leaning back in his chair and fiddling with the end of his tie. He looked up at everyone. "We've got this murder investigation going on here, and I gotta tell you, finding out the victim was an international spy really complicates things. We're not exactly set up for that kinda stuff."

Inverness slid her eyes over to him, and for a moment I thought laser beams would shoot out and cut him in half.

"Your investigation is important to us, detective," she said. "Let me assure you."

Ross caught me mouthing the word "bullshit."

"Ernesto Mazzotti is still our suspect in the murder of Victor Bollings," said Frost. "The larger issues of national security cannot change that."

Inverness didn't like this at all, but she let him go on.

"I, for one, do not want to allow this recent publicity to derail our prosecution, which will proceed as planned," he said. "The defense is free to enter mitigating circumstances in open court. And let the chips fall where they may."

The other special agent snorted.

"Chips," he said.

"And dip," I said.

"What?"

"Chips always go with dip," I said. "Unless you're on some kind of health kick."

"Sam," said Ross, in that paternal, scolding way I always hated.

The special agent studied me as you would a slab of roast beef about to be thrown in the deli slicer.

"Let me ask more directly," said Inverness to Jackie. "Did you speak to Roger Angstrom of the *New York Times* about Victor Bollings?"

"Why would I do that?" said Jackie.

"That isn't an answer," said Inverness.

They stared at each other, a dance of implacability.

"Anyone feeling claustrophobic?" I asked, looking around the room. "I know I am. Too many people in here."

"So get the hell out," said the other special agent.

"I was thinking the other way around," I said. "You get the hell out along with the rest of this gang so Jackie and I can talk to Special Agent Inverness in peace."

Nobody moved. Inverness looked alert, her focus ping-ponging between Jackie and me.

"Very well," she said. "Clear the room."

Ross said, "I think you meant, 'Would you please excuse me so I can have a confidential conversation with Ms. Swaitkowski and Mr. Acquillo.'"

She gazed over at him.

"Would you? Please?"

Ross gave it a few beats, then stood up with the rest of the group and they all left. Except for the other special agent.

"You too," I said.

"I'd prefer to have Special Agent Roselli hear this directly," said Inverness.

"I'd prefer to be sailing on the Little Peconic Bay. Which I'll go do if this dickless jerk stays in the room," I said.

Jackie would normally be swatting my shoulder and telling me to shut up, but she just sat and waited.

"Albert, I can handle this," she told him, and he left, slow as can be.

During which I said, "Albert? You're kidding me."

"Okay, I'm listening," said Inverness, as soon as the door clicked shut.

"We will not discuss the *New York Times* article," said Jackie.

"I'll go to the grand jury," said Inverness. "Compel testimony."

"Go ahead," said Jackie, and she was about to say something else when I cut her off.

"I got a better idea. Let's quit with all the tough talk and just have a conversation."

"You lie to me and you'll be disbarred," she said to Jackie, "and you'll both go to jail."

"You see, I find that sort of thing just not useful," I told her.

"No one's going to lie," said Jackie.

"Is Albert from Washington?" I asked.

She looked like I'd just asked if she was wearing panties.

"In other words, yes, he is," I said. "There's the problem. I think you got some bad eggs in that basket. Mauricio of the guayabera tried to warn us off this case. Not a lie. And you're the one who told me he was a phantom. Also not a lie."

"I regret that conversation," said Inverness. "I didn't know it would lead to a breach of national security."

"Give me a break," said Jackie. "Bollings is dead. No one is surprised that an international businessman was working for the government. Nothing's been compromised unless you count the opportunity for my client, who's accused of Bollings's death, to get a fair trial."

Inverness was good at keeping her reactions under control, but something unsure passed across her face.

I've heard that kids who grow up in abusive households get good at reading body language and unspoken thoughts. A good defense against the surprise smack on the head, or swift kick in the ass. Maybe that's why I suddenly realized what was going on with Special Agent Inverness.

"You don't know anything about Bollings," I said. "You're out of the loop. Just a field rep sent here to scare the local bumpkins into coughing up the goods."

She sat there silently, so I said, "A couple weeks ago, a team of special operations types in black jump suits landed on the beach outside my house. They tossed the place and shot at me. I'd probably be dead if the cops hadn't shown up when they did."

"That's ridiculous," said Inverness.

"So you really don't know anything," said Jackie.

"I know you two are in very big trouble," she said. "And making up stories about mysterious men in Latino shirts and teams of black ops won't make it any better."

Jackie huffed.

"Not another word, Sam," she said. "We're done here."

"You won't much like the next people who come calling," said Inverness.

"What are they going to do, put cigarettes out on our foreheads?" I said.

She looked offended, but didn't reject the possibility.

"Here's the deal," said Jackie. "We will cooperate, but only with immunity from prosecution. We talk to the highest-ranking FBI official you can drag out here, and only with a witness of our choosing."

She repeated what Jackie was asking for, without agreeing to the terms, then got up from her seat.

"I don't think this is going to go well for you," she said, more an opinion than a threat. "Someone will be in touch."

The others were standing around the hallway outside the muster room when we came out. We ignored the quizzical looks and left without comment. I looked over my shoulder before leaving the area and saw Inverness herding everyone back into the muster room.

"We'll cooperate?" I asked Jackie, when we were clear of the building.

"I don't know. I just wanted to get the hell out of that room."

"You think we fucked up?"

"I don't know that either," she said.

Chapter Twenty

Jackie and I met back at my place. We went out to the Adirondack chairs where Jackie sent a text to Roger Angstrom. He called a few minutes later. Jackie put the phone on speaker.

"What did you tell them?" he asked, without preamble.

"Nothing," she said. "I assume the same for you."

"I assume as well, since my editor handled the meeting, and we are the *New York Times* after all. It took some convincing to get them to run the story. Contrary to popular belief, we're careful about outing spooks. But this one is dead, so it's in a different category. More importantly, we tried again to get the CIA to confirm or deny, warning them of the upcoming story, but they held to their denial. It's hard for the government to jump on us after we gave them an opportunity for a conversation."

"Have they made a statement?" I asked.

"Nope," he said. "Not a peep."

"And nobody else has come forward?"

"No, but if they did, I might not tell you. Sorry."

"I get it," said Jackie. "But let us know what you can. I'll ruffle your hair."

"I wish."

NOT SURPRISINGLY, Rebecca Bollings was the next in line to pester me with questions I couldn't answer. I was in my shop, trying to move several backlogged projects along and nearly achieving my preferred state of delusional oblivion. Eddie was with me when the phone rang, and he looked at me as if warning against picking up the call.

"How dare you not tell me," she said.

"Tell you what?"

"You know very well."

"I only know what I read in the papers," I said. "I'm just a cabinetmaker."

"These accusations. The media has lost its mind."

"So you didn't know."

I could hear her breathing. Not light, anxious little breaths, but big full gulps of air, as if she'd just run a marathon.

"My life is ruined. This will never go away. I'll be a pariah."

"I'm sorry, Mrs. Bollings. I'm not the one to be talking to about this. Way out of my league."

There was so much dead air on the line, I thought she'd hung up. Till she said, "Bullshit."

Sometimes I think carefully about what I'm about to say. Sometimes I overthink it. Other times, it just comes out, and only much later on I understand why.

"You're the bullshitter, Mrs. Bollings," I said. "We both know it."

I had to listen to a lot of heavy breathing before she said, "My apartment. Tomorrow. Bring the dog."

AT THE end of the day, I heard Amanda's truck rattle down our common drive. I left my work in good order and went upstairs to take a shower, after which Eddie and I strolled over to see how Amanda was doing.

Turned out not so well.

The shades were drawn and all the lights were off. I looked around the first floor, then went upstairs to her bedroom. It was even darker up there, since the windows were covered in heavy curtains. She was on her bed, on top of the duvet, still in her work clothes—dusty T-shirt, jeans, and boots—and curled up into herself.

"Hey," I said, "what's up?"

"Don't really see the point," she said, her words muffled by the bedclothes.

"Okay, which point?"

"All this. What good comes of it? Fixing up houses to sell to rich assholes."

"They're not all assholes," I said. "In fact, you like most of your buyers. More importantly, they like you."

"You're right. I'm the asshole. Have you noticed how many jellyfish we have in the bay this year? They never show up this early. The climate is going to kill us."

I sat on the bed and stroked her hair.

"How long has this been going on?" I asked.

"Beginning of time? I don't know. My head hurts."

I felt my chest contract, and heard a fuzzy sound in my ears. I took a deep breath and tried to let my body unclench.

"How bad?" I asked. "Need an aspirin?"

"No, I sort of like it. Gives me something to do. I like you, Sam. I really do. You're good company. I was never good at making friends. Have you noticed? I don't have any. Except for you. My mother was my friend, but she's dead. I like your daughter, but she's in France. I don't want to keep you. You're probably busy."

I got up and walked around to the other side of the bed, where I could slide my arms under her and pick her up. She didn't resist. I carried her downstairs and out the door, across the lawn and out to the Adirondacks. She held on to my neck when I set her into one of the chairs, and I had to pry her fingers loose.

I sat in the other chair.

"About an hour till sunset," I said. "What can I get you?"

She laid her head back and closed her eyes.

"They told me I should be careful with wine."

"Fuck that. Red or white?"

"Why's everything so dark?"

"You got your eyes closed."

Before I went to get her some wine and myself a tumbler of vodka and ice, I told her a few jokes, which she'd heard before, but I told her anyway. They made her smile, but then she started to cry, so I guess they weren't that good after all.

When I got back, she said, "I'm sorry. I'm stuck in all this gummy black."

"Open your eyes. Come on, open up."

She did, and before her was the Little Peconic Bay, all windy water, glazed with tiny waves and brittle scintillations. The sun was off to the left, close to the horizon, but still ablaze between cottony balls of clouds.

I left my chair and knelt in front of her and started to undo her jeans.

"What are you doing?"

"We're taking a swim."

"We are?"

I untied her boots and pulled them off, along with her damp, white socks. Then I dragged off the jeans by both legs, taking her panties along with them. I grabbed her hands and pulled her to her feet so I could strip off the rest of her clothes. She stood there on the lawn, naked, her summer tan lines a display of vivid contrasts. Her hair covered half her face, but the half I could see had a jagged smile.

"You're a nut, you know that?" she said, as she watched me strip down as well. I took her hand and led her to the breakwater. I had her sit on the edge with legs dangling, then I clambered down, and had her fall into me so I could hold her, and carefully place her on the pebble beach. I took her hand again and we walked without hesitation into the salty bay.

When the water was up to our waists, she let go of my hand and dove in. I followed and gathered her up, sliding over her slippery wet skin. She stared at me, as if trying to divine her own thoughts.

"What planet are you from, Sam Acquillo?"

"The Bronx. It's close to the sun. On our good days."

"Is it like Krypton?" she asked.

"Sort of."

"What are your super powers?"

"I never give up," I said. "Don't you do it either."

"Okay," she said, laying her head with its sodden wad of hair on my shoulder, and closing her eyes again, blocking the relentless descent of the sun.

JACKIE HAD me meet her at the Suffolk County lockup on my way into the city to see Rebecca Bollings. Ernesto had been moved from the hospital into a private cell, where he was still recuperating. Jackie was waiting at the jail's check-in exchanging banalities with the benighted guards. After clearing the metal detector, we were shown to an interview room, where soon after they brought Ernesto in a wheelchair.

Though still a big man, he'd shrunk a little into his orange jumpsuit, his eyes deep in dark hollows. When the guard left we asked how they were treating him.

"Very good," he said. "Who else gets wheeled around like a king?"

He said his wounds were healing well, but the recovery was a lot more painful than he expected. They were giving him two Vicodins a day, examining his mouth each time to make sure he swallowed. Opioids were like gold in the underground prison trade.

"Like I'd take the pain to make a few bucks," he said.

Jackie told him how various court motions were going, including a plea for more time based on his physical condition. He seemed bored by it all, but was polite as always.

"Now for the bad news," said Jackie. He gripped the arms of the wheelchair. "Your wife and kids are still safely hidden away."

"What's bad about that?"

"Somebody burned down your house. Total loss."

"*Madre santo*. Who did this?"

"We know it was arson, but not who did it," I said. "They used a foam mattress as accelerant, not an amateur move. Though easy to learn about online."

"Are you able to keep up with the news in here?" Jackie asked.

"I was before those guys jump me. Nobody anymore to talk to but the guards, and they all just listen to the radio."

She took a folded section of the *Times* out of her bag and handed it to him.

"Look at the right column on the front page," she said, referring to the article on Victor Bollings.

Ernesto read for a while, his lips moving along with the English words. He went to the jump page and finished reading. Then he looked up at us, his already ashen face a lighter shade of grey.

"Do you believe this?" he asked.

"Why shouldn't we?" said Jackie. "It's in the paper."

He shook his head and tossed the paper so hard it hit the table and slid off the edge. We left it there.

"When are you gonna come clean, Ernesto?" said Jackie. "I'm your lawyer. Everything between us is confidential. Unbreakable. We're going to get there eventually, with or without your help. Why not save us some time?"

"You know a guy named Tomas Maldonado?" I asked him, helping to prove Jackie's point.

Ernesto opened his mouth, then snapped it shut.

"I talked to him. Or rather, I encouraged him to talk to me. He told me Bollings was working counterinsurgency, focused on Los Rastrojos. What do you say?"

"My family," he said.

"I told you they're safe," said Jackie.

"He was my friend," he said, finally. "For many years. Since I was in the army training soldiers to fight hand to hand. They put me on a team that worked with the Americans. I became DAS."

"*Departamento Administrativo de Seguridad,*" I told Jackie. "Colombian secret police."

"You sure you want to hear all this?" he asked. "Once you know, you can't unknow it."

"We'll take our chances," I said.

He closed his eyes as he told the story, as if not wanting to witness his own words.

ERNESTO COMMANDED his DAS team, working with his counterpart, an American colonel, who led a special forces unit that operated outside the US military. Unofficial. Ernesto never learned where their funding came from, but to him and his men, their American mates were essentially *mercenarios*, guns for hire.

The combined teams grew together during long training and ugly operations in the remote jungles and villages that sheltered a smorgasbord of Farc revolutionaries, drug cartels, common criminal gangs, and lunatic political factions, the worst of which was Los Rastrojos.

"*Rastrojos* are what remains after you cut away the jungle, slash and burn everything into the ground," he said. "The leftover life is too tough and crazy to die."

They had their own fanatical faith, part Marxist, part Zen, part Zoroastrian, and utterly incoherent. Their activities were equal opportunity, preying on civilians, insurgents, military, and any other group that crossed their paths. They never sold drugs, but helped themselves to others' supplies to use for personal consumption.

"They were feared because they fought as if trying to die. Like the Arab martyrs, though I think it's because they were so stoned they didn't notice people were trying to shoot them," said Ernesto.

Victor Bollings never went on these missions. He was strictly planning and strategy, and a reliable source of intelligence, Ernesto assumed by way of US surveillance satellites and human assets tucked away inside the various targets. The Colombians and Americans both liked and respected him, and as far as Ernesto was concerned, he was their field commander, even if he never entered the field.

"He planned more for getting us out than getting us in. It's not hard to fight for a guy like that. And he spent time with us drinking and eating our food, learning our culture, respecting us as equals. There is nothing more important than respect."

Over time, Bollings became convinced that the leader of Los Rastrojos, a man they called *El Primero Entre Iguales*, or El Primero for short, was the glue that held the anarchic group together. With no command structure to speak of, no organizing objective or stated goals, Bollings thought it was a pure cult of personality.

"The snake had a head. We needed to cut it off."

The problem was getting close enough to El Primero, who rarely led his troops into battle, had never been identified, or even photographed. None of Victor's officers had a plan, until Ernesto came up with the obvious. They'd have to infiltrate.

Ernesto didn't bother to ask for volunteers. He just volunteered himself. Having grown up in a farming village, he knew the rural ways of the group, and well-educated, he felt he could talk his way into their harebrained religious faith. Lastly, no one among the combined force was a more effective, ferocious killer.

"I'm not proud of this, but it was the truth. Everybody knew it."

It took Bollings nearly a year to develop convincing intel that located the general whereabouts of Los Rastrojos. Ernesto had been letting his hair grow out, had a spider tattooed on his forehead, and even had a false tooth in the front of his mouth removed.

"There was never any meaner looking motherfucker than your friend Ernesto, excuse my bad language."

Appropriately dressed and armed, a chopper dropped him in a field many miles from Los Rastrojos, they hoped. And for the next month, he lived off the land—mostly the fruits of farmers' labor—and searched for the merry band of sociopaths.

His luck came when two Rastrojoitos rode a Toyota Land Cruiser into a village looking to buy a woman. Or more accurately, convince a young prostitute that coming with them was better than being carved up with a machete. He asked the men if he could join up, which made them laugh and tell him they'd be glad to bring his head back to the camp, but the rest of him would have to stay in the village. Ernesto divested them of their weapons, and while holding them on the ground by their throats asked if El Primero would be happy if they came back without the woman.

Thus a general agreement was reached.

When they got to the camp, Ernesto handed over the two caballeros, their weapons, the woman, the Toyota, and himself, in that order. They stripped him down to his skivvies, hand-cuffed him, and brought him to somebody slightly more equal than the rank and file, who grilled him for hours while they sat cross-legged on the ground. Ernesto never lost control of his cover story, and felt at peace with the situation, which at any moment could mean instant death. He thought his offer to show how he so easily disarmed the two Rastrojoitos tipped the scales.

They uncuffed him and brought over two men. Ernesto said to make it four. Or six. They accommodated him. He told one of the men to come close, but the others to stand well away. They looked at him like he was an idiot, but complied. Then he knocked the one man to the ground with a single punch, grabbed his rifle, and pointed it at the hapless five, standing in a neat row. He had them drop their weapons and lie facedown on the ground.

Everybody laughed. He was in.

"For another six months, I ran with the Rastrojos. I won't tell you what happened, what I did," he said to me in Spanish. "This belongs in a safe in my heart. I will not take it out."

"That's okay," I said back in English. "You can cut to the end."

During that six months, he saw El Primero about a dozen times. He was clearly Amerindian, though taller than average, a member of one of the forested indigenous tribes, and spoke flawless Spanish with a lispy touch, like a European. He wore polo shirts and Dockers khakis, and a pearl-handled six-shooter in a low-slung holster, like Wyatt Earp. No entourage, just an attractive middle-aged white woman in cargo shorts and Birkenstocks who stood silently at his side.

The couple lived in a camouflaged RV, equipped with a satellite dish that rumor said brought in HBO and Turner Classic Movies. Occasionally they would emerge and call for the camp to gather around outside the RV, where he would give four-hour lessons in Rastrojo doctrine, which Ernesto was sure no one understood, aside from the intermittent praise of the followers' bravery, enlightenment, and purified souls.

Ernesto did recognize references to Cervantes, Sun Tzu, Aristotle, and Billy Joel, though the connective philosophical tissue was hard to make out. Didn't matter to the audience, who spent the lesson lounging around the jungle floor smoking crack and fondling the women who roved through the crowd handing out drugs, wine, *Hormigas Culonas*—big-assed roasted ants—and perfunctory sexual ministrations.

"I mostly laid off the crack, though the ants were tasty, I have to admit."

Over time, Ernesto was able to creep his tent within a few dozen feet of El Primero's RV. Given the generally chaotic social order, this wasn't difficult. Though there was an inner circle of Slightly More Equal Rastrojoitos that created a kind of moat and barred further progress.

It was the morning after one of El Primero's more extended sermons. Dawn was imminent and the only movement came from the feral dogs that haunted the camp and used this dead time to scour the grounds for cast-off food. Ernesto stuffed some food and water into his backpack, along with a map, tiny flashlight, compass, and a stolen handheld radio with a built-in GPS, and put on a pair of high-top basketball shoes he'd stripped from a dead combatant, and left his tent with only a small, semiautomatic pistol.

He moved silently through the guardian tents and walked right up to the entrance of the RV, opened the door, and climbed in, shutting the door quietly behind him.

Though not quietly enough.

He heard a woman say, in English, "Darling, did you hear something?"

He followed the sound of the voice to the rear of the RV and an open door revealing a king-sized bed in which El Primero was lying asleep on his back, the woman propped up against the backboard, a sheet pulled up to her throat.

"Fuck you," she said, before Ernesto put a bullet in her forehead, and another in the temple of El Primero as he struggled toward a wakefulness never fully achieved.

Ernesto went out a window on the other side of the RV and walked casually through another row of tents and into the dark jungle. He heard voices behind him, confused and questioning. As he moved deeper into the tangled foliage, he heard other voices sounding alarms, a scream, gunshots, all of which faded away as he used the compass to strike a path toward the extraction zone, miles ahead.

They almost caught him a half-dozen times, but Ernesto knew how to flatten himself into the thick brush and lie still as death.

In a few days, he reached what he hoped were the proper coordinates. He took a chance and used the handheld radio for the first time. Trained in the lingua franca of the US military, he used the term for taking out a targeted individual.

"Tango down. I'm here, amigos. Would love you to come get me."

A few tense days later, as the radio's battery slid into oblivion, a chopper appeared in the air above Ernesto, and he admitted to a few tears of gratitude and relief.

"You think you're dead for sure, and then you're not, it gets emotional."

Chapter Twenty-One

J ackie might have had some tears of her own, but instead she cleared her throat and thanked Ernesto for sharing what she knew was a very difficult story. He just shrugged and said his life was over anyway, so why not talk about anything he wanted. Jackie took exception to that.

"No, you have given us the path to your acquittal. Do not go all existential despairy on us. Do not."

He looked at me and asked, "She always like this?"

"Yes."

"Thanks for those thoughts, but you don't tell nobody what I told you," he said. "You can't count the number of people who will be offended. Victor always told me, 'Nowhere is safe. Just do the best you can and keep a low profile.' That's what I did, and it was going fine until someone whack him with the golf club. You try to make this my defense, you have the whole government land on your head like an avalanche. I'm telling you, you don't know these people."

I noticed some of the blood had returned to his face. He looked much more vigorous than when they first brought him in, as if telling the story had captured lost power.

Jackie took a deep breath, then asked the question that swirled around the room.

"Does this mean you know who killed your friend?"

Ernesto raised his handcuffed hands.

"No. Could be Rastrojos, Colombian DAS, or your CIA, authorized or not. Who knows? Just try making that your defense. They laugh you out of the court."

"Let us worry about that," said Jackie, stretching across the table to lay her hand on his forearm. "Your job is to get healthy and strong. We won't say or do anything without your prior consent. I promise."

"They bug this place?" he asked, looking around.

"No," she said. "This is still America."

I hope, I said inside my head, fighting the urge to look around the room myself.

THE TRIP into the city to see Rebecca Bollings went quickly, probably because I had a lot to think about. I was never a person who expected life to follow an inevitable arc toward better things. Quite the contrary. I'd proven my own point by screwing up more than once, snatching despair from the jaws of serenity. But I was still angry at myself for the disappointments that crowded my mind.

I hated to admit this trouble with Ernesto was bigger than my imagination could quite contain. I'd prided myself on having control over the world, without appreciating that the world in front of me was so small, so confined. The largeness of the great beyond was giving me vertigo, trembling the ground beneath my feet.

I wondered, was it age? I couldn't control that either. Through all my loony experiments with natural boundaries, I'd never doubted my ability to punch through, often literally. Even when I was ground to a pulp, by circumstances often self-inflicted, I had this arrogant notion I could change reality to suit my mood. Now I wasn't so sure.

I was disappointed that I'd been through so much, and learned along the way, yet the learning had so little effect on how I felt. It seemed wasted.

Then I realized, as I drove down the Long Island Expressway, it was Amanda. I'd let myself give in to unconditional love, and look where that got me. Imminent tragedy. Out of my control, beyond my reach.

What a cruel joke.

REBECCA BOLLINGS answered the door to her second-floor apartment wearing a silk robe that fell about midthigh and socks with little rubber dots on the soles she said came from a night in the hospital getting tests for a possible heart attack. Turned out it was just a panic attack, exaggerated by an excess of wine and spicy burritos. But she got to keep the socks, which came in handy in her over-air-conditioned apartment. Not her fault, she said, since all the cold air sloshed down from the rooms above.

She'd just completed her yoga routine, followed by a shower, and was about to dive into a fresh liter of Australian red wine. Did I want some?

"Sure. Eddie is fine with a bowl of water."

I sat in a dining room chair, swiveled around to face the sitting area. I hated overstuffed couches that hurt my back and threatened a poor response in the event of an attack. Irrational, I know, but that's what I'd evolved into.

Rebecca took another chair a few feet away, where she curled her feet up off the floor. We toasted our drinks.

"Do you believe it?" she asked, kicking things off.

"What?"

"That Victor was a spy? You should know the man gave money to gun control initiatives, and dropped twenty-dollar bills in beggars' laps. Cried all night when his mother died. Adopted lost kittens and dogs. Foisted them off on me, but what the hell. I found them homes. On the other hand, someone once broke into the apartment and stole our stereo, my laptop, the good silverware, and some jewelry I'd forgotten to put in the safe. A week later the doorman said some guy left him with a hand truck stacked with boxes, then took off. It was all there."

"People can surprise you," I said.

She smiled too big a smile.

"You are so right about that. I've had to change my phone number and e-mail address, suspend business operations, take my website and Facebook page offline, hire a security service to watch the front door of the building and follow me around when I go shopping. So far I've resisted the urge to buy a firearm to put under my pillow in direct defiance of Victor's sentiments. All because people read newspapers."

"There's a lot of nuttiness out there."

"You think?"

"So you had no idea Victor was involved in something other than international management consulting?" I asked.

She looked like she was gearing up for a fight, but then settled herself back in the chair.

"I never knew what he did. He didn't tell and I didn't ask. We led mostly separate lives, I told you that. Happily."

Eddie chose that moment to go visit her. She scratched his head, then he walked back to me and lay at my feet, letting out a deep sigh.

"Sorry, but I don't believe you, Mrs. Bollings," I said. "It's too perfect a picture."

"That's a rude thing to say."

I sat very calmly, my hands in my lap. She stared at me, I kept my eyes on the oriental carpet before me, bending down to give Eddie a scrunch behind the ears.

"You've wanted to say something to me from the moment we first met," I said. "You'll feel better if you just do it. I can keep a confidence as long as it doesn't mean life or death for someone else."

"How am I supposed to judge that?" she spat out.

"You're not. That's just the deal."

She put her foot up on the chair in a way that caused her short robe to open, showing the inside of her legs and a glimpse of what was in between. In a quick movement, she was covered again. It wasn't purposeful, and I didn't think she noticed me noticing.

"I've researched you," she said. "You're certainly not just a humble cabinetmaker."

"I've heard all that before," I said. "I tell everyone, don't believe what you read on the Internet."

"Right."

She swirled her wine and watched the glass like it would tell her something she didn't know.

"Do you think a man who stayed at world-class hotels would acquire a foot fungus that cost a few toenails?" she asked. "Would he return from a business trip with a gash in his thigh stitched up with common thread? Who sleeps and lies awake in two-hour shifts? Who can grab a pickpocket's hand in Rockefeller Center and break his arm, stuff a baseball cap in his mouth, and be two blocks away in the time it takes to recite the Pledge of Allegiance?"

"You knew."

She held the wine glass in the air again and swirled, the only gesture available at the moment.

"I'm not stupid," she said.

"Hardly."

"No, I'm really not stupid. I have a doctorate in theoretical mathematics. I've lived inside the Internet almost from the day it was born. I make a ridiculous living working two hours a day. The rest is mine to play with as I please."

It was a prideful boast, though it didn't sound like she was all that proud of herself. More exhausted with the whole thing.

"I heard you never visited when he was abroad," I said.

"Who told you that? It doesn't matter. It was common knowledge. I never visit anyone I can't reach in less than a day by car, assuming no bridges. I've never flown in an airplane. Or lived higher than this second-floor apartment. I can manage a short stay at three stories if I can use the stairs. I haven't traveled in an elevator after my parents forced it on me when I was nine years old. They said they were sorry when I regained consciousness. I still don't forgive them."

"What are you telling me?" I asked.

"Like you said, I knew. The way wives know there's something about their husbands the husbands don't want to share. And he never did."

"Maybe for your protection," I said.

"Maybe."

I let that sit for a while, then changed the subject.

"I still don't know why I am sitting here," I said.

"The FBI wants to interview me. They're all full of politeness and consideration, bordering on obsequiousness, which makes me that much more suspicious. Nicey-nice often precedes a punch in the gut," she said.

"They always interview the spouse in a murder case. It's routine."

"I did that already. This is about his little side business. They called the day the *Times* article came out."

"Interesting."

"That's what I thought," she said. "They're the counterintelligence people. Why the hell would they want to talk to me?"

"Are you going to talk to them?"

"Fuck no. Follow me."

She slid out of her chair and walked across the room. I followed her to a bedroom. She crossed the room to a dressing area next to the master bath. She opened a closet door, and after rummaging around beneath a row of dresses, dragged out what looked like a mangled piece of furniture. Mahogany, probably antique.

"I don't know why I kept it," she said. "It's only part of the chair. It was my great-great-grandmother's. Sentiment?"

"What happened?"

"I don't know. I came home one night when Victor was here, passed out on the living room rug. Empty fifth of Jack Daniel's on the kitchen counter. The remains of the chair scattered all over the apartment. A coffee table and lamp did worse, but I just threw them out."

"This happen often?"

She shook her head.

"Occasionally. I had the superintendent patch up a few holes in the Sheetrock."

"He never hit you."

She looked shocked by that.

"Heavens, no. He treated me like I was made of fine crystal. I'm not, by the way. More like Yankee hardwood. No bend, no break."

She took my hand and led me out of the intimate spaces. I didn't like the touch, but went along, till we made it to the living room, where I gently pulled away. She sat in her chair and I went back to mine.

"Why show me all this?" I asked.

She felt around for her wine glass, abandoned on a side table, then went to refill. She held up the bottle, but I took a pass.

"I didn't know whom to trust," she said, once settled back in. "But then I thought, who else but a PI working on defending my husband's murderer?"

"Ernesto didn't do it," I said. "He and Victor were friends, back in Colombia."

"You know this for sure."

"No one knows anything for sure, but it's what I think."

She was silent for so long, I almost thought she didn't want to talk anymore. But then she said, "He was just back from a year's posting in Brussels when they changed his job. He was to write a strategic plan for restructuring the domestic practice. No more travel outside the states. Twice the salary. With a personal assistant and bottomless expense account. A plum assignment. They set his retirement date, at only sixty-two, and gave him a big bonus. Big enough to build that house in the Hamptons, a dream of his I honestly never shared.

"The night he told me was the night he went away. Not physically. He just withdrew into himself. Stopped talking and started decorating the walls with fist-sized holes. Three nightly cocktails instead of one. Hour-long walks around the neighborhood before going to bed. In the guest bedroom. Never touched me again. You know the rest."

"Not really. I just know someone killed him."

"That is the rest. I'd always looked forward to him being home full-time, foolishly. I liked my life, but I was ready for some steady companionship, even it was out there away from the city. I thought he was too. He was a very interesting man, as I've tried to tell you. But then the person I knew disappeared and this stranger moved in."

"Did you talk to anyone about it?"

She shook her head.

"All marriages have their rough spots. I kept waiting for him to snap out of it. We were very private people. I think you know that."

"So why tell me?"

She didn't seem to know for sure.

"I don't know. Maybe you remind me a little of Victor. Secret strengths and weaknesses. Self-contained. A smoke screen of clever bullshit to cover the anger that's right below the surface. Not afraid of anything. No, scratch that. Only afraid of one thing."

"What's that?"

"Yourself."

CHAPTER TWENTY-TWO

I got Rebecca Bollings to agree, if she did talk to the FBI, to have a lawyer in the room. Specifically, one of Burton Lewis's people from his Manhattan practice. The serious money-making practice that helped make Jackie's good works out in the Hamptons possible.

On the way back to Southampton I got a text from Tony Cermanski. He wanted me to stop by the Town HQ to look at some video taken by the arson squad at Ernesto's house. He wrote that Joe Sullivan would be there. I wrote back to say sure.

I called Amanda, who was just coming home from one of her job sites. I asked how she was doing.

"Better."

I told her I needed to meet with Cermanski and Joe Sullivan. Then about my conversation with Rebecca Bollings. I said I'd learned some things, but it didn't make me feel any better. She asked me why. I said I'd learned a lot more about Ernesto as well, but it was too big a story to tell over the phone. It could wait until we regrouped back on Oak Point.

"Perhaps after another swim," she said.

"Perhaps."

CERMANSKI, SULLIVAN, and I gathered around a flat-screen monitor that displayed the digital video recorded at Ernesto's house while the fire department was still trying to put it out. A young video engineer had downloaded the files into software that allowed her to manipulate the images—zoom in, zoom out, split the screen, and so on.

Sullivan explained arsonists were notorious for hanging around to enjoy the result of their fun, that often as not, this held the greatest rewards. The cops had been through the video a few times, but thought I should take a look.

The engineer had isolated all the faces in advance, freezing the frame, and zooming in as close as possible before the resolution degraded. Each face was in a little box, numbered and organized by the time code.

The onlookers reflected the neighborhood. Men, women, and children, blacks, Latinos, and Anglos. It was a big crowd, so there were plenty of faces to examine. Including the firefighters. I asked why.

"Just in case," said Cermanski. "Arsonists like to join all-volunteer departments like ours in the Hamptons. Setting a fire, then joining your buddies to put it out is not unheard of."

I recognized some of the faces. Tradesmen and laborers you'd see around job sites and lumberyards. I wrote the names I remembered and the engineer's corresponding ID.

It was a tedious process and came to naught until we had run through the faces, and the engineer went back to the raw footage and just let it roll. That's when I saw the cab of a dark pickup.

"Stop," I said. I pointed to the truck and asked if she could zoom in. It was well in the distance and lights from the emergency vehicles flickered on the windshield, obscuring the driver's face, which is why she hadn't captured the image. But I had her slow down the video to where there were milliseconds of partial clarity. In one of these you could see the outlines of a cowboy hat.

"There's our boy," I said. "The Lone Ranger."

"Damn, we missed it," said Cermanski.

"Fresh eyes," I said. "Don't blame yourself."

"I'll put out another APB, but I wouldn't expect anything," said Sullivan. "And we'll go have a chat with these guys Sam identified."

"I can check the license database to see who from Kentucky has moved up here," said the female tech. "I'm thinking of the alleged cousin. It's a long shot, but you never know."

"Good idea," said Sullivan. "While you're at it, contact Kentucky and get a list of registered dark blue duallys. Can't be that many of them. You don't happen to remember the make, do you Sam?"

"Had a big grill, does that help?"

WHEN I got back to Oak Point, Amanda and Eddie were waiting for me out on the breakwater. This time I was armed with steaks and vegetables intended for the grill. She was in bare feet wearing a floor-length flowing thing. The setting sun deepened her Italian complexion as the day inched toward twilight.

"I know you," she said.

I built a hearty vodka out of the cooler and sat in the neighboring Adirondack. Eddie gave me a brief hello, then lay at Amanda's feet.

"You owe me Ernesto's story," she said, sliding down a bit in her chair and closing her eyes. "You talk. I'll listen."

So I did, and as advertised, it took a long time to tell, especially with all the asides I was lured into by the complexity of the tale. Amanda mostly stayed silent, only interrupting to get clarification. When I was finished, she took a heavy breath.

"I feel bad for Querida," she said. "She knows nothing of all this, I'm sure."

"I'm sure you're right," I said.

"So what are you going to do?"

"I don't know. Maybe Ernesto's cover is blown, maybe not. Did the CIA waste Bollings? Who knows? Why would they? Why did O'Connor sideline him? Are they in cahoots with the government? Where's the FBI in all this? They're in charge of domestic counterintelligence. Why interview Rebecca? What the fuck is happening with the world anyway?"

She dropped her head toward her lap, nearly disappearing under an excess of wavy hair.

"Probably collapsing under the weight of our manifold sins and foolishness," she said. "Maybe we shouldn't care as long as we're allowed to sit here and enjoy the breeze over the bay and look at the sailboats. Maybe we should stop trying so hard."

"I'm working on that. Though first I need to feed you. Don't argue with me and hold the criticism until I'm too senile to notice."

"I might beat you to it."

AMANDA ALMOST passed out soon after that, so I led her back to her house and put her to bed. Then I climbed in the Jeep and drove over to Mad Martha's, which on a Friday night was likely packed with the local crowd of aging tradesmen and a few regular city people who'd been coming there so long no one knew the difference.

I waited for a place at the bar, and when it opened grabbed it like a drowning man grabs a life preserver.

The bartender stood there and looked at me as if he didn't know what I would order. I went along.

"Glass, ice, something clear, and a cocktail napkin to soften the experience."

"Comin' right up."

He was very busy, so it took some time, and several reorders, to get him into a conversation. As he wiped up the bar in front of me I asked, "What's your position on the Latinos working here in construction?"

He tilted his head back and forth, a mime of his conflicted thoughts.

"Never bothered me. Keep their heads down. Work hard. Afraid to come in here, but I'd serve 'em like anybody else. Most of 'em have gone home since the boom, and the ones left pretty much mix in, so I don't get the fuss." He looked out over his clientele. "Still, some of the people here are naturally resentful, of everything. Easier to throw blame than to look at themselves."

He moved away down the bar, as if fearing being overheard. But then came back a few minutes later.

"Oh, and by the way," he tilted his head toward the kitchen, "who do you think's cooking the food and cleaning the dishes back there?"

I nodded and let it go for a while, watching the game on TV and metering out my drinks. When the crowd thinned out, I had another chance to talk to him.

"Any of the people who drove in for the protest come in here?" I asked.

"Some. How come?"

"I'm looking for a guy from out of state. Wore a cowboy hat, western sort of outfit. Shaggy hair, big moustache. He'd stand out."

"Maybe. Why so curious?"

"If I told you, then you'd know."

He put both hands on the bar and leaned in.

"You was always hard to figure out, Acquillo. Some attribute it to that Ivy League education."

"MIT isn't an Ivy. No scientist would let vegetation crawl over old masonry walls."

"That's just what I'm talking about."

"So?"

"Came in here a half-dozen times. Big fucker. Lot of confidence. Haven't seen him lately."

"Said he had a cousin living here," I said. "Anybody you'd know?"

He threw down his bar rag and moved away. I pretended not to notice and focused on the game, occasionally swiveling around in the barstool to look around at the packs of bulging men and their sometimes-bigger wives, dolled up for the night out and talking a little too loud, adding to the increasing din inside the place.

Jimmy Watruss, the owner and a sort of friend, appeared before me.

"Hey, Sam."

"Jimmy. What's up?"

"I'm here to ask the same thing."

"Just enjoying my drink."

Jimmy was a vet who wore the honor overtly. Long, grey hair in a ponytail and cut-off shirt baring strong arms with tattoos commemorating Middle Eastern conflicts the rest of us had forgotten, or never knew about in the first place.

"That's good to hear," he said. "Not looking for trouble then."

"Never looking for trouble. Only looking for a big fucker in a cowboy hat who claimed to have a cousin here in the

Hamptons. I think he's blown town, but maybe I can talk to the cousin."

I had to nearly shout the words, since the music in the place was doing its best to compete with the clamor. Jimmy had to lean in with his left ear, since his right ear was dead to the world after an Iraqi rocket intersected with his Bradley fighting vehicle.

"Does this have anything to do with Ernesto Mazzotti?" he yelled in my ear.

"It's got everything to do with Ernesto. Somebody burned down his house. This guy might know something about it. I just want to talk to him."

I had to add that last bit, because in Jimmy's world, looking for someone often didn't end that well for the one being looked for. We had some history, Jimmy and me, not all of it so sweet, but there was still a shred of trust.

"You see the pudgy white-haired guy behind me?" he asked. "White shirt, no chin?"

I gazed that way and nodded.

"Sort of looks like a fish?" I asked.

Jimmy smiled and nodded.

"Derrick Reinhart. Writes a blog about the East End. Not a big fan of our immigrant community. I saw him in here with people from out of state during the protests. Don't know if your cowboy was one of them. Drank free all night. He might know something."

"You let assholes like that in here?"

"It's a democracy, Sam. Get used to it."

I put my hand on his rock-hard shoulder.

"You're right," I said. "Sorry."

"Don't fuck him up."

"I won't. I promise."

Instead, I asked the bartender what he was drinking—a single malt bourbon—and brought a glass over to where he was sitting with a fleshy, grey-haired woman and a skinny little rodent of a guy in an oversized hoodie, defying the summer weather.

I stuck the drink in front of him and said, "Mind if I sit?"

He looked a little hesitant, but the free booze did its work.

"Certainly," he said. "There's plenty of room."

I pulled up a chair and sat across the table.

"I'm looking for a guy," I said to Reinhart. "Maybe you can help me."

"He owe you money?" asked the skinny guy.

"No. I just want to ask a few questions."

"I know who you are," said Reinhart, which surprised me. "Sam Acquillo. Former professional boxer, ex-corporate bigwig with the late, great Con Globe. Accused of murdering Robbie Milhouser. Acquitted. Star witness in the Alfie Alder-green case."

"You know a lot," I said.

"I make it my business to know a lot. I read every paper published on the East End, prosaic as they are. And remember everything. MIT," he said, pointing at me. Then he pointed at himself. "Princeton. Not that anyone cares."

"At least you do," I said. He took a self-congratulatory sip of his bourbon. "All that remembering must be a burden. I try to forget most things."

"That's why you need people like me. Well, maybe not you. Only the thoroughly benighted."

He sipped his drink again, enjoying his own repartee.

"Thanks, I think."

"You know what I mean," he said. "We're being swamped by a tide of catabolic degeneration. It's the dawn of a new dark age, utterly unanticipated by the self-satisfied progressive coterie."

I looked at the grey-haired woman.

"What do you think?" I asked her.

"Damn right," she said.

I turned back to Reinhart.

"You probably know all about the Bollings case, since you seem to like murder trials," I said.

"The Mexican killed him," said the skinny guy. The woman nodded quick agreement.

"He's Colombian," I said. "And guilt is for the courts to decide."

"That is our justice system, alas," said Reinhart.

"You might like that system if you were in Mazzotti's shoes," I said. "Especially after getting jumped by a bunch of Neo-Nazis who were probably inspired by your blog."

"First off, I'm a citizen, not an illegal alien," said Reinhart. "If our courts were any good he wouldn't have been here in the first place. Maybe this will finally wake everybody up."

My temper started to assert itself, but I called upon my better Zen self to settle it back down.

"Everyone's entitled to their opinion," I said.

"What's yours?" he asked me.

"I don't think Mazzotti did it. Even if I didn't know the man, I'd wonder what kind of dumbass assassin would choose a golf club as a murder weapon, then toss it in the woods with his prints and DNA all over the handle. Whatever happened to poison umbrella tips and sniper rifles?"

"Yeah," said the skinny guy. "The whole world's going to fucking hell."

Reinhart smiled indulgently.

"This man you're looking for," he said to me. "Do you have a name?"

"No, but he wears cowboy clothes and drives a blue dually pickup with Kentucky plates."

The skinny guy started rocking in his seat, but kept his eyes on Reinhart, who said, "Why the interest?"

"Somebody burned down Mazzotti's house. He was there. Might have seen something."

"Isn't that a matter for the police?"

"If he talks to me, maybe there doesn't have to be any police," I said.

"Hmm," said Reinhart. "Very circumspect response."

I found a dry cocktail napkin on the table and picked a pen out of Reinhart's shirt. I wrote down my phone number.

"Have him call me," I said. "Ask how his cousin's outboard is running."

"My, so cryptic," said Reinhart.

"What is it you do again?" I asked him.

"I write the *East End Examiner*, the best-read blog in the Hamptons. You knew that."

"No, sorry, I didn't," I said, and tossed the napkin across the table.

I went back to the bar and ordered another drink. The bartender asked me how it went with Reinhart. I told him Jimmy made me promise not to fuck him up.

"Too bad," he said.

An hour later, I saw the skinny guy slipping out of the bar. I dropped down a wad of bills and left right behind him. I saw him swaying through the parking lot, searching his pockets for his keys. A Japanese compact chirped and flashed its lights and the skinny guy went right to it. He was about to open the door when I grabbed him by the scruff of the neck and spun him around.

I got him by the throat with my right hand, shoved him into the car and patted him down with my left.

When I was done, I whispered in his face. "Where is he?"

"Who?"

"The cowboy. I saw how you reacted when I asked about him."

He shook his head as best he could with my hand gripping his throat.

"How the hell am I supposed to know?" he choked out.

I gripped harder, lifting him off his feet.

"I'm really not in the mood to argue with you. In ten seconds you'll have a broken nose and I'll be on my way home to curl up with a good book. Ask yourself if it's worth it."

"I can't tell you nothin'," he said. "Even if you break all of me."

"He's stayin' with Reinhart," said a woman's voice. I turned my head around and saw the grey-haired woman. "Let him go. He's a piece of shit, but he's the only piece of shit I got."

I set the skinny guy back on the ground and eased up on his throat, though not all the way.

"You know his name?" I asked.

She said no, but she'd seen the cowboy at Reinhart's house two days before. They were partying and all drunk on bourbon and hateful talk about the collapse of Western civilization.

"Why are you telling me this?" I asked.

"So's you don't strangle my man like you was going to do. I want that privilege for myself."

I moved my hand from his throat to his shirtfront, then shoved him into her arms.

"He's all yours," I said. "I wouldn't have hurt him."

She put her arms around his tiny, shaking body.

"So you want to tell yourself."

ON THE way back to Oak Point, I woke up Sullivan to make him a deal. I'd reveal where the cowboy was if Jackie and I could talk to him, after he and Cermanski had the first whack.

"No deal and you'll tell me anyway," he said.

"I will."

"So why try to bargain?"

"I'm experimenting with cooperation. I could have just gone over there and grabbed him myself."

"But then you'd be breaking the law. You'd lose your spanking new PI license and Ross would never let you near an investigation again."

"Okay, I'll just go to bed and you can enjoy waking up, getting dressed, and hauling the guy in."

"Not me. This is why we invented police officers. Where is he?"

I told him to look up the address of Derrick Reinhart, and filled him in on Reinhart's self-anointed role as the defender of truth and justice on the East End.

"I hate all that shit," said Sullivan.

"Can you bring Reinhart in too? I would love that."

"No probable cause. Maybe he'll do something stupid and give us an excuse."

"Don't count on it," I said. "Guy's a worm."

"I think you should take two stiff vodkas and call me in the morning."

"Will do."

Before taking his advice, I woke up Jackie and briefed her on the situation.

"I wish you'd called me first," she said.

"It's so hard to please everybody these days," I said.

She hung up on me.

I made it to Oak Point a few minutes later, and went right to Amanda's, where I found Eddie on the couch and a deep, quiet house. I crawled into Amanda's bed and she pushed up against me and sighed. The moment cleared my mind of all its clamoring anxiety, and after only an hour I drifted off, giving the morning permission to take care of itself.

Chapter Twenty-Three

I'd known Danny Izard since he was a teenager who ran with a pack of kids that included my daughter. Since Allison wasn't speaking to me at the time, classic fallout from the divorce, Danny's proximity was a welcomed thing. There was no conspiracy; I knew the young man was forthright, level-headed, and responsible almost to the point of self-righteousness.

I didn't know at the time that Allison had a serious crush on him, another happy situation, since she stuck close to him and let him look after her, a privilege not afforded her parents, most especially me.

It was no surprise he became a Southampton Town police officer, taking over Joe Sullivan's North Sea beat when Sullivan made detective. He was the one who caught the assignment to pick up the cowboy.

When he got to Reinhart's house he pulled in the driveway with his lights out. He started with the garage, shooting a flashlight through a window in the side door. The blue dually was in there, dwarfing Reinhart's Prius. He went back to his patrol car and lit up the full light array. Then went to the front door of the house and rang the bell.

Reinhart answered in his boxers and T-shirt.

"What the hell is this about?" he asked Danny.

"Are you the owner of a blue pickup with double rear wheels?"

"I don't have a pickup."

"There's one in your garage," said Danny.

"Do you have a warrant?"

"Is the owner of that pickup in the house?"

"You haven't told me what this is about," said Reinhart.

"He's wanted for questioning. Is he in the house?"

Something happened after that, but Danny was fuzzy on the details. He remembered Reinhart stepping back into the house, and then waking up on his back looking up at the night sky. Then Reinhart's face came into view. He was saying "Officer? Officer?"

Danny heard the sound of the truck roaring out of the driveway. He tried to stand, but the ground tipped around too much, and he fell down again. Reinhart took his arm to help him, but Danny shook it off. He pulled his handheld radio off the utility belt and called dispatch. His words were slurred, but he got the report out. He pulled out his service weapon and told Reinhart to lie facedown on the ground.

This time he was able to get up on his feet, and once he felt steady enough, had Reinhart put his hands behind his back so Danny could slap on a set of handcuffs.

"Give me his name," he said to Reinhart.

"Ron Haley. I had no idea he was going to do that. Honestly. I'm as shocked as you are."

"No you're not," said Danny, before taking out his cell phone to give Joe Sullivan the bad news.

I GOT my wish, on two counts. I got to see Derrick Reinhart sitting in the police interview room wearing an orange jumpsuit, and after Sullivan and Cermanski were done with him, he agreed to talk to Jackie and me. Sullivan had told him he didn't have to, though cooperating with Ernesto Mazzotti's defense attorney would help tamp suspicion about his role in the house fire.

Apparently Reinhart jumped at the chance.

"This situation is beyond absurd," he said, opening the discussion. "I had no role in the attack on Officer Izard."

"Except harboring his attacker," said Jackie.

Reinhart squeezed his lips together, as if stifling what he wanted to say.

"As I told the detectives, I was merely giving Mr. Haley a place to stay. You might have noticed it's high season in the Hamptons. You can buy a car for the price of a hotel room."

"How do you know him?" I asked.

"He came for the protest. I met him at Mad Martha's. We shared interests. I offered him my spare room. That is the beginning and end of it."

"So you're not cousins," I said.

That took him aback.

"Of course not. He's from Kentucky, for Lord's sake." As if a blood connection with anyone south of the Mason Dixon was beyond the pale.

"What sort of interests did you share?" asked Jackie.

"Have you read my blog? Secure borders, employment for citizens first, a muscular American military, strict adherence to the Constitution. These are legitimate positions," he added, defensively, though he didn't have to for my sake. I meant it when I said everyone's entitled to their opinion. And in his case, distributing those opinions online. Though unlike Jackie, I hadn't had a few hundred people besieging my home with ugly signs.

She told him the police had yet to apprehend Mr. Haley.

"Any idea where he went?"

"I went over this with the detectives. No idea whatsoever. And not a word about Mr. Mazzotti's house burning down, or any mention of violent acts."

"You've proven you're a smart man, Reinhart," I said. "What's your read on this guy?"

"Thank you," he said, as if relieved that someone had finally acknowledged his superior intellect. "Clearly a primitive. It's obvious from the clothes and ridiculous truck. But not unintelligent. He asked me very thoughtful questions. And never indulged in racist or demeaning characterizations of immigrants, or homosexuals, or liberal democrats, which I don't enjoy hearing, no matter what you think of me."

I took from Jackie's fixed expression she'd need more convincing than that.

"Did you see him attack Izard?" I asked.

He shook his head.

"No. He yanked me back into the house. I just heard what sounded like a baseball bat hitting a sandbag. The officer grunted, and he was flat on his back when I ran out. Haley was running for the garage, and I ducked back inside. I didn't want to be seen watching him flee."

"You were frightened," said Jackie.

"Wouldn't you be? I immediately tried to give the officer assistance, which he refused, though that should count for something."

We pressed him on what else he knew about Haley, but it turned out to be very little. My guess was Reinhart did 90 percent of the talking, making it easy for Haley to keep his own story to himself.

I gave him one more chance to speculate.

"Why do you think he did it?" I asked. "What was he afraid of?"

"The police, obviously. Why? Not a clue. Though I wouldn't use the word fear."

"What's the right one?"

"Expedience."

SULLIVAN CONFIRMED the cowboy was still missing, despite a higher-grade APB, extending down the East Coast and points west. He said Danny Izard was in the hospital with a mild concussion from a blow to his head and a bad case of embarrassment, partly derived from ignoring Sullivan's request that he bring along backup when he went to collar the cowboy.

I asked what they were going to do with Reinhart.

"Kick him. Being a gullible, self-important jerk is not a crime."

"It should be," said Jackie.

"Not enough jails in the world to hold them," said Sullivan. "You'll be shocked to learn there is no Ron Haley that fits our guy's description, in Kentucky or anywhere else. And no owners of a blue dually. We have his prints and DNA taken from the stuff he left at Reinhart's house. No hits on IAFIS. It takes a lot longer to process the DNA. Fingers crossed on that. Our tech is reviewing about eight hours of video taken at the protest. We'll probably need you to confirm or deny," he said to me.

"Maybe he taught that truck to grow wings and fly to South America," I said.

Sullivan tried not to look insulted, without success. Though he took the higher ground.

"You were right to call us with the information," he said. "Okay, he got away, but you earned points with Ross Semple."

"That'll be a big comfort to Ernesto," said Jackie, spoiling a moment of camaraderie.

I GOT an e-mail from Justin Pincus at O'Connor Consulting saying he hoped I'd have a conversation with his management. I wrote back and said conversing was fine, but not with his management, and not in the city. If he wanted to talk, it would be out on Oak Point, and I'd make it as pleasant as possible, depending on the tone of the conversation.

He wrote back that it was a deal, and offered up a few dates. I gave him my address and phone number, and said to bring a swimsuit in case he wanted to jump in the Little Peconic Bay, as most reasonable people do once they've seen it from the breakwater that separated the pebble beach from my cottage's backyard.

"I can't swim," he wrote back, "but I'm a highly accomplished wader. Will be equipped."

When I picked him up at the train station he was wearing a blue Oxford cloth shirt, slacks, and loafers, carrying a leather duffle bag.

"No tie?" I asked him. "Really roughing it, huh?"

"This is the provinces, am I right? Want to fit in."

I was driving my father's '67 Grand Prix, giving it a little exercise.

"They don't make 'em like this anymore," said Pincus, looking around the cavernous interior. "How does it run?"

"Great. Occasionally have to pick crushed Hondas out of the chassis. Don't even hear a bump."

He'd timed his arrival nicely, right before the sun went down over the Little Peconic Bay. I took him straight to Amanda's, where we'd be assured abundant food and refreshments would be waiting on the patio.

"Nice to see you again," she said to Pincus, then introduced Eddie.

"Your dog?" he asked her.

"No, but he'd prefer it," I said. "Used to live in the woods, and now looks disgusted at anything short of pâté de campagna served on fresh crostini."

Pincus petted his head and accepted an unsolicited handshake.

"Nice place you have here," he said to me, after gazing out on the water.

"It's Amanda's. My shack is next door. A quarter the size, but I get the same view. And I own the driveway, sort of."

"He likes to lord that over me," said Amanda.

As we settled in, I identified the strips of land on the horizon across the bay while it was still light enough to see. I pointed out Nassau Point, where Albert Einstein wrote the letter to Roosevelt warning that the Nazis might be developing an atomic bomb, igniting the Manhattan Project, and changing world history. Most assume, I think rightly, he'd pondered this while sailing on the Little Peconic Bay.

"So you're saying big things can happen in small places," said Pincus.

"That wasn't what I meant, but you're right," I said. "Perfect little places think they're apart from the bigger world, but that's an illusion us little-place people choose to believe."

He looked down at his crisp business shirt and brushed off invisible crumbs.

"Thanks for letting me come visit," he said. "O'Connor management is keen on hearing your perspective on the Bollings matter, if you don't mind sharing it."

"I'll bet they're keen. How's the international business doing?"

"I'd say in freefall, but that suggests too leisurely a descent."

Especially in those parts of the world where business and government were inextricably entangled, which was to say, most of it. It was a true test of the salesmanship skills of off-shore directors. First, convince their clients they themselves were not agents of US intelligence, second, that the organization itself wasn't just a nest of spies. It should have helped that the CIA denied Bollings was a covert operative, but for some reason, confidence in the agency's truthfulness wasn't overwhelming.

Pincus pointed out the Darwinian nature of the situation, wherein the best at O'Connor would survive a massive down-sizing, and be left to manage a much smaller slice of the pie.

"Not much I can do to help them with that," I said.

"Of course. They're just hoping you could shed some light on Bollings himself."

"What about you, Justin? You knew him better than most."

"Can we have some rules of engagement here? No bullshit?"

"Sure. I just can't say anything that would compromise our defense of Ernesto Mazzotti," I said, telling myself that included anything that might also get me sent to a federal penitentiary.

"Okay, then I think it makes sense that Bollings had a secret life. He was a secretive guy, as I told you, even with his friends at O'Connor, including me. It never raised suspicions because introversion seemed a natural part of his personality. He also took a lot of private meetings with local VIPs, and socialized at their houses and favorite haunts, so ample oppor-tunity to recruit and handle assets, and exchange information."

"So what do they want to know from me?"

"You obviously don't think Mazzotti killed him."

"If you think innocence is a criterion for defense attorneys taking a case, you don't know much about how the law works."

"So you think he did it."

I laughed, I couldn't help it.

"For a smart guy, you don't know much about this. If I thought he did it, I wouldn't say. Even if I'm just a PI, if a prosecutor heard that, it'd be exhibit number one."

"I thought we were being candid," he said.

"I am. And lucky for this conversation, I don't think he did it. I thought he was innocent at the beginning, and think more so now."

"So you've learned a lot."

"I have. Some of it I wish I hadn't."

"What do you mean?" he asked.

I wasn't sure, though it probably began with a late-in-life loss of faith. I used to believe you could know things just by trying. Get to the truth, the bottom of the story. Now it felt like reality was entirely fungible, that facts existed only as manifestations of different people's perspectives. The political world was bad enough, but once you slipped into the alternate universe of covert operations—nesting eggs of disjointed elements, reflexive lying and myth making, unaccountability and deceit—rationality itself seemed to splinter into brittle shards and blow into the wind. It wasn't just a world of shadows, it was a world without light, distinguishable only by subtle shades of dark grey.

This wasn't a lunatic fringe, it was dark matter that permeated everything and explained nothing. A thing without a head, serving the greater good or spreading malevolence in random, mindless spasms. The fearful symmetry. Rage and chaos lurking in the dark, mocking our delusions of order.

It made me feel like a sap. My lifetime of punishing experience, what I thought was hard-won wisdom, signifying nothing.

"I thought I knew, more or less, how the world worked," I said. "Turns out I was mostly wrong."

"Should it concern me that a cynic like you hasn't been cynical enough?" Pincus asked.

I laughed again. Why should existential crises be so funny?

"I know Ernesto didn't do it, because I still believe in free will, logic, and reason, despite all the evidence to the contrary,"

I said. "Which means somebody else did. It's my job, even though Jackie doesn't pay me anything, to learn who that is."

I had a flashback to my time at the company when I was swept into discussions with O'Connor people, Pincus and others, driven by their Socratic training at Harvard Business School, and the like. There's a reason why psychoanalysts and elite professors ask a lot of questions—it's just so seductive to the ones being asked.

"Is this what your bosses want to know, if I have knowledge of the actual killer?" I asked.

Pincus got up from his chair and walked a few steps out onto Amanda's lawn. Eddie jumped up to follow, thinking something fun was afoot. And it was, sort of. Pincus assumed a golfer's pose and started making phantom drives into the bay. Eddie hurtled himself toward the breakwater, since we'd often play this game for real—me refining my congenital slice, Eddie shagging balls off the beach, and sometimes out of the water.

"He's going to be really disappointed if there isn't a ball," I said.

Pincus stopped swinging.

"Sorry. Didn't know. What do I do?"

I pointed to a tennis ball partially tucked under a side table.

"Heave it out there. He'll forget it was supposed to be a golf game."

Pincus threw the ball hard, then sat down again.

"So do you know who actually killed Victor Bollings?" he asked.

Eddie saw the bouncing ball out of the corner of his eye, made an immediate course correction, and caught it a few feet from the breakwater. He trotted back, mouth stuffed and triumphant.

"No," I said. "Though why should they care? It'll do nothing to improve their business prospects."

"They just want to know. I want to know."

And there it was. True candor at last, however veiled. Maybe credibility wasn't the only thing paralyzing O'Connor's overseas operations. Or maybe some of it was fear.

"Theresa Woodsen, Bollings's boss, gave him a new assignment," I said. "Ostensibly a promotion, with no international travel, bigger salary, bonus, administrative support, and a generous expense account. Did you know that?"

Pincus nodded, a kind of cautious nod.

"How come?" I asked.

"Standard procedure. Give the high production people a nice bump at the end of their game, while making room for the upstarts needed going forward."

"Like you," I said.

"Like me," he said, without hesitation, or insult.

"Did you know it threw him into a massive depression?"

For the first time, he looked thrown off balance.

"I didn't. He seemed fine to me."

"Of course. That was his super power. Feel one way, act another."

He bowed his head, as I've seen other people do when processing a complicated new thought.

"I don't get it," he said. "Maybe because I look forward to that day myself. We make so much money no one cares how hard we work, but that doesn't mean the jobs aren't hard. None of us reach sixty with our nervous systems intact. We call it PCSD. Post Consulting Stress Syndrome."

I just sat there and looked at him. My own Socratic consulting technique: make the client arrive at his own conclusion.

"He didn't want to stop," said Pincus. "He wasn't ready. Felt cast aside in the full bloom of his career. Losing his role was a loss of identity, a loss of purpose."

"Or?" I asked.

Pincus struggled with that for a moment, then said, "Something bigger was at stake. Something bad would happen if he left that job."

I liked playing Socrates, just asking questions, the easy part. "Such as?"

Pincus frowned at me, as if angered by the effort I was putting him through.

"His covert operations," he said. "He'd lose his cover."

"Close, but not quite," I said. "What else?"

Pincus looked out at the darkening skies above the Little Peconic Bay.

"O'Connor knew," he said. "They were in on it, and for some reason, decided to shut him down."

I let the silence build in the air as a form of confirmation.

"Fuck," he said. "I gotta get me another job."

Chapter Twenty-Four

I was just walking into Jackie's office when she got a call from ADA Andy Frost, telling her the US attorney was considering bringing charges against her for making false statements to the FBI. He said it was a courtesy call, so she'd have a chance to review her conversations with federal officials, and be aware that the New York Bar association had been informed, and would be kept privy of the investigation.

She put her finger up to her lips and put the call on speakerphone.

"You know this is bullshit," she told him. "You were there."

"Actually, Jackie, I wasn't. Your PI convinced Special Agent Inverness to clear the room."

"What false statements did she say I made?" said Jackie.

"I don't know. That's with the US attorney. You know it's a felony, which on conviction would result in instant disbarment. And prosecution for your Mr. Acquillo."

"Of course I know," said Jackie. "You don't think I'm that stupid."

"I don't think anyone convicted of these charges in the past was stupid."

"Unfucking believable."

"The US attorney's office did have a suggestion. Given this shadow hanging over your own behavior in the Mazzotti matter, that you transfer the case to another lawyer so as not to compromise his defense. It would be just too big a distraction."

"Have I been charged or not?" she asked.

"I said they're just considering it."

"And will giving up the Mazzotti case have any bearing on their decision?"

"I don't know, though for your own sake, that might be the best path to take," he said.

"I used to like you, Andy," said Jackie. "Now I just feel sorry for you. If you have a conscience, you're never going to sleep again. If you don't, God will notice."

"I'm only trying to help."

"Okay, so can you pass along my statement to the US attorney and the FBI regarding this issue?"

"Absolutely."

"Good. Then here it is. Fuck you, fuck them, fuck the air you breathe and the ground you walk upon. Did you get that? Should I repeat for clarity?"

"No, I hear you."

"Well then, I guess we're done here," she said, and hung up the phone.

She sat behind her desk with both hands in her lap, and said, "Oh, my God."

"It's not true," I said. "You didn't do it. Nobody lied."

"That doesn't matter. The charge is enough to take me down. My word against hers."

"When did they put Kafka in charge?"

"When responsible people were asleep. Fat, dumb—so terribly refined—and happy," she said.

"What are you going to do?"

She looked at me, incredulous.

"Defend Ernesto as long as he'll have me, fight the good fight, and go down with the ship. What did you think I'd do?"

"All those things. I just needed to confirm so I can manage my schedule."

She got up from the chair behind her desk and walked over to a couch crammed up against a far wall, where she flopped down and put a forearm over her eyes.

"Let's go take a ride," I said. "Get some air."

She thought that was ridiculous, but she came along without a fight, and once we were underway, agreed it was a good idea. I took her down to a town beach and we walked out on the sand. There was only a scattering of beachgoers, and it was easy to find a spot to drop down and look at the ocean. A northwesterly blowing offshore was bringing in cooler than normal air for that time of the season. The breeze flattened the surface of the water and formed the waves into tidy curls. The morning sun, still low on the horizon, turned the spray into flickering grains of glass. A flock of birds in loose formation skimmed the water, then sharply banked and headed back in the opposite direction, rising to a higher altitude. A big power boat, its flying bridge and topsides bristling with fishing rods, made easy way over the calm seas.

"You're right," said Jackie. "I don't do this enough."

"I didn't say that."

"I take it for granted, and then when I'm here, it's like the first time I've ever seen the ocean or felt the wind."

Sitting cross-legged, Jackie picked twigs and shell fragments out of the sand and tossed them into the air where they flew a short course toward the sea. Her ball of strawberry hair, shoved by the wind, hid her face, protecting her thoughts.

"I have an idea," I said.

"One I'm not going to like."

"Don't say that till you hear me out. We have to bring this to Burton. He won't let it stand. He'll make a few calls, shake a few big trees, but they'll be expecting that. They'll be conciliatory, but nothing will change. Instead, I think he should take over the lead on the Mazzotti case. Personally. You can still work behind the scenes, not completely out of harm's way, but they'll have to go directly through the big dog. They're not going to do that."

She threw a whole handful of sand in the air.

"He hasn't practiced in years," she said. "He won't want to do it."

"He will if you ask him."

"It feels like I'm quitting. The weak woman running to the sheltering arms of a powerful man."

"Smart strategy isn't failure. It's using all the resources you have available. The only weakness here would be pigheadedness. Caring about what other people might think, losing perspective on what really matters. Which is beating these bastards and saving your client."

She pulled back her hair so she could look at me.

"Lovely idea," she said. "Thanks so much for thinking it up."

"What happened to Jackie?"

"She agrees with you. It can happen. Let's go barge in on Burton."

We were walking back to the Jeep, when I felt Jackie pull on my sleeve. I turned around and she wrapped her arms around me, burying her face in my chest. She held on long enough for me to recover from the surprise and tentatively hug her back.

"I don't know how to be looked after," she said. "I never had a chance to learn. Doesn't mean I'm not grateful. Even though I do all I can to push people away."

I patted her back.

"Knock it off. We look after each other. We have to, since nobody else will. And who can blame them."

She let out a tiny laugh, then squeezed hard.

"This is a tough one," she said, pulling back so she could look at me, though still holding on.

"It is."

She stuck her face back on my chest and said, "Okay."

"Okay."

IT WENT better than I thought it would. Burton not only agreed to our request, he looked excited by the prospect. It helped me remember he was still a young man, in that he was nearly ten years younger than I. People think inherited wealth is an automatic path to success, but most inheritances are squandered. Burton had turned his family's modest fortune into a massive empire, through privilege for sure, but also strength of mind and will.

He'd been building birdhouses because he wanted to, not because he'd retreated from useful life.

He literally rubbed his hands together when Jackie dropped the case files on a coffee table in front of him.

"I'll call Frost first thing in the morning," he said. "When's our next court date? What's our plea?"

The two lawyers then dove into legal strategy, expressed in an exclusive, incomprehensible patois, so my mind started to drift, and then my body, until I was out on Burton's vast backyard, where I could hear the ocean waves grumble, the pre-nocturnal insect chatter, and unfortunately, my own querulous thoughts.

I lay flat on my back on the grass and took stock.

Chaos theorists maintain that a natural order exists within seemingly random occurrences. The trick is to extract that order, put it on a test bench, and turn it into a system that operates in the real world.

The Mazzotti case had challenged that belief beyond anything I'd experienced. It seemed totally haphazard, pinballs bouncing around on heedless trajectories. It offended my sense of the world, and rattled me in ways I hadn't felt since I was a boy let loose in the Bronx, full of fear disguised by snarling rage.

I wondered if it was age, a creeping infirmity too subtle to announce its arrival. Probably, but not the whole story. I knew I had the physical strength of far younger men, a gift borne of genes and hard labor. I asked the black sky above me what I was afraid of, and the answer drifted over me like weightless silk.

Loss. I'd tried so hard not to care about anything, or anyone, and now there I was. Caring so much that I'd sacrifice myself to assure another's survival. Yet for Amanda, even that wasn't enough. There was no quid pro quo. There wasn't a god I could negotiate with, to offer myself up in exchange.

Darkness was coming, and there was nothing I could do to stop it.

Amanda didn't go to work the next day, because I wouldn't let her. I insisted we go out on the boat, the first time since she went for that impromptu swim. Tide, wave height, and weather conditions were good, just enough wind to loaf around, my favorite sailing experience those days. I'd consumed my fill of nautical adventure—wouldn't replace it, but didn't bear repeating.

Amanda brought food along in a big wicker picnic basket. I had the potables awaiting on board. Eddie ran across the topsides eyeing seabirds he was fully confident of snatching, even though this had never happened.

We motored out of Hawk Pond and through the twisty channel to the Little Peconic, where I set a full complement of sails that filled nicely in the light breeze, and killed the engine, replacing the mechanical burr with a subtle swoosh against the hull and occasional flap of the canvas. We had the bay mostly to ourselves, nearly empty as it usually was during the weekday, even in the high season. I noted one open fishing boat, and bore away, not tempting mischievous fate with an absurd probability.

A small private plane hummed overhead, catching my attention. Far above a contrail dissipated into a strip of cloud, slightly curved. It was painted yellow by the sun rising in the east.

Amanda used two crossed hands to pull her sundress over her head. She slapped on generous palmfuls of sunblock, even though her Italian skin had long ago reached peak olive brown. When I first saw that body it was all stringy muscle, long thin fingers and toes. The extremities hadn't changed, but her shoulders had taken shape from general construction and menial chores around her job sites. And time had softened the curves, just enough to bring her on par with the average, healthy woman twenty years her junior.

I told her as much.

"I've had enough trouble in my life," she said. "A little compensation is only fair."

I had to agree, though I reminded her that most people get no such bargain.

"Luck is capricious. We've already established that," she said, her face peering out from a tumble of hair.

I fiddled around with the sails, and the autopilot, until I had a reliable equilibrium, then sat down across from her in the cockpit.

"What's wrong?" she asked.

I spread my hands, offering up the perfect day.

"With this?"

"With you."

There was a time when I would have deflected the question, jollied and charmed her into ignoring the signals of distress I unconsciously conveyed. This time, I didn't feel like it.

"It's a mental problem," I said. "Whenever I feel life is where it should be, and I let down my guard, something terrible happens. It makes me wary of contentment, as if the feeling is a lightning rod for catastrophe. That relaxing my hypervigilance brings it on."

She put the cap on the sunblock, took off the top of her bikini, dropping the garment onto the cockpit sole, and crawled into my lap. She gathered me into a hug, somewhat awkwardly, and squeezed.

"You're a good man, Sam Acquillo," she said. "And it's a good life. Let's live it day by day, and when it's over, it's over."

A big tern chose that moment to fly through the running rigging, squawking in alarm, as if suddenly aware of a bad decision. Eddie erupted, barking like a dog possessed. A sudden puff pushed the boat to starboard, causing Amanda's coffee cup to slide off the seat and crash onto the cockpit floor.

The boat cruised on, unaffected by the clamor.

Chapter Twenty-Five

We returned to the marina just as the night settled over North Sea. I secured the boat and got everything shipshape, and found Amanda out cold on one of the settees. I carried her to the car, and drove us to Oak Point. After I got her tucked into her own bed, I went back to the cottage so I could brood in the privacy of my own home. As we crossed the common lawn, Eddie peeled away toward the water on an undertaking with no clear objective.

I stopped at the kitchen to mix up a hearty aluminum tumbler of vodka and ice, and headed out to the screened-in porch to read and try to pound my jittery mind into some semblance of sleep.

The only furniture on the porch was a daybed and a round table with two chairs. When I flicked on the light, I saw a man sitting at the table. He held a smooth, dark grey black pistol in his lap. His feet were flat on the ground and his shoulders loose. He wore a billowy silk jacket, khakis, and technical-looking running shoes.

Despite the clothes, and even absent the shaggy moustache, I knew who he was.

"Howdy, partner," I said.

He flicked the gun toward the daybed.

"Have a seat," he said. "As far from me as you can get."

I raised my tumbler.

"You want a drink?"

"I'm all set."

I asked him what happened to the Kentucky accent.

"Must've lost it somewhere."

I sat on the daybed and took a swig of the vodka. I wished I had a pack of cigarettes stowed out there somewhere, an impulse I felt at least once a day.

The cowboy looked older and leaner without the hat and long brown hair, now a dark shade of grey, cropped close to his head. Bright blue eyes.

"Tomas Maldonado says hello," he said, in Spanish.

"I wouldn't think he was your type."

"He took your suggestion and resigned from the embassy, after spilling his guts to embassy staff. Very inconvenient for a lot of people."

"Including you?" I asked.

"Especially me. I still have an apartment in Bogotá. Wanted to go back some day. I blame Maldonado, by the way. Piece of crap. He told me about your visit. And what he said to the embassy. I don't know how much to believe. Disappeared after that. Afraid I'm going to slit his throat. I might. Pussy."

"Who set fire to Ernesto's house?"

"A friend of Derrick Reinhart. I have a recording of him admitting to the crime. Bragging about it, actually."

"And Reinhart knew?"

He shook his head.

"No. Before the friend could tell him, Reinhart wrote a blog post condemning the act. The guy thought it better to keep his mouth shut after that. I have his bag of leftover memory foam, but there's not much else in the way of forensics. Will be tough to convict."

I asked him if he was planning to shoot me.

"Fair question," he said. "I was going to ask you the same thing."

"I'm sure you've already searched the house and found my old Colt .45 in a drawer in the shop. You can see I'm not carrying, but you're welcome to frisk me anyway. Then you can put that thing away."

"Sure. You take it."

He tossed the gun onto the daybed, within easy reach. I left it there.

"What about Reinhart's friend? Are you telling the police?"

"Maybe. Why did you blow Bollings's identity to the *Times*?"

"I didn't. And I don't know who did, or why. Jackie Swaitkowski and I talked to the reporter, but didn't give him anything but Maldonado's name. He told me his source wasn't in the government. It was a quid pro quo."

"Swaitkowski knew the reporter," he said. "He'd written a profile of her a few years ago. Coincidence?"

"No. I think whoever dropped the dime wanted it to look like it was Jackie and me. Someone really wants us off this case. Would that be you?"

He sat back in his chair, folded his arms, and stuck out his legs.

"Not me. I like you just where you are."

I picked up the gun. It was blocky, but remarkably lightweight. He unfolded his arms and tapped his wristwatch.

"It won't fire unless you're wearing this," he said.

I asked him who killed Victor Bollings.

"You're convinced it wasn't Mazzotti," he said.

"You know it wasn't. Why mess around with a golf club when the edge of a hand will do the job?"

He closed his eyes and scratched the back of his neck.

"Will that be your defense?" he asked.

"You haven't answered my question."

"I don't know who killed Bollings. I was hoping you could tell me."

"Did O'Connor Consulting know about his moonlighting gig?" I asked.

"Just one of them. A woman, recruited him early in his career."

"I don't know who killed him either," I said. "If I had to guess, I'd say someone from the intelligence community."

He chuckled at that.

"I love that word 'community.' Makes it sound like this cute little suburban neighborhood, with all these spies cutting the grass and walking their dogs. Communal is the last thing those people are."

"Those people include you, Colonel," I said.

He squinted at me as if to get my face in better focus.

"I don't know what you're talking about," he said, in mock affront.

"I don't care who you are, or what you do, how you do it, or where. I don't care who actually killed Bollings. Or why. The only thing I care about is proving Ernesto's innocence."

Before answering, he asked me to toss back the gun.

"It wasn't anyone in the organization I worked for in Colombia," he said, catching the gun by the handgrip. "By the way, that organization doesn't exist, never existed, and will stay nonexistent forever. Hell, I don't exist."

"Rastrojos? There are plenty of Latino gangsters on Long Island. They could have done it for sport."

"Probably not," he said, after some hesitation. "They'd sure want to. The original Rastrojos leadership is all dead. Either killed each other off, or got visited by some of our fancy toys after Ernesto located their position. Not sure who'd be left to care, much less chase down El Primero's assassin, even if they knew who he was, or where he was, which is as close to impossible as a thing can get."

"Secrets have a way of sneaking out."

He looked unconvinced.

"We tore them to ribbons. Best intel says they've never fully reconstituted much less secured proxies in the states. And why bother framing Ernesto? Just kill him along with Bollings."

"Someone else in the happy community?" I said.

"A big maybe. They tell the citizens the intelligence silos were broken down after 9/11. Maybe at the top, but operationally, everyone's a silo. Chain of command is more like an Escher drawing. Nothing connects, everything is a misdirection. Turf wars happen all the time, by people who are bred to fight in the dark. But I don't waste a lot of time thinking about it. Politics are outside my mission parameters."

"But not infiltrating the anti-immigrants."

"Personal initiative. Gave me an excuse to hang around town. They had no idea who Bollings was. Their killing him and framing Ernesto makes less sense than the Rastrojos."

I asked him again if he wanted a drink. He said, all right, what the fuck.

I brought him into the kitchen and had him pick a beer out of the fridge. Eddie had been lying on the rear stoop, and when he saw the colonel, went slightly batshit. I introduced them.

"You did a nice number on one of my squad," he said. "Concussion. On two months' sick leave, minimum."

"He was unauthorized," I said. "By me."

"He fucked up. Good training exercise."

"Tell him it was a kid's baseball bat. That'll help his self-esteem."

I let him drink some of his beer before saying, "The local police are very interested in finding you."

"Not going to happen. I'll give them the arsonist. As for the cop I took down, another training exercise. In my mind, one for each of us. We'll call it a draw. And I'd prefer if you didn't tell them about our conversation."

I'd already decided not to tell anyone, so it was easy to agree.

"Just don't underestimate those detectives," I said.

"I don't. I fucked up myself, otherwise I'd still be looking like Wyatt Earp."

I watched him finish his beer. He used a paper towel to wipe down the bottle and fastidiously dab his mouth. He told me he'd be around, I just wouldn't know it.

I asked him if he learned anything I could use to let me know. He said he would, and if I had anything, to text him. He wrote the number on a fresh paper towel. It was only five digits long, plus a pound sign. We didn't bother to shake hands, he just slid out the back door and dissolved into the night.

Ross Semple called me the next day and asked if I could trouble myself to visit him at Southampton Town HQ, no online appointment necessary. I said I'd be honored.

"What's up?" I asked.

"Come in. We'll talk."

The pleasantness aside, I knew he meant "get your ass in here."

So I did.

As promised, the woman behind the glass window let me through as soon as I walked in reception. She escorted me to the windowless room where I'd watched the video of the crowd around Ernesto's burning house. Ross was there with the young tech, who sat cross-legged on her ergonomic chair. He thanked the receptionist and asked me to sit.

"We've discovered a technical error," said Ross, "thanks to the careful work of this young lady. That said, it's put the department in a rather awkward position, since it raises a host of legal and procedural issues, so I have to ask for complete confidentiality."

I got the feeling this speech was meant more for the tech than me, at least the style of delivery.

"Sure, Ross. What happened?"

"You might not know we have recording devices in select locations around the station, not just the interview rooms. Nothing nefarious, there're lots of practical reasons for this. For example, we just had a forensics class in the muster room put on by the county chief of detectives. It's a refresher our people have to take to maintain their certifications. Recording the class is routine, so we can include it in ongoing training and review. All done with prior consent by everyone in the room."

He turned to the tech.

"When the device is on, it records automatically when it detects a sound," she said. "I got busy and must have forgotten to turn it off. As soon as I discovered the error, I alerted the chief."

For some reason, Ross didn't seem disturbed by the error, nor the tech particularly chagrined.

"You'll remember when we all met at the station with the two FBI special agents, the ADA's office, and people from the village, we had to use the muster room to fit everybody. Damned if we didn't manage to record the whole thing."

I could see the implications.

"I've contacted the ADA," said Ross, "and assured him the recording was impounded, in case of disciplinary action by internal affairs. As a further courtesy, we're sharing this with everyone who was recorded that day without their consent. We ask in return that no one discuss this with anyone outside those involved."

I think I held on to my poker face until we were out of the room and Ross was walking me back to reception.

"All this new technology is a tricky thing, eh, Ross?"

"Hard to get it perfect."

"How did Inverness take it?"

"Remarkably restrained."

WE DROVE to our meeting with Andy Frost at the Suffolk County District Attorney's Office in Hauppauge in Burton's 1966 Jeep Super Wagoneer. Usually in service around the grounds of his big house on various rough tasks, he'd had it cleaned inside and out, and the fake wood veneer on the sides polished to nearly wood-like authenticity.

He felt it was important the lead attorney arrive at the county lockup in command of the car, and the Wagoneer was the only car he owned. He was wearing a dark grey, three-piece suit about the same vintage as the Jeep, with a yellow dot tie bunched neatly above the vest. It went well with his untrimmed, soft brown hair—the hair of a teenager—and his sun-damaged complexion, which added mightily to those years.

Jackie and I were the slobs we usually were.

Burton took the indignities of security at the front entrance with reticent poise. We'd prepped him, realizing he'd rarely, if ever, encountered post-9/11 impediments.

Frost greeted him just beyond the metal detectors.

I looked to see if they had a secret Anglo-Saxon privilege handshake, but it seemed pretty conventional. Jackie and I followed behind, hands unshook.

I'd been in CEO offices of billion-dollar companies that were smaller than Frost's. Raised walnut paneling covered the walls and a floor-to-ceiling bookcase held only books with leather spines. More leather was spent covering giant overstuffed

Chesterfield sofas, where he guided us to sit. The sofas formed a U around a massive fireplace, well-used. A stately oak desk was about a mile away, the surface clear but for a black desk pad, a small stack of papers, and a picture frame, turned toward the desk chair.

"You might remember the DA who went to jail about ten years ago for rank corruption," said Frost, raising his hands to present the room. "This is his legacy. The ADAs drew straws. I won."

Burton unbuttoned his suit jacket, leaned back in the Chesterfield, and crossed his legs, completely at home.

"Thank you for seeing us on such short notice," said Burton. "We want to catch you up."

"Of course."

"I'm assuming the lead on the Mazzotti case," he said. "For continuity and legacy knowledge, Ms. Swaitkowski will assist. You're free to inform the US attorney's office, or whoever else is attempting to coerce our firm into relieving Ms. Swaitkowski of her responsibilities that we're prepared to bring counter-charges of official misconduct for impugning the integrity of our trusted counselor, and by extension, the firm itself."

Frost waited to be sure Burton was done talking.

"Well," he said. "Consider that done. What else can we do for you?"

"Drop all the charges against Mr. Mazzotti?"

"Fat chance, Burton. All this dancing around with federal agents and national security fanfare has zero material impact on our prosecution. The facts are clear, the evidence overwhelming. The charges stand, the trial will proceed."

"Hey, you can't blame us for asking," I said, and this time Jackie did swat me on the shoulder.

CHAPTER TWENTY-SIX

Amanda's Audi A4 blended in a lot better with the cars in Scarsdale than my weathered Jeep. To complete the camouflage, I wore a blue, pin-striped suit and brought along a classic leather briefcase. The sun had just set, and when I made my first pass by Theresa Woodsen's house, the windows were mostly dark. So I took a little ride around town, before making a second pass, and it looked like she'd gotten home.

There wasn't a Mr. Woodsen, so I assumed she was alone. I parked the Audi on the next block and walked back carrying the briefcase. I went to the front door and rang the bell.

I put the odds at about fifty-fifty she'd answer. A woman alone with a stranger at the door would be sensible not to answer, even if the guy looked like he lived in the same neighborhood. But she did, though with the door held by a security chain as a precaution.

"Yes?" she said.

"My name is Sam Acquillo, and I'm an investigator for the team defending Ernesto Mazzotti. I know about your covert activities with Victor Bollings. I'm here to make an offer."

"That's preposterous," she said, but didn't slam the door.

"I have detailed information on your operation in Colombia. It's safe with me for now, but it doesn't have to stay that way. This is your only chance to make a deal. If you don't let me in immediately, you'll be reading about it in the media tomorrow."

The door closed for longer than it took to remove the chain, so I figured that was that. But then the door opened.

"I don't hold meetings at my private residence," she said. "Especially without an appointment."

"Time to make an exception. You'll want to hear what I have to say."

She stood back and let me in. She led me from the foyer to a small sitting room lined with books. She looked older than her head shot on the O'Connor website—easily midsixties, but still attractive. Shoulder-length, silvery blonde hair with minimum styling, as tall as I am in her flat-heeled shoes, slight build. She pointed to a love seat and chose a chair at an antique desk for herself.

"You're a persistent fellow," she said. "Though I don't think you have any idea what you're meddling in."

"I do. That's why I'm here."

"You know nothing," she said.

"I know Bollings joined your international unit at O'Connor about twenty-five years ago, and you recruited him into the CIA soon after that, once you got to know him and trusted his skills and temperament. It was a team, you on the inside, Victor out in the world. Assignments flowed through you, as did the intelligence Bollings gathered in the field. A straight line. As long as you and Bollings were solid, the connection with Washington was secure."

"Quite the imagination," she said.

"I don't care if I got it all right. I just know it's true, which means others who have the time and wherewithal can prove it. Once they know where to look. In fact, after the *Times* article, that process is already underway."

Her face stayed impassive, even slightly bored—her eyes, a shade not unlike Amanda's, half-lidded.

"That reporter may find himself on the end of an ugly investigation," she said.

"Not likely. He checked the Bollings story with the CIA and they denied everything. So the *Times* is in the clear. You'd just be an interesting add-on. You'll deny everything as well, but that won't spare the agency and O'Connor from further damage control. I don't know what that would entail, but if it was worth killing Bollings to keep him quiet, it's worth killing you."

She took in a deep breath, but didn't flinch.

"Ernesto Mazzotti killed Victor," she said.

"Jesus, I wish people would stop saying that," I said. "It's really tiresome. Do you really think I'd be sitting here if that were true?"

"You wouldn't be sitting here if you could prove it wasn't," she said.

"I am the proof," I said, pointing to my head. "It's all up here. I have the connections, I have the story line. I'm the only one. I want to save Ernesto, but not at any cost. I've taken a page from your playbook. Closed systems, need to know only. Legitimate deniability. You fuckers are crazy dangerous and there's a lot of damage you can do to people I care about. They don't even know I'm here, for their own protection. We can all handle ourselves, but I have to admit, this time we're outgunned."

She nodded agreement.

"That you are indeed," she said.

The door opened and Mauricio of the guayabera walked in, only this time, he wore a black jacket and blue jeans. And the weapon wasn't concealed.

Woodsen held her palm open, showing me a little grey fob with a red button.

"I'm surprised they gave you another gun," I told Mauricio. "The way you keep losing them."

He didn't seem to be his old jovial self.

"I only make the same mistake once," he said. "Facedown on the floor."

I did as he asked.

"He learned this from me," I said to Woodsen, as he patted me down. "I've got other pointers I can share if you want."

He had me sit up so he could pull back my arms and put on a pair of handcuffs.

"You didn't give me a chance to make my offer," I said.

Woodsen stood up from her desk chair.

"Not that it matters," she said, "but I'm telling you no one at the agency had anything to do with Victor's murder. We have information that would prove beyond a reasonable doubt that Mazzotti's responsible. But due to national security, it cannot be exposed in open court. If for some ridiculous reason he's acquitted, we will take immediate custody and deal with him ourselves."

"I think it matters," I said.

"Not to you, I'm afraid," she said. "Your part in all this is about to come to an end. Please get this man out of my house," she said to Mauricio.

He closed his hand on the back of my suit jacket and gave a little tug. I wrenched free, and pushed back into his knees. He gathered a tighter grip.

I said, "Now would be good," and the colonel stepped through the doorway behind Woodsen and put his slick little automatic, equipped with a muzzle suppressor, at the back of her head.

"Go ahead and shoot him," he said to Mauricio. "I can take both of you out before you remember to blink."

Nobody moved.

"Okay," said the colonel, "I'll start with her, then you." Mauricio let go of my collar and dropped his gun on the floor. "Uncuff him."

Mauricio helped me stand and I felt him undo the cuffs. I picked up his gun and told him to hand over the key. When he did, I put the cuffs on him and said to sit. Then I got out of the line of fire.

"Go ahead and shoot him?" I said to the colonel.

He said, "Frisk her."

Neither of us enjoyed that very much, but I could say with confidence that she was unarmed. I put her panic button in my pocket and the colonel forced her back in her chair.

"I know who you are," she said to the colonel.

"Good," I said, "so you know what we have. The whole Colombian operation."

"You took an oath," she said to him.

"You killed my boss."

"I did not."

I brought a chair in from the dining room so I could sit in front of her.

"I'm still ready to talk about my offer," I said.

The accretion of self-control gripped her in its bond. Training, procedure, indoctrination, and belief. Silence. I could see her ready herself for the bullet through the brain.

"I can't stop you from speaking," she said.

"I only want to know one thing," I said. "In return, we leave here and that's the end of it. If you try to hurt any of us, my friend here will find you and finish the job."

"Gladly," said the colonel.

"And the media stays out of it," I said.

She was thinking about it, though you wouldn't know from the set of her face.

"So what's your question?" she asked.

"Why did you shut Bollings down and send him into retirement?"

I didn't know Theresa Woodsen very well. Our relationship thus far had consisted solely of defiance, coercion, and fear. We sat knee to knee, the muzzle of a gun pressed to her skull. That she would have flicked away my life with no more concern than killing a bug was left unsaid. And yet the brightening in her hazel eyes showed something I hadn't seen before. Amusement.

She coughed out a little laugh, and I laughed back, despite myself.

"I didn't fire him," she said. "O'Connor did. They found out he'd been carrying on with some woman for the last twenty years, routing his travel through London so he could meet her, flying her and putting her up at his postings on the corporate credit card, running his admin costs through her at extraordinary rates and generally fucking the company so he could fuck her. It wasn't the CIA who busted him. It was an internal audit. Like a lot of smart guys, he thought he could get away with it, the arrogant bastard."

I exchanged glances with the colonel. He also looked amused, but kept the gun where it was.

"Burton Lewis knows people on the board of directors," she said. "You can easily confirm this." She looked up at the colonel. "There was nothing I could do to stop it from happening. I would never harm Victor. He was my best friend. And he loved you, and Ernesto, which makes it all the worse. He loved all the men and women we sent out there to do the things we asked you to do. Victor was in agony whenever you were deployed. It was our own private hell."

Then she scowled at me, as if daring me to disagree. I didn't oblige, but I did call Burton Lewis, taking Woodsen up on her suggestion.

"I was told you know people on the board at O'Connor," I said when he answered.

"I know the chairman," he said.

I filled him in, and he told me to stay on the line while he used another phone. The four of us in Woodsen's house waited silently. It wasn't the easiest fifteen minutes I ever spent.

Burton came back on the line and told me what I wanted to know. And then some.

"Really," I said.

"This is what I was told."

I thanked him and hung up the phone, then said to Woodsen, "Okay, it's a deal."

The colonel looked like he wanted to shoot her anyway, out of general principle, but he stepped back. I left Mauricio cuffed and told him I'd keep his gun to add to the collection.

"You might want to find another line of work," I told him. "You're not very good at this."

I was about to follow the colonel out the back door when Woodsen asked, "How will I know you'll hold up your part of the bargain?"

I thought about it.

"When you notice you're still breathing?"

THE SOUTHAMPTON police force shared its building with the local court. There was a lot of milling around by traffic violators, harried lawyers, and the stern, but patient, village cops there to keep order.

They had their own receptionist behind bulletproof glass, more in the mold of surly Janet Orlovsky, maybe because it was court day and she was tired of repeating instructions to the motley crowd.

"Is Tony Cermanski here?" I said.

"Who's asking and why?"

"Sam Acquillo and the why is for the detective."

She looked over my shoulder at a skinny, white-haired cop standing at the metal detector defendants passed through on the way to the court. Then she looked back at me.

"You can sit over there," she said, pointing to a low wooden bench. She waited until I backed away to make the call. I saw her speak into the phone, look at me, and nod. She hung up and went back to whatever she was doing.

Cermanski walked out a door behind reception with his usual teenage strut. I stood up and shook his hand.

"What's up, Sam?"

"I want to run something down, but I think you should go with me. Save the back and forth."

"I can do that. Just give me a second."

We took my Jeep. On the way to the Bollings's construction site he pressed me on what I was thinking. I told him it was better if he just listened and stayed objective. He said that was bullshit, but I held firm.

Frank Entwhistle's truck was in the muddy driveway, to my great relief. The house had progressed a lot since I'd seen it last. I asked Cermanski to leave his service weapon in the Jeep.

"If something goes wrong, the chief will have my ass," he said.

"I'm asking you. It'll help the cause."

"You ask a lot."

"I could do this without you," I said.

He wasn't happy about it, but he undid his belt and slid off the holster.

I recognized one of the crew that I'd known for a while and asked about Entwhistle. He pointed at the house.

"In the TV room with the electricians," he said in Spanish.

Frank looked a little troubled when he saw us walk in the room, but he quickly broke off with the electricians, apologizing, and led us to a sunporch off the back of the house.

I reintroduced Cermanski, and both said they remembered each other. Frank asked what was going on.

"The crew that was here the day Bollings was killed, how many are still around?" I asked.

He pursed his lips and pondered.

"Most of them," he said. "The framing was done, so we had the finish guys underway. Ernesto's boys." He looked at Cermanski. "They're still on the job finishing up the trim before installing Sam's cabinets."

"Who's running Ernesto's crew?" I asked.

"Sanchez. The guy who found Bollings."

"Tell him it's nothing bad," I said. "We just want to talk to him."

Frank still looked bothered, but he left the room. I asked Cermanski to sit on the floor with me.

"Really?" he said.

"No chairs," I said. "And it's a lot less threatening. You can afford to clean those khakis."

"You are going to tell me what this is about," he said.

"Just hang in there and look benevolent."

He dropped down to the tile floor and leaned against a paneled knee-wall.

"You know I work hard at looking tough," he said. "You would too."

He pointed at his face, which could pass for a high school senior's.

"I could rough it up for you if you want," I said, pointing to my own busted nose.

"I'll pass."

Sanchez followed Entwhistle into the room, looking wary but eager to please. I offered the floor across from us, and he sat, joined by Frank, who took awhile to get his hefty body settled down.

We spoke in Spanish. Entwhistle and Cermanski knew enough of the language to follow along.

"You're not in any trouble," I told him. "But I need you to be completely honest."

"I will, Mr. Sam. I have nothing to hide."

"I know," I said. "The day before Mr. Bollings was killed, who was here with him?"

He looked over at Frank, and took a moment to say, "He talked to the boss. He was always with the boss."

Frank nodded.

"That's right, Sanchez. We met on the site."

Sanchez looked relieved.

"Anybody else?" I asked.

Sanchez wiped his finger across the newly installed tile, leaving a clean streak.

"Ernesto and Señora Bollings."

Frank nodded again.

"She was here late that day," he said. "We'd see her every few weeks. Made it tense on the site. She never looked exactly thrilled."

Sanchez smiled.

"The señora was good at pointing out things she didn't like," he said. "We were glad the boss left before she really said what she thought," he added, looking at Entwhistle.

"Anything else happen that day?" I asked him.

He looked at our faces, one at a time.

"Tell them, Sanchez," said Frank. "It's okay."

"Señor Bollings was talking to Ernesto and the boss in the kitchen. This seemed to make the señora angry and she stalked out of the house and stood around the trucks until Ernesto and Señor Entwhistle left. When the señor came outside, the señora yelled at him, but he just talked in a quiet voice, trying to calm her down, I think."

"What was she saying?" asked Cermanski.

He looked pained.

"She called him a liar. And other things. My English isn't perfect, but I know what 'asshole' means."

Cermanski glanced over at me.

"What else did she say?" he asked Sanchez.

"I heard her say something about 'teaching that wetback to play golf.' Or something like that. That's when Señor Bollings got mad, too, and they both started screaming at each other. I was embarrassed for them."

Cermanski asked if he'd told this story to the police the day he'd found the body.

"The lady police just wanted to know our names and where we lived," he said. "But nobody came to ask me anything."

Cermanski suddenly looked like he'd spent the day in the sun, but his voice was steady when he asked, "Sanchez, did you see or hear anything else?"

"I always check to see if the crew is gone before I leave. The señora was outside again, walking around the muddy yard and talking to herself. Señor Bollings was in the house, sitting like this on the floor. He asked me if I was married. He spoke this pretty Castilian Spanish, like Mr. Sam, only better. Sorry, Sam. I told him yes, that I loved my wife, which I do. He started crying. It was very uncomfortable for me, so I just left."

"That's all?" Cermanski asked.

"That's all. Mr. Bollings was alone in the house when I left."

"Thanks, Sanchez," said Cermanski. "We're good for now."

He thanked us and helped Entwhistle to his feet. When the two of them left, Cermanski said, "You knew."

"Not exactly. Educated guess."

"Who did the educating?"

"I can't tell you. I made a deal and I have to honor it. Don't hold that against me. You do it all the time, otherwise nobody would talk to you."

One of the things I knew about cops is they like to hold all the cards and leave you with none. I didn't blame them. I'd do the same thing if I was in their situation.

"Prints and DNA on the golf club?" I asked.

He wasn't done being pissed at me, so it took awhile for him to answer.

"Bollings and Mazzotti, and one unknown. We assumed contamination. It happens a lot."

"And no one got elimination samples from Rebecca Bollings," I said.

He shook his head. "Nobody thought it was worth it. The Mazzotti case was a slam dunk."

"But you're still getting the samples," I said.

"Oh, yeah."

"Can you do me a favor?" I asked.

"Depends on what it is," he said.

"Give it a day."

He looked reluctant, but said he would.

"I'll make it worth your while."

I WASN'T happy about driving back into the city, but it couldn't be helped. When I reached Rebecca Bollings's building, the doorman told me she was home, as far as he knew.

"Normally is," he said. "One of the more popular tenants with the local delivery people."

I told him I wasn't expected, but he let me work that out with the front desk, though he waited until I got cleared.

"She said to go on up," said the woman at the desk.

Rebecca met me in a long bathrobe and flip-flops. I wondered if she ever wore street clothes in her apartment.

"You're maybe the second person to ever drop in on me without calling ahead," she said.

"It's a habit of mine. Why waste time with all that formality?"

"Politeness?"

"Overrated."

"You can come in anyway," she said.

I followed her into the kitchen where her Australian shiraz was in full deployment, along with a half-eaten salad. She offered me the shiraz, but I demurred.

"Still have to drive back to Southampton."

She filled her glass.

"The girl at the desk said you had something to share with me," she said.

I told her that was partly true, though I also had a few more questions.

"Let me hear the sharing part first."

"Fair enough. Mind if I pee?"

She pointed to a door off the kitchen, saying the powder room was on the right. I thanked her and she said she'd be in the living room. I did what I wanted to do and went back to the book-laden living room where we reestablished our prior seating arrangement. She kicked off the flip-flops and sat in her desk chair wrapped in the big bathrobe.

"I know why O'Connor took Victor out of the field and assigned him to a new job here in the states," I said. "I know you two didn't talk about his work, but I'd like to hear your opinion."

"Really? That's a refreshing change. To be valued."

"People value your data analytics," I said.

"That's true. Outside of that, I'm just a woman. If you were a woman, you'd know what I mean."

"You're probably right. Ever been to London?"

She leaned back in her chair.

"What the hell does that have to do with anything? And of course not. I told you I've never been inside an airplane."

"You did. I forgot."

"I thought you were a skilled investigator," she said.

"Just got my license. Still working out the kinks."

She seemed satisfied with that, and asked what I'd learned from O'Connor. I told her it was going to be hard to hear. She said she was a big girl, and as a researcher, ready to hear anything.

I said, "Okay. Victor was having an affair. Maybe more than that, since he'd been seeing the woman for about twenty years."

She looked down into her glass, swirling the wine.

"What do you mean, 'more than that'?"

"A long-term relationship. She lived with him on his assignments. Based on what you've told me, she spent more time with him than you did. Some might call her his other wife."

She stared at me, hard.

"Is that what they said?" she asked.

"No, that's what I'm saying. I'm an engineer. I can also crunch the numbers."

"You're not a very diplomatic person," she said.

"People have told me that. I keep trying anyway."

She drained off about half her wine glass.

"Has the FBI come around yet?" I asked her.

"No. Perhaps they've forgotten."

"Probably not. Are you going to tell them about your husband's Englishwoman?"

"That hardly seems necessary," she said. "Even if it were true."

"You thought it was necessary enough to tell O'Connor," I said. "Just as you thought it necessary to tell the *Times* about Victor's clandestine operations. You always knew what he did. His secret was safe with you, until you discovered his other secret."

She pointed at me with the nearly empty wine glass.

"What a preposterous thing to say."

"You told me the last time I was here that you were smart," I said. "I have to agree. Wicked smart. With lots of time to figure out what you were going to do and how you were going to do it. And it pretty much worked out according to plan. You hated O'Connor for owning Victor's time and loyalty, and providing the wherewithal for him to establish his alternate life. You hated the intelligence world for the same reasons. You hated your own phobias for making you feel weak and helpless, even as you achieved great professional success. And finally, you hated Victor for his betrayal. But hate is a funny thing, especially when practiced alone, in your own self-contained bubble. You're so busy wreaking havoc on the hated that you think you're above it all, that no one will look in your direction. You forget about persistent, undiplomatic assholes who look anyway. Like me."

She seemed frozen in her chair, but had little trouble telling me to get the hell out of her apartment.

I stood up and asked if she'd ever played golf.

"Ridiculous waste of time," she said, without hesitation.

"I figured that," I said, and left with her toothbrush in my pocket, helping Cermanski collect his prints and DNA samples.

CHAPTER TWENTY-SEVEN

You want everything to work out perfectly, but of course, it never does. The cops determined that the unknown prints and DNA on the golf club that killed Victor Bollings belonged to his wife, Rebecca. They were also able to use her phone records to determine she'd called me, pretending to be a *Times* reporter, and the newspaper itself, and O'Connor Consulting, at times that lined up with subsequent events. Though with no recording of the conversations, it was still circumstantial.

Burton was able to use his pull with FBI people above Special Agent Inverness to prove that Rebecca had traveled to London, and through GPS tracking on her smartphone, been in the vicinity of a flat rented by a woman long associated with Victor Bollings. Also circumstantial, but telling.

I wondered what it took for her to make the trip. A triumph of fury over fear.

ADA Frost was focused on building his case against her, since the state and federal government decided it was better to deport Ernesto than hold him as a suspect. Burton told me his family followed him to Colombia. We hadn't heard what happened to them, but I held out hope.

Dr. Ng, Amanda's neurosurgeon, gave her another MRI and said her brain was clear of malignancies. There was no guarantee they wouldn't come back, but he said there was also no guarantee she wouldn't fall afoul of the New York City bus system. He said exhaustion and mood changes were common in cases like hers, and probably not permanent, provided she returned to the life she'd had before the surgery.

We didn't quite follow that prescription, doubling down on our time sailing over the Little Peconic Bay and staring at it from the Adirondack chairs above the breakwater. Amanda introduced some new recipes to our food stock, but I stayed with vodka to assure continuity. She also shouldered more responsibility for heaving stuff for Eddie to chase, which meant receiving a variety of soggy objects dropped in her lap.

Fall was sneaking up on us, so we were under cozy wool blankets when she told me, as a precaution, that she'd added my name as joint owner of all her assets, saying it would simplify things should something happen to her.

I told her I couldn't accept that.

"Just give me half your boat and that cottage behind us, and I'll consider it even," she said. "The dog is all yours."

"Apparently not," I said, looking down on him lying at her feet.

"I'm not marrying you," she said. "But since it looks like you aren't going anywhere, we might as well tighten up the relationship. And if I suddenly pop off, all my stuff has somewhere to go."

"I could never benefit from your demise," I said.

"Consider it an incentive to keep me alive."

The Little Peconic Bay didn't enter into the debate. It just continued on with its restless preoccupations, concerned by neither bad nor good.

ACKNOWLEDGMENTS

My Colombian friend, Alexander Giraldo, was an invaluable source of information about his country and its favored Spanish idioms. Gracias, Alex.

As always, Death Investigator Michelle Clark helped me with my dead body and mode of expiration, and Detective Art Wisegerber guided me through the crime scene.

Martin Steiger, CEO & Lead Investigator at the Culper Investigations Group, retired police lieutenant in the NYPD Counter Terrorism Division and army veteran of the wars in Iraq and Afghanistan, provided crucial information derived from his full life experience. Law firm Cohen, Forman, Barone helped out on immigration law and the dynamics of the immigrants' life on Long Island.

Jill Fletcher, longtime beta reader and now professional book doctor, was along for the whole ride. Thanks, Jill. Barbara Anderson, The Permanent Press copy editor, also did a stellar developmental read with many excellent saves and suggestions. Other beta readers at various stages were Marjorie Drake, Dan Pope, Carolyn Brenier, Lynn Wilcox, Randy Costello, Bob Willemin, and Al and Mary Jack Wald.

Thanks to Marty and Judy Shepard for everything, including the wonderful Permanent Press crew—Emily Montaglione and Nick Collins, Barbara Anderson, cover designer Lon Kirschner, and production artist Susan Ahlquist.

And to my wife, Mary Farrell, who mostly recognizes me by the back of my head.